Please return/renew this item by the last date shown.

To renew this item, call **0845 0020777** (automated)
or visit **www.librarieswest.org.uk**   22. NOV 10

Borrower number and PIN required.

Libraries West

The Old
Man's Friend

The Old Man's Friend

Andrew Puckett

ROBERT HALE · LONDON

© Andrew Puckett 2008
First published in Great Britain 2008

ISBN 978-0-7090-8520-1

Robert Hale Limited
Clerkenwell House
Clerkenwell Green
London EC1R 0HT

www.halebooks.com

2 4 6 8 10 9 7 5 3 1

Typeset in 10/12½pt Plantin
by Derek Doyle & Associates, Shaw Heath
Printed and bound in Great Britain
by Biddles Limited, King's Lynn

For three friends

Joan and Lesley Nichols and Betty Gadsby

Acknowledgement

With thanks to Dr Simon Cooper for indispensable help and advice

CHAPTER 1

As Fraser gazed down at the old man's body, tiny as a London sparrow beneath the hospital sheets, he was swept by a wave of desolation, and then by a fury so intense that he could feel the blood pricking at his eyeballs.

Pneumonia – again. They were wrong – *again*.

' 'Scuse me, Doc.' Wally the Trolley, the mortuary technician, had come to collect the body.

He turned and walked quickly away, out of the brightly lit ward, out of the hospital. He found a bench, sat down and breathed deeply as the breeze rustled the leaves of the young tree beside it.

Somebody had deliberately killed the old man. Not just let him die, but quite deliberately put him to death, murdered him. And he was not the first. All the others had been murdered too and now he, Dr Fraser Callan, was going to have to do something about it. But what? Tell someone? Philip? He wouldn't believe it. The police? They'd ask a lot of questions, find nothing and leave him to stew in the resulting acrimony.

It came to him that there was only one thing he could do. He didn't like it, but he had no choice.

He stayed there on the bench until he'd calmed down enough to control himself, then went back inside, hoping that no one had noticed him. He went to his room, shut the door and looked up the old man's medical record on the computer: '*Friday: Chest infection, put on ampicillin ... Saturday: Stable ... Sunday: Developed into pneumonia, erythromycin added. ...*'

But too late, all too late. He'd died early this morning.

Fraser sat back in his chair and thought, his mind icy calm now. To know that murder had been done wasn't enough, you had to be able to prove it, or at least show evidence for it. Aye, gey and easy – when he hadn't the least idea who was doing it, never mind how it was being done.

Figures. It would come down to figures.

He spent the next two days gathering them, and then keyed in the phone number he'd never thought he'd need again. If Marcus was surprised to hear from him, he didn't show it and told him to come up the day after tomorrow, Friday.

He begged the day off from Edwina, his immediate boss, saying his sick mother needed him again, and caught the early train to London on Friday morning. As the fields of Wiltshire and Berkshire slid by, he thought about Marcus, and Tom. . . .

Marcus Evans was a civil servant with a difference. He ran a small section in the Department of Health whose purpose was to investigate allegations, or even rumours, of wrongdoing in the NHS that couldn't be looked into in any other way. Not many people knew about it. Fraser only did because he'd been on the receiving end of its attentions the year before.

He was shown into Marcus's office in Whitehall at 9.30. Tom was there as well. They both stood and Marcus came across to shake hands.

'Fraser, come and sit down. Would you like some coffee?'

'Aye, I would please.'

As Marcus busied himself pouring it, Fraser glanced round the room. It somehow managed to be both light and formal at the same time, the lightness accentuated by the cream carpet and pale walls, the formality by the dark furnishings and prints of old London.

'Before anything else,' Marcus said as he handed him a cup and saucer, 'may I say how sorry we were to hear about your wife.' Tom nodded and murmured his agreement.

Fraser had to clear his throat before he could reply. 'Thanks.'

Frances had died six months earlier of leukaemia. He knew Tom and Marcus had both been at the funeral, but they'd left without speaking to him.

'Now, how can we help you?' Marcus said.

No point in pussying around it . . . 'I've been working as a locum staff grade at a hospital for older people in Wansborough for the last couple of months, and I think—' he broke off, then continued: 'I know fine well that someone's systematically bumping them off.' His accent, noticeably Glaswegian, became more pronounced as he finished.

In the silence that followed, the curious thought went through his head that Marcus had been held in a time machine since he'd last seen him; he seemed to be wearing exactly the same dark suit and tie, with the same shine to the bald dome of his head above the heavy walrus moustache.

'I see,' Marcus said at last. 'You say *you* know – do you mean you have evidence?' He spoke softly as always, with a faint London twang to his voice.

'Statistical evidence,' Fraser said.

'You know what they say about statistics?' said Tom, speaking for the first time. He hadn't changed much either, Fraser thought – leather jacketed, sharp featured and hard – and there was nothing faint about his London accent.

'Lies and damned lies, you mean? I've no reason for either.' Tom didn't reply and Fraser continued. 'I've compared the death rate at Wansborough with other community hospitals and it's significantly higher.' He reached down to undo his briefcase. 'If you'll just take a look. . . .'

'We'll look at your figures in a minute,' said Marcus. 'You say patients are being killed – any patients, or a particular type or category?'

'Aye. Those whose lives some might say were not worth living.'

'That's subjective, to say the least.'

'I don't mean vegetative cases being allowed to die naturally – that happens, of course – I mean mentally alert people with two or three or more months left to live being deliberately killed.'

'So you're talking about involuntary euthanasia?'

'I am.'

'How's it being done?'

'I don't know. I only know that it *is* being done, and that it's being made to look natural. The victims seem to be dying of pneumonia.'

'Any idea who's doing it?' Tom again.

'No, I don't know that either.'

Marcus regarded him for a moment. Fraser had changed; even with his beard, he could see that his face was thinner, darker, the brown eyes deeper in their sockets making him look more than his thirty-three years. 'Perhaps you'd better tell us from the beginning,' he said. 'How did you come to be working there? It's not really your line, is it?'

'No,' Fraser agreed. He began haltingly: 'After Frances died, I didna know what I wanted to do. . . .'

Although he'd been expecting it, even almost willing it at times, her death had shaken him more than he could have imagined.

He'd tried to lose himself walking over Dartmoor and Exmoor. He dreamed strange dreams in which Frances spoke to him, then woke up crying because he couldn't remember what she'd said. Guilt rode him like a vulture: he was alive, she was dead, it was his fault and he had to atone in some way. Which is why he'd volunteered to go and work in Africa for a year for a charity.

It hadn't worked.

It wasn't the heat, or the flies or the disease, and he liked the people, whom he thought the happiest he'd ever met, despite their poverty. What he couldn't stand was the corruption of some of the petty officials and one day he'd told one of them exactly what he thought of him. It hadn't been well received and his sacking was the price for peace.

'I told you so,' Mary, his mother-in-law, said when he got back. 'So what are you going to do now?'

'I don't know,' he confessed. Fortunately, his house had only been let on a short lease and was empty, but he needed money to pay the mortgage.

'Wait there a minute,' she said, and left the room, coming back a few minutes later with a sheaf of newspaper cuttings. 'I've been meaning to show you these for a long time, but then what with Frances and everything else. . . .' She tailed off. 'Anyway, look at them now while I make some tea.'

It was a series of articles, mostly from the *Telegraph*, on the state of care for older people in NHS hospitals. There were case studies of elderly but relatively healthy people going into hospital for trivial complaints, then dying from the treatment they received there; being found by relatives in urine-soaked bedclothes that hadn't been changed for days; food put out of reach so that they couldn't eat; bedsores you could put your fist into; instructions such as *Not For Resuscitation* and *Nil By Mouth* surreptitiously attached to their notes.

'If you want to help ease the suffering of humanity,' Mary said, 'why don't you go and work in one of those places?'

He looked at her. 'I do remember hearing about this, but I thought they'd sorted it out now.'

'I thought so too, but then last week, I saw this.' She handed him another cutting. The headline said: 'Why did Mabel have to die like this?' Mabel Fisher, a healthy woman in her seventies, had gone into hospital for a minor operation and died there from malnutrition. This was followed by a report from the charity Age Alert claiming that six out of ten older patients in hospital were at risk of malnutrition and dehydration because the nursing staff were simply too busy to feed them properly. This meant that not only were they taking longer to get better and thus exacerbating the bed shortage, but some, like Mabel, were actually dying.

'Six out of ten,' he repeated to himself, 'I knew there was a nursing shortage, but I never thought it was that bad.'

'Well, why don't you go and find out for yourself?'

So, a couple of days later, when he saw the advert for a locum staff grade to cover maternity leave at Wansborough Community Hospital in Wiltshire, he rang the consultant in charge, Dr Armitage, and arranged to go and see him the following afternoon.

Philip Armitage was a smallish man of about fifty, with sandy hair, a goatee and mild grey eyes behind glasses.

'I'll show you round, then we'll have a talk,' he said. He was gently spoken with a faint Midlands accent.

The hospital, which was in the grounds of the Royal Infirmary, was in the form of a misshapen T, with beds in the long stroke and admin in the short. It looked as though it had been built that way to fit into a leftover piece of land (which he found out later was the case). It appeared very cramped from the outside, and yet inside seemed airy and spacious – a bit like an NHS tardis, Fraser thought with a smile.

'How many patients?' he asked.

'Forty-five all together, thirty women and fifteen men.'

It was freshly painted in blue and yellow, clean, well equipped and, so far as he could see, well run. There was also very little smell.

Many of the old hospital wards he remembered, especially those for older patients, had held what he'd thought of as the miasma of the infirm. It's a smell that hits you straight in the nostrils and when you stop noticing it, then it's time to worry, because it's impregnated your clothes.

Fraser commented on it.

'Having a new purpose-built unit helps, of course,' Armitage told him. 'Although good nursing and cleaning staff may have something to do with it.' They walked back to his office. 'Not quite what you were expecting?' he enquired of Fraser with a twinkle.

Fraser had to admit that it wasn't.

'Perhaps you shouldn't believe everything you read in the papers.' His steady gaze and faint smile seemed to be mocking him.

'Perhaps not,' Fraser agreed, reluctantly smiling.

'Oh, I know there were some places that were frankly vile,' Armitage continued, serious now. 'This hospital replaced one of them, in fact. There are still some which, er, leave something to be desired, shall we say? But this isn't one of them.'

'Obviously not,' Fraser said.

There was a knock on the door and a secretary brought in some tea. While Armitage poured, Fraser glanced round the room. It was austere almost to the point of starkness – no photos, no pictures or plants. The only thing of interest was a bookcase that seemed to contain old medical books and Fraser wondered if he was a collector.

'Sugar?'

'Oh – no thanks.'

He handed Fraser his tea and then questioned him about his medical experience. He asked him why he wanted the job.

'The truth is,' Fraser said, 'I'm not sure what I want to do with my career at the moment.' He told him briefly and unemotionally about Frances.

'My dear man, I'm so sorry.'

Fraser couldn't remember the last time he'd been called that, yet there was no doubting Armitage's sincerity.

'Thank you.' He paused. 'I need time, but I also need some money.'

'I can understand that.' Armitage regarded Fraser for a moment. 'I think you're the right person for this post.'

Fraser looked at him in surprise. 'You're offering it to me?'

Armitage nodded. 'Yes.'

'Do you not have other people to interview?'

'Only one other person has showed any interest and I didn't think they were suitable. We were about to re-advertise.'

'I see.'

'Perhaps I should have told you earlier, there's a flat in the doctor's quarters that goes with it.'

Accommodation had been one of the two things worrying Fraser. He now gave voice to the other.

'You mentioned earlier I'd be working under one of your associate specialists, could I meet him – or her?'

'I was about to suggest that,' Armitage said, standing up. 'And it *is* a her – Edwina Tate.'

He took Fraser a little way along the corridor to an open door. The woman working at the VDU swivelled round in her chair and stood up. She was tall and slim, a bit younger than Armitage, with a thin face and long dark hair shot with grey.

'Hello.' She held out a soft hand, then, at Armitage's prompting, outlined what she wanted. She had a somehow otherworldly manner and Fraser neither liked nor disliked her. He felt he could work with her.

As they left, Armitage said, 'While you're here, you'd better meet Ranjid, our other associate specialist and also my deputy.' He tapped on another door, marked Dr R Singh, and pushed it open. 'Oh – I'm sorry, Ranjid, you're busy.' He quickly pulled the door shut and they moved on.

'So you'll think about it and let me know?' he said to Fraser as they returned to his office.

'I'll do that,' said Fraser.

'Tomorrow? I'm sorry to push you, but if you don't want it, we're going to have to look for someone else.'

'Of course,' Fraser said. 'Tomorrow.'

He had thought about it as his MG roared throatily back along the motorway to Bristol. Wansborough itself was possibly the most unappealing town he'd seen in his life, viciously ugly office blocks and windswept car parks and shopping malls, but he'd rather liked Armitage and felt he could rub along with Edwina.

He also thought about the scene he'd witnessed in the second before Armitage had pulled the door shut of Ranjid Singh's office – two faces, the one behind the desk clearly Asian with good-looking, regular features now twisted in anger, the other swivelled round towards them, startlingly beautiful, the beauty accentuated by the flush over the high cheekones and the twin tear trails.

As Armitage had observed, they'd been busy – a new variant of doctors and nurses, perhaps?

Was it any concern of his? No.

Besides, he'd thought, it was only for four months.

CHAPTER 2

Philip Armitage had that quality in common with all the best doctors Fraser had known of regarding every patient as an individual, someone for whose well-being he was personally responsible. Of course, he reflected, all doctors should have it, but some have it more than others.

Armitage did four ward rounds a week, two with Edwina Tate's patients, two with Ranjid Singh's. They both had an equal number of patients and all three senior doctors were present on every round.

'How are you feeling, Mrs Hobbs?'

Martha Hobbs, aged seventy-five, was recovering from a hip replacement and her wound site had become infected with MRSA.

'Better than I was, thankee, doctor,' she said in ripe Wiltshire. 'Still hurts here, though.' She indicated the infected site. Her face was round and wrinkled, haloed with fluffy white hair, her eyes like a pair of blackcurrants.

Armitage examined the wound site. 'You're feeling better because the antibiotics are working,' he said. He felt her forehead. 'Your temperature's coming down.' He knew this already from the chart. 'And so is your pulse rate. The discomfort may last a little while, but you're on the mend, Mrs Hobbs. Tell Sister if the pain goes on bothering you and she'll give you something for it.' He patted her hand and they left the single room – most of the rooms in the hospital held six beds, but MRSA patients were nursed in isolation.

They stopped outside. There were eight of them: Armitage, Singh, Edwina, Fraser, Helen St John, who was the senior sister, another sister and a couple of house officers. Fraser had to make an effort not to stare at Sister St John, for she was the woman he'd glimpsed crying in Ranjid Singh's room.

'That antibiotic is taking its time,' said Tim Oakley, one of the housemen. 'Should we add another?'

'I don't think so,' Edwina said. 'The lab said the organism's sensitive to

Vancomycin and I think we—'

'Excuse me,' a soft voice behind them said – they were blocking the corridor and a young healthcare assistant with a loaded tea trolley was trying to get past.

Armitage smiled at her and backed against the wall. When she'd rattled by, he turned to the houseman. 'It may seem to be taking its time, Tim, but it's clearing the infection.'

Next was Edith Underwood, eighty-three, and suffering from Multi Stroke Disease. Armitage spoke gently to her, but she was deeply unconscious. He briefly examined her, then ushered them out.

'You've spoken to her family?' he asked Edwina.

'Yes. They know she's on diamorphine and fluids only, and they're fully in agreement.' She hesitated. 'She hasn't spoken for a month and they know she's not going to.'

Fraser had no trouble in believing it; there had been a blankness about her face, a sense of something missing.

Armitage nodded and they moved on. In another side room lay Stanley Oglevy, seventy-nine, with Lewy Body Dementia, a disease similar to Alzheimer's, but more aggressive. He'd been admitted with a broken hip after falling out of bed. He'd been made comfortable and his daughter had agreed that it would not be in his best interest to treat any further condition that might arise.

'I think he has pneumonia,' Edwina said quietly.

Armitage sat by the bed. 'Mr Oglevy?'

There was no answer, so he carefully undid his pyjama jacket and listened to his chest, painfully thin, as it slowly rose and fell, rose and fell.

'I think you're right,' he said, rebuttoning the jacket and replacing the bedclothes. He stood up and turned to the staff nurse. 'Continue intravenous fluids and keep him comfortable.'

'Do we treat the pneumonia?' Tim asked.

'I don't think so,' Edwina said.

'I agree,' Armitage said.

After the ward round was finished, Fraser went with Edwina back to her office. It was almost as spartan as Armitage's.

'We've got ten minutes before Referrals Clinic,' she said. 'Perhaps you'd like to give me your thoughts on what you've seen so far.'

'Well, I'm impressed.' Realizing that more was required, he went on. 'I like the way you all act as a team, I like the way Philip leads from the middle, and I especially like the way every patient is treated with respect – Mr and Mrs – rather than with false chumminess.'

She smiled. 'What about the decisions we made not to treat?'

'I think in those two cases they were right.'

'Good,' she said. 'After all the bad publicity we've been having, I know some places have started treating cases like Mr Oglevy again. In his case, I think it would be cruel.'

'I'm glad you have the courage of your convictions,' Fraser said.

She smiled again and nodded as if to say: You'll do.

In the Referrals Clinic, as with the Out Patients' Clinic later in the day, he thought she handled the patients briskly and competently. Her policy seemed to be to keep them out of hospital for as long as possible.

'You've probably noticed yourself,' she said when they'd finished, 'how some people seem to give up the moment they're in hospital, especially older patients. It's as though it's a signal to them that their time's up.'

At six he walked back to his flat, which was in an uninspiring grey block about a hundred yards away. Even to call it a flat was euphemistic, he thought as he let himself in – it consisted of a single room with en-suite loo and bath.

He showered, then went back to the canteen for a meal – he didn't feel up to taking on the shared kitchen yet. Then, back to his room, where he immersed himself in the book Armitage had lent him, studying especially Multi Stroke Disease and Lewy Body Dementia. Edwina was right, he thought – the prognosis was grim in both cases.

By ten, he'd had enough and decided to visit the doctors' bar. He had a bottle of whisky in his case, but thought the walk and fresh air might do him good.

The east wind had teeth and he was glad of his coat – spring was late and the site was on a hill on the outskirts of the town. The doctors' bar was in the main hospital and very quiet by the time he found it, just a couple of small groups of people talking in low voices. He had a pint by himself at the bar, then the deadness of the place got to him and he left.

His flat was beside a playing field and, across it, he could see a brightly lit entrance and caught a gust of laughter on the wind – the social club bar.

On a whim, he followed the dimly lit path that led round the perimeter of the playing field. A copse ran along the far side with a high wall behind it.

There were perhaps a score of people in the bar, some playing darts, some chatting, two or three sitting on their own. Tobacco smoke layered the air. He bought a beer and joined the loners – by not joining them. He'd had a solitary nature since his youth, even more so since Frances had died. So why did he feel more comfortable in this smoky, grubby, noisy den than in the doctors' bar, he asked himself? Were they more his kind of people? Maybe. Or maybe it was because for all its vulgarity and soon to be banned smoke, it was somehow more authentic.

He finished his pint and bought another. His mind went back to Frances. He'd been thinking about her after his talk with Edwina, how precious those last few months had been – in fact, he thought now, some of those days and evenings before she died had even held a kind of happiness; watching TV with her, reading, playing chess, just *being* with her.

Life is precious, he thought – and yet only that day he'd agreed about allowing the two vegetative patients to die. But those decisions had been made with respect, a love of humanity.

He was being maudlin. It was time to go. He drained his glass and left. No one paid him any attention. This time, he walked slowly across the playing field, needing the aloneness and anonymity the black hole in the middle gave him.

The sheer mass of the main hospital block reared in front of him, the non-pattern of the lighted windows making it look like a giant computer. Tears stung his cheeks before being whipped away by the wind. What the hell am I doing here, he wondered?

Time passed as he absorbed the unit's routines. In the evenings he read in his room, sometimes went over to the social dub. Weekends, he went back to Bristol.

By and large, he got on well enough with Edwina, with only one blip. Patients with dementia were usually moved on to a nursing home as soon as their acute condition had been treated, but there were some borderline cases – like Mrs Chambers. Her dementia was partial, caused by cerebral atherosclerosis, but she'd clearly never be able to look after herself again. Sometimes she could speak quite lucidly, more often not. Her only visitors were her care worker and a welfare officer. She had to wear a nappy and had no modesty about it whatsoever, lying on her bed with flaccid white legs and nappy on full display. She was always pressing her bell for attention and when the harassed HCA put it out of her reach, she would pester the other patients and their visitors in her reedy, penetrating voice until she got it back. Then she'd press it again. She was terminally pathetic, Fraser thought. Helpless but unlovable.

She got a chest infection and Edwina put her on ampicillin. The next day Fraser was called by the staff nurse to look at her. He thought she had pneumonia and his inclination was to add another antibiotic, but felt he ought to check with Edwina first. She'd always told him she had an open door policy, so he tapped on her door and went in. She had company – a large, slightly florid man in a baggy tweed suit and a smartly dressed woman with short blonde hair.

'What is it, Fraser?' she said abruptly.

'Ah ... sorry to interrupt you, Edwina – it's Mrs Chambers in room three, I think her chest infection's developed into full-blown pneumonia.'

'I'll come and see her when I've finished here.'

As he turned to go, the blonde woman said, 'Aren't you going to introduce us, Edwina?' Edwina did so – reluctantly, it seemed to Fraser. 'This is our local MP, Patricia Matlock.' She was thirty-five going on fifty, attractive with vivid blue eyes. 'And this is George Woodvine, Chairman of the Trust.' He was around sixty, with thick white hair, a tanned face and military moustache.

'You're a long way from home, Dr Callan,' the MP observed, appraising him as she did.

'And also a very busy man,' Edwina said firmly before he could reply.

She came looking for him fifteen minutes later and together they examined Mrs Chambers.

'Should we add another antibiotic?' Fraser asked.

'All right,' Edwina agreed. 'Erythromycin. Oh, and Fraser,' she said as they walked away, 'for future reference, if you find my door open, come in. If you don't, don't.'

Mrs Chambers died that night.

He hadn't made much effort to get to know any of his colleagues socially, so when a few days later he saw Ranjid Singh sitting at a table in the canteen on his own, he went over to him.

'Mind if I join you, Ranjid?'

Ranjid looked up. 'Sorry, but I'm expecting company,' he said. It was a small table, too small for three.

'Sure,' said Fraser. He was moving away when Helen St John arrived.

'Were you going to join us, Dr Callan?'

'It's all right, there isn't really room.'

'For goodness sake, we can move.'

She took her tray to an adjacent table. Fraser followed. Ranjid joined them with evident ill grace.

They began eating. She said, 'How are you settling in, Dr Callan?'

'It's Fraser,' he said. 'Well enough, I think – although maybe you ought to direct the question to Edwina.'

'I'd have thought the confidence she's displaying in you answered that.'

'Thank you,' Fraser said with a cheesy grin.

There was a silence while they ate. Aware of the awkwardness, he said, 'Have you worked here long – er – Helen, isn't it?'

'Helen,' she agreed, a smile dimpling her cheeks. 'Since the hospital was opened, about eighteen months ago. Before that, I was in London.'

'D'you prefer it here?'

She made a mouth. 'In some ways. I don't have a problem with London. You, I take it, are from Glasgow.'

He grinned, genuinely this time. 'Is it that obvious?'

'It's . . . distinctive,' she said. Her own accent was pure Home Counties and hockey.

He glanced at Ranjid, who seemed to be concentrating on his food. 'How about you, Ranjid?' he asked.

Ranjid looked up. 'How about me – what?'

'Have you worked here long?'

'Since the hospital opened,' he replied, staring back without expression. 'Before that I worked at St James', which was formerly the hospital in Wansborough for older patients. Does that answer your question?'

'It does, thank you.' *And sod you too, Ranjid – or do I mean Rancid?*

'Good,' said rancid Ranjid. 'And you, Dr Callan, did you work for long in Glasgow, or did you perhaps have a problem with it?' He put down his knife and fork although his meal was barely half finished. 'Forgive me, I have work to do.' He got up and took his tray over to the stacker.

Helen watched him with compressed lips; her eyes glittered and her face flushed as it had that time he'd seen her in his room. 'Excuse me,' she said abruptly, getting up. She caught up with Ranjid, spoke to him angrily as she followed him out.

'Weird,' Fraser muttered to himself. But it was none of his business.

CHAPTER 3

Fraser got to work the next morning to find that Frederick Allsop had died during the night. He'd been admitted the week before with a broken arm after a fall – he was seventy-six and had Parkinson's Disease. He'd been made comfortable, but had got a chest infection and been put on ampicillin. What surprised Fraser was that the infection hadn't responded to the antibiotic and had developed so quickly into pneumonia.

'Mind if I join you?'

He looked up to see Helen St John.

'No, of course not.'

He was lunching alone in the canteen. She put down her tray and sat opposite him. She said awkwardly, 'I wanted to apologize for yesterday.'

'You don't have anything to apologize for.' He carefully avoided putting any stress on the 'you'.

'Mm.' After a pause, she said, 'I take it Philip hasn't said anything to you about Ranjid?'

He shook his head.

'Then I suppose I'd better.' She paused, picked up her fork and picked at the food on her plate.

She said, 'Ranjid hasn't had much luck in life recently. His wife left him and he was involved in a long drawn-out custody battle for the children. She won and took them back to India.'

'I'm sorry,' Fraser said without expression.

'It would help if you'd try and be patient with him.'

Fraser nodded as he put down his knife and fork. 'I'll do that. Thanks for telling me.'

She gave the slightest of shrugs. 'Someone had to.'

After a moment he said, 'Can I get you a tea or coffee?'

'That would be nice, but if you'll wait till I've finished, we'll go to the coffee lounge. More comfortable.'

'OK.'

He glanced covertly at her. She really was beautiful, he realized, not just attractive. It was the combination of her high cheekbones, widely spaced grey eyes and full, almost bee-stung lips. How old would she be? Mid-thirties? A bit older than him, he thought, and at the pitch of her beauty . . . she looked up suddenly, smiling as she put her fork down, the smile instantly banishing the slight look of petulance to her mouth.

They took their trays to the stacker.

'Where is he now?' he asked as they went out.

'Ranjid? At a meeting somewhere.' She led him to the lounge and found an armchair while he bought the coffee.

'Thanks,' she said as he handed it to her.

He sat beside her. 'I couldn't help noticing,' he said, fishing, 'that he seemed a wee bit sensitive when I asked him how long he'd been here.'

'Mm. It's not-so-ancient history, part of the baggage we carry around.'

'I'm listening.'

'You don't remember hearing anything about St James' hospital a couple of years ago? It was a national scandal.'

He shook his head.

'It was the old workhouse – appropriately. I say *was*, but it's still in existence – some imbecile's trying to have it Grade Two listed. Anyway, it was the worst type of geriatric hospital – out of sight, out of conscience so far as the public were concerned. Then the aged parent of some TV celebrity died there – she'd gone in with a urinary tract infection and ended up more or less starving to death. The TV celeb, who probably hadn't given dear old mum a thought in years, made a cause célèbre out of it.'

'Exaggerated?'

'Not entirely, no.' It really had been a terrible place, she told him, standards of hygiene non-existent, nursing not much better and food that had to be seen to be believed because the catering staff stole all the decent stuff.

'Not that it made much difference, nobody bothered to feed them properly, so they all suffered from malnutrition.'

Not knowing what to say, he grimaced.

'They probably didn't suffer as much as you'd think,' she said, 'since they were all dosed to the gills with diamorphine.'

He said slowly, 'I don't know whether that makes it better or worse.'

'To tell you the truth, neither do I.' She sighed. 'Anyway, our TV celeb managed to blow it into a major scandal. I'm surprised you didn't hear about it.'

'I'd have still been in Scotland at the time.'

She looked at him curiously. 'You Scots aren't kidding about being separate, are you?'

He grinned at her as it occurred to him that he was in no great rush to get back to work. 'What do you mean by major scandal?'

'Oh, it was all over the national press and TV. There were demands for heads to roll – our local MP, Patricia Matlock, was a junior minister in the DOH, an *ambitious* junior minister. She'd been banging on about health standards, so it really was embarrassing for her.'

'I've met her,' Fraser said.

'Really?' She looked genuinely surprised and he explained how he'd seen her in Edwina's room. 'Well,' she continued. 'She managed to retrieve the situation by forming a committee with some of the trust managers to sort it out. Philip was headhunted and redesigned the new hospital. While it was being finished, he got a team together of people he knew or had worked with before – including me and Edwina – then the staff at St James' were mostly sacked or moved away.'

'I see. Why wasn't Ranjid sacked or moved away?'

'He'd been preoccupied with his custody battle. Also, he had tried to warn the trust about the place, but no one had taken any notice. Anyway, some of the fallout did stick to him and he's still rather bitter about it.'

Fraser said, 'I'm surprised Philip wanted him on his team.'

'Philip's a rather remarkable man.'

'I'm beginning to realize that.'

'You know he's giving a talk here tomorrow night?'

'No, I didn't.'

'You could do worse than go. The Postgrad Centre at seven.'

'Are you going?'

'I might.'

That night, Alice Steel died of pneumonia. She'd been seventy-three and suffering from breast cancer with perhaps only two or three months to live, but she hadn't been ready to die and was determined to make a fight of it. Fraser had liked her for her gutsiness – it was he who'd put her on ampicillin for a chest infection.

He found Edwina and told her. 'We seem to be having a lot of fatal pneumonia at the moment,' he said.

'Well, it is a common cause of death in old people.'

Fraser thought for a moment. 'It would have to be either Haemophilus or pneumococcus, wouldn't it?' he said, naming the two types of bacteria usually responsible.

'Probably,' she agreed.

'Well, if it was Haemophilus, it wouldn't have developed into pneumonia so quickly, and if it was pneumococcus, it would have been sensitive to ampicillin . . . wouldn't it?'

'Haemophilus can be virulent in older people,' she said. 'And we do sometimes come across resistant pneumococci.'

'Is it worth trying to find out which?'

'Oh, I don't think so, do you? It wouldn't have altered anything.'

There were about forty people in the Postgrad Centre when Fraser got there, mostly housemen and nurses, he thought. He spotted Helen by herself towards the back and went to join her. She was wearing a pink top that heightened her complexion. Armitage was on the platform with a man in an immaculate dark suit and Fraser asked who he was.

'Patrick Fitzpatrick. He's director of community medicine.'

The chatter died away as Fitzpatrick got to his feet and introduced Armitage in a flamboyant Irish brogue. There was polite applause as he came forward.

'I wonder if it might have been better if you'd waited until I'd finished,' Armitage said, 'To see whether you felt I was worth applauding.'

There was a ripple of laughter.

'When I was a houseman,' he began, 'geriatrics, as we called it then, was regarded as the fag end of medicine. By the time I retire, I hope that Care of the Older Patient will be regarded as one of medicine's most important as well as most rewarding areas.' His voice was light and intimate and he had a way of looking round that made everyone there feel as though he was addressing them personally.

People dreaded old age, he told them, which when you thought about it was ridiculous – it ought to be the most pleasant stage of life, the time when you can take stock and take the time to enjoy your family and friends.

'So why do people dread it so much?' he asked, looking round again.

Because for some, there was good reason to dread it – sickness and incapacity of both mind and body, and as if they weren't bad enough, a lack of proper care.

'I'm sure you've all heard of the death wards where old people were incarcerated until they died – the irony is that they weren't only appallingly cruel, but uneconomic as well. By treating older patients humanely, you can actually save money. We've proved that here. How? By keeping them out of hospital for as long as possible and, when they do have to be admitted, making their stay as short as possible.'

He went on to describe the practical means by which they'd achieved this. He finished to solid applause and Fitzpatrick took questions. There were a lot, and by the time the meeting broke up, Fraser was surprised to find that over an hour had gone by.

'He's a good speaker,' he said to Helen. 'He made it interesting.'

'Why don't you tell him that?'

'I will.' He stood up, paused. 'D'you fancy a drink afterwards?'

She hesitated, then: 'All right,' she said.

They made their way down. Armitage thanked Fraser for his comments, then introduced him to Fitzpatrick.

'A fellow Celt, if I'm not mistaken,' Fitzpatrick said, shaking him heartily by the hand. 'Patrick Fitzpatrick. I'm the original Irish joke.'

'Fraser Callan,' said Fraser, not quite knowing how to take him. He was about five feet nine, an inch shorter than Fraser, with a round face, very blue eyes and dark hair beginning to go grey.

'So what brings you to the land of the Sassenachs, Fraser?'

'Er – gainful employment, I suppose.'

'Ah,' he said sonorously. 'Another who has had to leave the land of his fathers in order to live.'

Helen and Armitage, who were standing together, exchanged resigned looks.

'Aye,' Fraser agreed. 'I've sold my birthright to the mighty pound.'

Fitzpatrick laughed, then said, 'Well, you couldn't ask for a better colleague than Philip – or indeed the fair Helen here.'

'Shut up, Patrick,' she said. 'Or I'll go.'

'Are you coming next week, my love?'

'I'll try.'

'Oh, do, *please*, my heart of hearts. And why don't you bring Fraser with you?' He turned to Fraser before she could answer. 'I've become a father and I'm welcoming the fruit of my loins into the world with an orgy. Tomorrow week, my house. Do come.'

'I'll – er – do my best,' said Fraser. He thanked Armitage again and they left.

'Is he real?' he asked Helen in a low voice.

'I'm afraid so.' After a pause, she said, 'I can never make up my mind whether he really is a fool, or whether he's fooling the rest of us.'

She led the way to a lift. As it rose, he said, 'You don't have to take me to his party, Helen.'

'I know. I haven't decided whether I want to go or not anyway.'

'Why don't I take you?'

She smiled. 'Because I might want to leave earlier than you.'

The lift stopped and the door opened.

'I'll be going back to Bristol, so I'll have to leave pretty early,' he replied.

'I'll think about it.'

The doctors' bar was crowded. He bought her a glass of wine and himself a beer.

'How old is Patrick?' he asked.

'About fifty, I think. Why?'

'Is this his first child?'

'Oh, I see ... No, he's got four daughters by his first wife. He only plucked up the courage to leave her when his girlfriend got pregnant. He's Catholic,' she added, as though this explained everything.

And so it did, to an extent, he thought – also perhaps the slightly desperate edge to all the badinage. He put the thought to her.

'You could be right,' she said with a shrug.

He wondered if her sudden coolness was due to Fitzpatrick's clumsy attempt at pushing them together, so he turned to neutral topics while they finished their drinks, then went with her to the entrance.

Strange how she blew hot and cold, he thought as he walked back to his flat. Why had she come to the talk? She must have heard Armitage speak on this before ... he wondered about their relationship – she clearly admired Philip Armitage and he'd felt their closeness earlier, even though they weren't obviously in each other's pockets. Close, yes, but platonic.

Not that it concerned him. It wasn't as if he fancied her or anything.

CHAPTER 4

Fraser got back after the weekend to find that Olive Spencer had died of pneumonia on Sunday. She'd been another 'faller', admitted with a broken hip. She was seventy-three and had Multiple Sclerosis, but it was under control and she'd been an intelligent woman, alert and impatient with herself for being so clumsy.

Fraser checked her notes. Chest infection Friday night, ampicillin prescribed by Becca Lake. It had developed into pneumonia on Saturday and by the time anyone thought to add another antibiotic, it was too late.

Exactly the same pattern as the others . . . Fraser drummed his fingers on his desk for a moment, then started going through the patient files on the computer.

In the four weeks he'd been there, six patients had died from pneumonia despite treatment. Six had been treated and survived. He went through Singh's patients and found a further five deaths.

Eleven patients in a month. This was a lot. Sure, pneumonia was common in older people, but this common? With this high a death rate?

He took down David's *Principles of Medicine* from the shelf and leafed through it, but could find nothing about epidemics of pneumonia. He wondered about discussing it with Ranjid since both Philip and Edwina were away that day, but his attitude to Fraser had been so offhand since the incident in the canteen that he decided not to. Instead, he went over to the hospital library, but couldn't find anything there either, other than information indicating that the speed of the infections meant they were almost certainly pneumococcal.

On the way back, he found himself passing Pathology and on impulse went in and asked to speak to the microbiologist. The receptionist phoned through and, after a couple of minutes, took him up.

'Dr Callan? I'm Roderick Stones.' He was a small, slender man with thinning grey hair and a rather abrupt manner. 'Have a seat. How can I help?'

Fraser explained. 'What I wanted to ask you is whether this could be some kind of epidemic?'

'Is this something Dr Tate has asked you to look into?'

'Well, not as such, no – she's away today. To tell you the truth, I came in more or less on a whim because I couldn't find anything in the library.' As he said this, he was aware of Stones' pale blue eyes watching him.

'I see. I have to say I'm rather surprised you should have come here without telling her.'

Thinking this more than a little pedantic, but not wanting trouble, Fraser said, 'I take your point, Dr Stones. Edwina's due back tomorrow, so I'll raise it with her then.' He made to get up.

'Oh, sit down – now that you're here. D'you have any names?'

Fraser sat down again and showed him the list he'd made. 'Only one actually had samples sent to the lab.'

'But they're all patients of Dr Tate?'

'Er – no, five of them are Dr Singh's.'

'I see. So he's away too, is he?'

Resisting the urge to squirm, Fraser said, 'No, he isn't. As I explained just now, I came in on a whim. But you're right, perhaps I should have spoken to them first.'

'Eleven in four weeks,' Stones mused. 'It may seem like a lot, but it's not what I'd call exceptional, bearing in mind their ages and the time of year.'

Fraser swallowed and said, 'I accept that, Dr Stones, but what about the fact that they're resistant to ampicillin? I didn't think that was common in pneumococci.'

'Oh, we don't use so passé a term as resistance with pneumococci anymore. True resistance *is* rare, but not insensitivity. Let me show you.'

He turned to the computer terminal on his desk and rattled the keys.

'Here's your patient, and look – the organism isn't sensitive to ampicillin, but nor is it truly resistant. By the time you started treatment, the infection was consolidated. He was an old man, the organism was insensitive ... I'm afraid it happens. Let's go back a little and find one who recovered. . . .'

Fraser watched, feeling more foolish by the minute.

'Ah, here we are – this one, you see, has a completely different sensitivity pattern, which knocks any idea of an epidemic on the head.' He swivelled round in his chair. 'Let me tell you something about the pneumococcus. Did you know it used to be called the Old Man's Friend?'

'No, I didn't.'

'It's a term not used so much now. It acquired the name before the widespread use of antibiotics, because it was probably the most common cause of death in the elderly then.'

'Why Friend?'

'I was just coming to that,' he said testily. 'Because it seemed to target those people whose life had come to a natural end, and also because, before diamorphine, it was probably the kindest way to die there was. The patient becomes drowsy, then slips easily into a deep sleep followed by coma. There's no pain or discomfort, just peace and rest. In some cases, it's positively cruel to treat with antibiotics.'

Fraser apologized for bothering him and saw himself out.

Ranjid summoned him to his office immediately after lunch.

'Shut the door, please and sit down. How *dare* you go behind my back, discussing my patients with Dr Stones?' He was actually shaking with rage.

Fraser tried to explain how it had come about. '. . . And when I noticed how you seemed to have as many cases as Edwina, I thought—'

'You told him we have an epidemic. . . .'

'I *asked* him, Rancid. It seemed to me—'

'*What did you call me?*'

'I—'

'You just called me Rancid – I heard you. You find that amusing, a racist pun on my name?'

Oh God, how could I have? 'No, of course not. . . .'

'Get out. Get out of my sight. There is no place for you here.'

'Ranjid, I—'

'I'm not interested in your excuses – save them for Dr Armitage.'

Fraser agonized through the afternoon whether to try ringing Philip in the evening; in the end he left a note on his desk explaining what had happened. The next morning, after clinic, Philip called him to his office.

'You know what this is about, of course?'

'Yes, and I'm very sorry it should have occurred.'

'So am I, Fraser.' He sighed. 'What possessed you to call him Rancid?'

'I don't know, Philip, it just slipped out. It was quite unintentional.'

'I'm sure it was. Unfortunate, though.' He paused for a moment, then continued: 'Ranjid is in rather a fragile emotional state at the moment, and these days, any charge of racism has to be taken seriously.'

'It wasn't meant to be racist. I'm not racist.'

'I'm sure you're not. However, taken with the other business. . . .'

'D'you want my resignation?'

'Oh, hopefully it shouldn't come to that.' He looked at him. 'Unless it's what you want. Is it?'

'No.'

'Well, let's look for a way around it. What made you go to Roderick Stones in the first place?'

Fraser explained and Philip let out a sigh.

'If you'd come to me with this, I'd have praised your observation and initiative. However, going to Dr Stones was a mistake.'

'I do see that.'

'Not entirely, you don't – he and Ranjid go back a long way and it was inevitable Dr Stones would tell him.'

Fraser groaned.

'Why didn't you go to Ranjid first, since he was here?'

Fraser hesitated. 'To be honest, because I didn't think our relationship was very good.'

'Professionalism should come before personal feelings, Fraser.'

'Yes, it should.'

Another pause. 'Are you still worried about the number of pneumonia cases here?'

'Aye, I am a bit.'

Philip steepled his fingers, pressed them against his lips. 'Pneumonia's probably the most common cause of death here, especially at this time of year – April isn't called the cruellest month for nothing.'

Fraser nodded. 'I realize that, but what's bothering me is that so many cases seem to be resistant to ampicillin – or insensitive, perhaps I should say. Is there not a case for using a different antibiotic?'

'Which would you suggest?'

'Well . . .' Fraser hesitated, realizing he'd been put on the spot. 'Tetracycline?'

'A lot of pneumococci and Haemophilus are resistant to it now.'

'Erythromycin, then?'

'Same problem, besides which, it's not as efficacious as ampicillin.'

'How about cefataxin?'

'Fine for pneumococci, not so good for Haemophilus.'

'Vancomycin? Gentamycin? Chloramphenicol?'

'All rather toxic. The fact is, ampicillin does remain the drug of choice, even though we are seeing some insensitivity to it. It's good that you're thinking about these things though, which is why I don't want to lose you. Unfortunately,' he continued, 'Ranjid wants his pound of flesh. I suggest we try and get him to accept an ounce. Would you be prepared to apologize to him in front of me and assure him it won't happen again? After which, so far as I'm concerned, it would be forgotten.'

What had he to lose? 'All right,' he said.

'Good. I'll go and put it to him now.'

But as they shook hands on it shortly afterwards, it was obvious to Fraser that Ranjid was neither going to forget nor forgive.

He went and found Edwina to apologize to her as well, but she gazed at him blankly and said she didn't know what he was talking about. He explained.

She said, 'So you're happy now with what Philip told you about the pneumonia cases?'

'Yes.'

She shrugged. 'OK then, fine. You've apologized and it's over. Forget it.'

He'd been expecting worse. She must live her life in compartments, he thought as he walked away; if something didn't directly concern her, she wasn't interested. OK then, fine.

CHAPTER 5

'Wow,' Fraser said. He was looking down the face of a scarp that dropped 500 feet into a broad valley below.

'That's Patrick's village there,' Helen said pointing, although all he could make out was a church tower poking up through the blanket of trees.

He'd forgotten about Fitzpatrick's orgy and hadn't understood what Helen was talking about at first when she'd told him she'd like to accept his offer of a lift.

'If you've changed your mind about going, don't worry,' she'd said.

'No, I'd like to take you,' he'd said.

He'd picked her up at her house and she'd directed him south to a narrow road that threaded its way up through the downs. Spring had sprung at last and it was warm enough to drop the car top. The trees and hedges were dusty green, lambs bleated and blackbirds warbled throatily as they reached the summit – and the scarp.

'I wouldn't like to come off the road here,' he said now as the MG's snout pointed down. The exhaust burbled gently in protest as he switched round a series of hairpins, then the road levelled out and after a mile, they ran into a village square.

'That way,' Helen said, and a few minutes later they pulled up in the gravel outside a long, low cottage.

Fitzpatrick came out to meet them. 'You look ravishing, my dear – or should that be ravishable?'

'Hello, Patrick,' she said as he kissed her cheek.

She did look good, Fraser thought. She was wearing a primrose-coloured shift dress over designer jeans.

Patrick led them down a stone passage and into a long living room split by a fireplace – the house was much bigger than it seemed from the outside. A score or so of people generated a low buzz.

'Come and have some punch,' Patrick said, taking them over to a drinks table. 'Don't worry, it's not strong.'

31

Philip, who was talking with Edwina and a couple of others nodded and smiled. A woman got up and came over to them.

'My wife, Marie,' Patrick said.

She was about thirty, startlingly pretty with red hair and milky skin. 'Hello, pleased to meet you,' she said. 'Love your dress, Helen. . . .'

Fraser had been expecting an Irish accent, but it was English, with more than a hint of estuary.

As Patrick ladled punch, Fraser became aware of another figure beside them. Patrick said, 'Ah . . . Fraser, may I – er – introduce you to Nigel Fleming, Chief Executive and also my boss.'

The head baboon, thought Fraser as they shook hands. The nerviness he'd noticed before in Patrick before had suddenly erupted again. And not a lot of love lost between them. . . .

'So, how long have you been with us now, Fraser?' Fleming asked him as Patrick smartly faded away.

'A wee bit over a month.'

'Are you enjoying it here?'

He might not look like a baboon, Fraser thought as they exchanged half a dozen meaningless sentences – he was about six foot, pale fleshed with a dark widow's peak – but he was without any doubt the tribe's dominant male, powerful enough to simply not care about what others thought of him.

'Well, I hope you enjoy your time with us,' he said, the shutters coming down as he judged Fraser, found him wanting and turned away to look for someone more interesting.

Helen was with Philip. Fraser was about to go over to them, but the intimate way they were talking made him hesitate. He mingled rather unsatisfactorily for a while – then a bell rang in the hall and Patrick hurried out. A moment later, a fantastic figure appeared in the doorway. It wore full evening dress with cloak, cane and top hat. The entire room was stunned to silence.

'Good evening, everyone,' the figure said in fruity tones, and resolved itself into George Woodvine, whom Fraser had last seen in Edwina's office with the local MP . . . What was her name? She was with him now – did they go everywhere together, he wondered? Matlock, that was it, Patricia Matlock – he remembered her now, with her short blonde hair and blue eyes.

'Are we to see the infant?' Woodvine enquired. 'Or is this a celebration in absentia?'

'As usual, your timing's impeccable,' said Patrick. 'Marie's feeding him now and he'll be down in a couple of minutes. Let me take your cloak.'

Woodvine handed him his accoutrements, then turned to greet

Fleming, who'd walked over to him. 'Good evening, Nigel.'

'Good evening, George.'

Not a huge amount of affection there either, Fraser reflected.

Philip and someone else came in with trays of champagne. Patrick returned with Marie, who was holding a baby.

'Would you do the honours, George?'

'Delighted.' He turned to the guests. 'Are your glasses charged? Excellent.' He turned back to the baby and solemnly addressed it. 'May you be blessed with the health, humour and comeliness of both your parents.' He raised his glass, and his voice. 'I give you Patrick Fitzpatrick the Second.'

As this echoed round the room, the baby let out an outraged howl and everyone laughed as Marie took him out again. Fraser found himself next to Philip Armitage.

'You decided to come then, Fraser?'

'Patrick made it difficult to refuse.'

Philip grinned at him, his expression saying it was good to see him socializing rather than sulking. They exchanged a few words, then he said, 'I think Nigel's going, I'd better go and say goodbye to him.'

Fraser looked round for Helen and saw her with Woodvine by the drinks table. He made his way over.

'George,' she said. 'This is Fraser Callan, our new staff grade.'

'We've already met,' Woodvine said with a smile, his white teeth and thick white hair accentuating the ruddy tan of his face. Holding up the whisky bottle, he continued, 'Will ye take a wee dram wi' me Fraser?' The accent was perfect and Fraser and Helen both burst out laughing.

'I'll take that as a yes,' Woodvine said.

'Noo,' said Fraser. 'I'd love to, but I'm driving.'

'My commiserations.'

'I enjoyed your speech,' Fraser said.

'For its brevity, I imagine.'

'And its felicity.'

Woodvine looked at him, his eyes grey and very clear. 'Now that is a compliment,' he said. 'Thank you.'

'George,' a voice called softly.

They looked round – it was Patrick, who'd come back into the room.

'I'll speak to you both later,' George said, and went over to him.

'I think you made an impression there,' Helen said quietly. 'It's usually George who does the impressing.'

'Oh, he did that fine well,' Fraser said. 'His entrance was something to behold.'

By common accord, they drifted over to the room's perimeter.

'Glad you came?' she asked.

'I wasn't at first.' He told her in a low voice about his time with the head baboon. 'He seemed to have a pretty negative effect on Patrick too,' he said.

'I know,' she said. 'It'll change now he's gone.'

'Why?'

She lowered her voice. 'He and Patrick don't get on. Well, actually, they loathe and detest the sight of each other, but Patrick had to invite him and Fleming had to come. Patrick always goes a bit flaky when he's around.'

'Why do they loathe and detest each other?'

'Ancient history. I'll tell you later.'

'Tell me now, no one can hear us here.'

She glanced round, bent her head closer. 'Remember what I was telling you the other day about St James'?'

He nodded, breathing in her musky perfume.

'Well, Fleming blames Patrick for not foreseeing it.'

'With any justification?'

'Patrick is director of community medicine, so in theory it was his responsibility.'

'Sounds to me more like Fleming trying to duck the buck.'

She grinned. 'Ah, but you like Patrick, don't you?'

'Don't you?'

'Very much, but. . . .'

'But what?'

She smiled, but shook her head.

Something has changed, he thought. She seemed . . . more alive towards him. Was it Ranjid's absence, he wondered? Ranjid was at a meeting in Wolverhampton for the day.

He said, 'Where does George Woodvine fit into all of this?'

'He's the trust's chairman.'

'So in theory, *he's* the boss?'

She shook her head again. 'Not even in theory. He's the non-exec chairman. Fleming has all the real power.'

'Then what's the point of him – George, I mean? Other than entertainment value?'

She smiled. 'He chairs the meetings and keeps an eye on things. Remember I told you how Patricia Matlock set up a committee to deal with the St James' scandal? Well, he, Patrick and Fleming were the other members. They were the ones with most to lose.'

'So they're all bound together whether they like it or not?'

'Something like that.'

'Ladies and gentlemen. . . .'

They turned as, with a flourish, Patrick pulled a cloth away to reveal a table of food. People oohed and aahed, formed an orderly queue, ate, and then drank some more. Patrick circulated, chatting with everyone, a happier man.

Helen said, 'What will you do when you've finished here, Fraser?'

'No idea. I've been wondering about going abroad again.'

'Again?' she asked, and he told her about his time in Africa.

'Yes,' she said, looking at him. 'I can see you burnt as a berry somewhere in shorts and a pith helmet.'

He laughed. 'Why d'you say that?'

'There's something restless about you.'

There was a roar of laughter from the other side of the room by the drinks table where a crowd of people surrounded George Woodvine.

'You're right about the atmosphere changing here,' he said, wanting to change the subject. 'Is it because Fleming's gone or Woodvine's arrived?'

'Both, I expect – plus the alcohol effect.'

'Speaking of which,' he pointed to her glass. 'Can I get you another?'

'Mm . . . some more punch, please. White wine if there isn't any.'

He'd just scraped enough from the bottom of the punch bowl to fill two glasses when Woodvine caught sight of him. 'Ah, Dr Callan, I presume – the very man.'

Fraser smiled, wondering what was coming.

'I've been telling all these good people here of the vicissitudes Patricia and I have undergone on our tours of the nation's hospitals.'

His ruddy face was certainly showing the alcohol effect, Fraser thought, although his diction was perfect. He listened along with the others.

'Last week we had to visit a hospital in – er – Warwickshire, I think it was . . . Anyway, the manager showed us in and I said to the patient in the first bed, who was swathed in bandages, poor fellow, "How are you feeling, my good man?" He said, "O wad some pow'r the giftie gie us to see ourselves as others see us".' His accent, as before, was perfect. 'Well, I stepped back, wondering if this was some kind of subtle insult and Patricia said to the next man, who was also covered in bandages: "Are you happy with your treatment here?" And he said, "Wee sleekit, cow'rin', timorous beastie O what panic's in they breastie?" Well, she wasn't too pleased about that, I can tell you, so I spoke very firmly to the next man, also well wrapped: "We'd like to know what you think about this place." And he said, "The best laid schemes o' mice an' men Gang aft a-gley."

Well, that did it. I turned to the manager. "What is going on here?" I demanded. And d'you know what he said to me?'

Woodvine paused and looked around.

'He said, "Didn't you know? This is the Burns unit".'

There were howls of laughter, from Fraser as well, although he'd seen it coming.

'You've heard it before, haven't you?' said a voice beside him and he turned to see Patricia Matlock.

'Aye, but it was the way he told it.'

'He has the giftie, then?'

'He has that. D'you really go round looking at hospitals?'

She nodded. 'All over the country, and we've had some pretty bizarre experiences, although nothing quite like that.'

'Why d'you do it?'

'To collect data, make contacts. Health's a special interest of mine.'

Aware of the drinks in his hand, Fraser smiled and said, 'I'm on an errand, so I'd better go.'

She smiled back at him. 'I think you might be too late.'

He stared at her, then over to where he'd left Helen – she was still there, but so was Ranjid Singh. They were both holding drinks and talking.

CHAPTER 6

'I . . . see what you mean,' Fraser said slowly. 'That's – er – very observant of you.'

'I find it pays to be observant,' she said. 'In every sense of the word. Don't you?' Her voice was husky, sexy, slightly pissed. Her blue eyes roved his face.

He put one of the drinks down and took a sip from the other. 'Now you're being enigmatic.'

'Well, you obviously haven't been drinking much if you can say that so easily.'

'Driving. How did you and George get here?'

'In a taxi, why? Oh, I see. You saw us arriving together and he, of course, *has* been drinking . . . but is it so obvious that I have?'

He made a mouth and rocked his hand from side to side. She gave a tight little smile.

'What I meant, Fraser, is that knowing things can prevent one making a fool of oneself.'

'Important in your job, I imagine.'

'In any job, Fraser. But just at the moment, important to *you*.'

'In what way?'

She considered him a moment, then said, 'I think you've blundered into deep and rather murky waters. T'were better you hadn't stepped in at all, but now that you have . . .' She leaned closer, entering his space unasked. 'Think about it, Fraser,' she said, and melted away.

What the hell was all that about? He looked round at Helen and Ranjid wondering whether to join them – then Ranjid caught his eye and walked over.

'Hello, Ranjid,' he said brightly. 'I thought you were in Wolverhampton.'

'I was. I came away early.'

'Interesting meeting?'

'Very, thank you.' He caught Fraser's eye movement, turned, and they

37

both watched as Helen went to the door that led to the passage. Ranjid turned back to him and said, 'It was *very* good of you to bring Helen here, but I shall be taking her home. Is that understood?'

'Does she know that?'

'She does.' He made as if to go, then turned back, took Fraser's arm and led him a little way from the drinks table.

'A word to the wise, Fraser – it might be an idea if you were to leave.' His grip tightened on his arm. 'By which I mean – leave the party, now, and leave the hospital . . . soon.' He gave a tight, sweet smile. 'Believe me, Fraser, you really are superfluous in every possible way.' He tapped the side of his nose, winked, then walked back to where he had been standing.

He's mad, Fraser thought. Raving, keening, howling . . . He felt as though people were staring at him, but they weren't. What the hell should he do? If he tried speaking to her, God knew what might happen.

Then Patrick emerged from the kitchen, caught his eye and came over. 'Can I get you anything, Fraser?'

'I'm OK, thanks.'

'A shandy, that's what you need – come with me.' It was Patrick's turn to grasp his arm and lead him firmly to the kitchen – where Helen was waiting. . . .

'What was he saying to you?' she demanded.

'That he'd be taking you home, among other things.'

'Like hell he is, we're going – now. Thanks, Patrick.'

'My pleasure and privilege, darling.' He opened the back door, kissed her cheek and shook Fraser's hand.

They hurried out across the gravel, he unzipped the tonneau and they got into the car. He reversed, then drove out through the gateposts.

'Should we find another way back?' he asked.

'There isn't an easy one. I don't think he'll follow us, if that's what you're worried about.'

'Is that so?' He looked into the mirror, but couldn't see any car lights. 'I think he's mad enough for anything.'

She looked at him. 'What else was he saying to you?'

He quickly told her. 'What's going on, Helen?'

She sighed audibly, 'I thought I'd explained it.'

He didn't say anything. The engine purred, the night was soft and warm, closing round them intimately. She said, 'We had an affair. It was stupid and I'm regretting it.'

'Had, or are having?'

'Had, so far as I'm concerned, but he's having some difficulty in accepting that.'

'What was he saying to you earlier?'

'What he always says, that we have to talk. It might have helped if you'd come back with the drinks,' she said pointedly.

'I saw you there with him and I didn't know what to think.'

'So I noticed.'

He changed down a gear as they started up the hill. 'He's mad, Helen.'

'He's neurotic.'

'Has he threatened you?'

'Not as such.'

'As *such* . . . does Philip know?'

'A little.'

'I think you should tell him all of it.' He concentrated on his driving as he went up through the hairpins, then said as they reached the top, 'He gives me the ghoulies apart from anything else.'

'Gives you the *what*?'

'Ghoulies – as in ghoul.'

'I thought for a moment you were being – *ahh*. . . !' She gripped his arm as from nowhere, a roebuck sprang high over the road in front of them, its eyes glittering in the headlamps . . . then another one followed. It hung above the car for a moment like an airship, then vanished into the night as though it had never been.

'Jesus,' Fraser said reverently as he straightened the car.

'Did one actually jump over us?' she asked faintly.

'Aye.'

'What a night.'

'Amen.'

The deer had driven Ranjid from their thoughts and they drove in silence down through gentle fields to the main road. Ten minutes later, he pulled up outside her house.

She said, 'You'd better come and have some coffee if you're really set on driving back to Bristol tonight.'

'I could use something stronger.'

'Well, you're welcome, of course, but. . . .'

'No, coffee'll be fine.'

They walked to the door, she opened it, shut it after him. 'Sit down while I put the coffee on,' she said, switching on the living-room light.

He sat on the sofa a few moments, then, unable to sit still, stood up, and pretended to look at the pictures on the wall.

She came back in. 'It won't be long.' She sat on the sofa, next to where he had been.

He hesitated.

'Sit down, Fraser. I won't bite.'

'You'll talk to Philip then?' he said as he sat beside her. 'About Ranjid.'

'Yes,' she said.

'He bothers me.'

'So you said.'

He turned towards her, intending to expand on why Ranjid bothered him, but found himself instead brushing her cheek with his lips. She turned, they tentatively nibbled for a moment, then he was kissing her mouth, her neck, her shoulders, nuzzling her through the thin dress . . . She put her hands behind his neck and pulled him to her, exploring him with her tongue. . . .

'Are you sure it's not too soon for you?' she whispered.

'Yeah. . . .'

Time passed. He broke off, knelt in front of her and slowly pushed his hands under her dress along the outsides of her legs. She groaned . . . He slid his hands over the seat of her jeans, round her waist, her ribcage. . . .

'Put the light out,' she breathed.

He was across the room in a stride, snapped the switch and was back. She raised herself as he eased her jeans and panties away, eased her to the edge and bent his head . . She was salty and warm, like the sea in September.

Suddenly, she cried out and pushing him away, got on her knees and clawed at his flies . . . His trousers went inside out as they snagged on his feet, she tore off his underwear and pulled him on top of her. He plunged wildly with no finesse whatsoever and they both came almost immediately.

'Oh, Fraser,' he heard her say as he spilled himself into her, and then the regrets began.

'Stay with me,' she said a little while later.

'I have to get back,' he said. 'I'm expected.' The truth was, he had to get away from her.

He pulled on his clothes, kissed her and left.

On the motorway, the wind thrummed tautly at the hood of the MG as the remorse ate into him.

'I'm sorry, Frances,' he said, over and over.

Only when he was at home with the first whisky inside him did it occur to him to wonder how Helen had known it might be too soon for him.

CHAPTER 7

They were together again and everything was all right, then he woke and like Orpheus could only watch as Frances faded away in front of him. He buried his face in his pillow and vowed he'd never touch Helen again.

So he avoided her when he returned on Monday, yet felt a perverse disappointment when she made no effort to speak to him. Then, just as he was leaving for the day, he ran into her in the corridor.

'You got back OK on Friday then?' Her smile dimpled the corners of her mouth and he remembered with a slight shock how attractive she was.

'Yes, thanks.'

'I was wondering whether you'd like to come to my house for supper tomorrow?' Her eyes, six inches below his, looked up so guilelessly that he felt himself hardening.

'Yes, I'd love to.'

So much for resolve, he thought as she walked away.

He was going into the social club that evening when he saw a familiar figure emerge from the Georgian building next to it.

'Patrick?'

'Oh, hello, Fraser.' His voice sagged with weariness, although he was as immaculately dressed as ever.

'Working late?'

'You could say that.'

'Fancy a drink?'

'In *there*?'

Fraser laughed. 'They don't bite.'

'Oh, all right. I'll take a quick one with you.'

The buzz in the bar fell away as they went in, then rose again. They took their drinks to a table.

Patrick said, 'D'you know, I've worked for seven years next door and this is the first time I've ever been in here.'

'All that time and you didn't know what you were missing.'

Patrick smiled weakly. 'So, what brings you here?'

Fraser explained that he lived just over the way. 'I wanted to say thanks for Friday.'

Patrick made an it-was-nothing gesture.

'Was there any bother after we left?' Fraser asked.

'From Himself, you mean? Not really. He had a little hunt round for her, a little rant at me when he realized the two of you were missing, then he left himself. What about you – have you had any trouble?'

'He just ignores me, looks through me as though I'm not there. But I think I can live with that.'

Patrick smiled again, a twist of the lips, then said, 'Forgive me asking, but are you and Helen . . . what's the expression now? An item?'

After a pause, Fraser said, 'The strictly truthful answer to that is – I don't know.'

'Well, whatever your relationship is – I wouldn't rub it in if I were you. I know he's difficult, but the world's too small and life's too short to make enemies you don't need.' He finished his drink. 'And now you'll forgive me if I leave – I've had it for today.'

After he'd gone, Fraser thought about what he'd said. Not the words he'd used so much, but the way he and the others all seemed to be in each other's pockets. It was incestuous, almost.

'Come in.' Helen shut the door after him and put up her face for a kiss. She was wearing an apron and her face was slightly flushed. 'Like some wine?'

'Why not?'

She showed him into the sitting room. 'I'll bring it to you here so that I can finish without any distractions.'

Something made him choose an armchair rather than the sofa they'd used before.

She came back in with a glass of white wine. 'It'll be about ten minutes.'

She was wearing a mini skirt under the apron and the different lengths accentuated the shape of her legs so that they seemed to twinkle at him as she went out.

He glanced around the room, at the pictures he'd pretended to look at on Friday. There were a couple of French impressionists, a Dutch landscape and a painting that was completely unfamiliar, not that he was any kind of expert. He got up for a closer look and found to his surprise that it was an original. It was another landscape, or rather, a shorescape – a stony, inhospitable beach in winter. A grey sea slopped sullenly over the rocks while the wind tugged at some scrubby bushes on the shore.

Ominous clouds scurried overhead. A figure, female and forlorn, gazed out to sea, her hair streaming from her head. The colours were muted but the detail and brushwork intense and the whole effect was disturbing, even depressing. At the bottom right-hand corner was the signature 'St John'.

Helen put her head round the door. 'It's ready.'

'Did you do this?' He indicated the painting.

'Oh, that. No. It was my mother.'

'Does she still paint?'

'She's dead.'

'Oh, I'm sorry.'

'It was a long time ago. You'd better come through, before it gets cold.'

The kitchen had a dining area set to one side. The dark wood table was laid for two with a glass vase containing a single red rose. She poured more wine.

'Cheers,' she said, raising her glass. He raised his and she touched it with hers to make a slight ring.

'Is it all right?' she asked a few minutes later. They were eating Lemon Chicken with rice and mange tout.

'It's wonderful,' he said.

'Really?'

'Really.'

He told her how he'd run into Patrick the night before, how exhausted he'd seemed.

'He works harder than people give him credit for,' she said.

He asked her how she'd got to know him and George Woodvine so well.

'Patrick's ubiquitous,' she said. 'You must have noticed that yourself by now.'

'What about George?' he asked. 'What does he *do*? The chairmanship can't bring in much.'

'He's got money of his own and he does all sorts of things. You know – Good Works.' She gave the last two words capitals.

'Landed gentry?'

'No, not really. His father and grandfather were more captains of industry, both knighted for services to the realm.' She explained how she and Philip had been to his house once and seen portraits of them hanging in the hall. 'Pillars of Victorian rectitude,' she said.

'But not George?'

'No. He's laid back, doesn't care for that kind of thing.'

They chatted about nothing very much through pudding (baked bananas in ginger sauce) and he waited until they'd finished before asking the question that had been nagging at him since Friday.

'Did you know about my wife?'

She paused a moment before meeting his eyes. 'Yes.'

'Who told you?'

'Philip.'

'He had no right.'

'No, I suppose he didn't.'

'So why did he tell you?'

Again she paused, then said, 'I was talking with him after he'd offered you the job. To be honest, I was sceptical as to why someone of your age and background should want it. I told him he'd been too hasty and that he should find out more about you. It was then he told me and I understood why he trusted you.'

'Why? Why should that make you understand why he trusted me?'

'Because Philip lost his own wife when he was about your age and never remarried. He would have felt it made a bond between you.' She paused. 'I'm only sorry I let it out when I did.'

He looked at her a moment before saying, 'It's all right.'

'How long ago did she die? Philip just said recently.'

'A bit over six months.'

'Leukaemia, I think he said?'

'Yes.'

Realizing he didn't want to talk about it, she said, 'What made you want to work with older people?'

He explained how he'd wanted to do something worthwhile, how Mary had shown him the newspaper articles after he'd come back from Africa. 'It seemed to come under the heading of *worthwhile*.'

'And has it been?'

'No, not in the sense I was thinking. Your hospital seems to be a model of how such places should be run.'

'Thank you, kind sir. Would you like some coffee?'

'Please. I'll try to savour it a bit more this time,' he added.

She laughed as she got up to make it.

He looked around. She'd managed to make the two parts of the room, the functional and the leisurely, distinct from each other, and yet somehow to blend together. Perhaps it was the pictures she'd chosen – yes, they were all on a theme of domesticity. His mind turned back to her mother's painting. 'D'you have any other pictures by your mother?'

'No, I don't.'

She had her back to him as she spoke, but he knew somehow she was lying. Why, he wondered?

'Did she paint for a living?' he asked.

'No.'

Knowing she didn't want to talk about it, he said anyway, 'I'm no expert, but I think she could have done.'

The silence hung for a moment, then she said, 'I think she'd have liked to.' She brought the coffee to the table.

'How old were you when she died?'

'Very young. Six. Hardly old enough to remember her, really.'

'That's sad,' he said, certain that she was lying again.

'As I said, it was a long time ago. What about your parents? You've never said anything about your family.'

He allowed her to change the subject and told her how his own father had died and his mother had brought him and his brothers up on her own. 'Not the easiest thing to do in Rutherglen.'

'It's that bad?'

'It was when I was a bairn. I was regarded as an academic star because I managed to become a lab technician.'

'How did you get into med school?'

'With a little help from some friends.' He told her how his boss, Dr McCloud had helped him become a doctor. She listened, leaning her chin on her folded hands, looking at him so demurely from under her eyelashes that he leaned over and kissed her.

'D'you want to go upstairs?' she whispered.

At the top of the stairs, he said self-consciously, 'I'll – er – just use. . . .'

'There,' she said, smiling and pointing. 'No,' as he tried a door that was locked, 'that's the junk room. The next one.'

Why lock a junk room? he wondered idly.

Her bedroom was light and fresh, cream on cream, duvet cover on carpet. She pulled the curtains.

He undressed her slowly. Her skin was smooth, supple, lightly tanned, her body ripe. She lay on the bed with one knee bent, her arms above her head so that the contours of her breasts were barely discernible, yet somehow more desirable.

'You look really good,' he said.

'You don't look so bad yourself,' she said.

He'd intended taking things slowly, to make up for last time, to savour her, but to his surprise, she made it clear she didn't want to tarry. She came quickly in a series of gentle gasps and he found himself left behind.

'Why don't you stay tonight?' she said later.

He pressed his lips together, said, 'I can't. I need time and space around me at the moment.' God, that sounds pretentious, he thought.

'I understand,' she said.

He was walking back from the social club the next evening when they came out of the shadows in front of him. They were always going to be bad news for someone but by the time he realized it was him, it was too late.

'Got a light, mate?' there were four of them, their faces hidden by hoodies, only their eyes gleaming faintly in the lamplight. He had to stop because the speaker had planted himself in front of him.

'Sorry, don't smoke.' He stepped to one side but the speaker stepped with him.

'Well, ya fuckin' well should then, shouldn't ya.'

Run for it . . . But two of the others were either side of him . . . *Play for time*.

Then a bottle smashed against the lamppost and the sweetheart holding its neck grinned at him. 'See, you're not wanted round here, mate.'

The others grabbed his sleeves as the shards of glass weaved and glinted in front of him – he ducked, slid out of his jacket and bolted head down for the darkness of the playing field.

'Geddim!'

They were just behind him, at his heels. One of them slipped in the mud. He heaved in air, tried to make his legs go faster. He risked a glance behind —the nearest was twenty yards back now but they weren't giving up, must think he was cornered.

And they were right – ahead lay the dark curtain of the copse, beyond it the high brick wall.

He burst into the trees, switched left, dodging trunks and bushes. A crashing came from behind as they followed – then his foot caught a root and he toppled through the air and sleighed into a clump of bushes.

He wriggled round, then lay still, winded. He pushed his white hands under the dead leaves, lowered his face into them.

They were running straight at him, they *must* see him, then they were running past. . . .

' 'Old it!'

They stopped, the speaker was just beside him . . . he could see his boots six inches in front of his eyes, knew he should shut them but he couldn't.

'Where is 'e?'

'Shaddup an' listen.'

Silence save the breath whistling in their throats.

' 'E's 'ere somewhere. . . .' The speaker shifted and his heel pressed on the tips of Fraser's fingers. 'Kel, gedover by the wall . . . Zit, over 'ere. . . .'

They moved away. Kel found a stick and prodded at the base of the wall. They tried staying still again, but got bored. One of them lit a fag and a few minutes later they started back over the playing field to the path.

Fraser crawled on hands and knees to the edge of the copse and watched them against the light of the hospital. They went back to where they'd left his jacket, went through the pockets and then made a big deal of tearing it into as many pieces as they could. Then they wandered off.

Just the flower of English youth having a few laughs, he thought. No point in going to the police. He limped back to the flat to get cleaned up.

CHAPTER 8

The old man arrived the following week. He was called Harold Carter and he had advanced bowel cancer with secondaries, some of them in the brain, which were making him vomit on top of the pain.

'How are you feeling, Mr Carter?' Philip asked him.

'Not too special, truth be told, Doc.' His speech was slurred but Fraser could tell he was a Londoner.

'We're going to treat you with dexamethazone,' Philip told him after he'd examined him. 'You should start feeling better by tomorrow. After that, we'll think about radiotherapy.'

'Thanks, Doc.' He swallowed and lay back. He was a small man anyway, less than five and a half feet, but was made smaller by his disease. His face was wizened, like a monkey's, his hair brittle white, his eyes dulled.

In the corridor, Edwina said, 'Can he stand another round of radio-therapy, Philip?'

'I'm not sure. As you know, he's specifically requested it – let's see how he is when his symptoms are under control.'

'He actually wants more radiotherapy?' Fraser asked.

'He thinks it might give him an extra few weeks,' Edwina told him. 'Which, of course, it might.'

'Is it worth it?'

She shrugged. 'He seems to think so.'

The next day, Harold Carter asked to see Fraser. He was looking a little better and Fraser told him so.

'I feel a bit better, thanks.' He swallowed. ' 'Cept my mouth's so dry I can hardly talk.'

'Haven't you got a glandosalve dispenser?' He looked on the bedside cabinet. 'Yeah, here it is. . . .'

Glandosalve was an artificial saliva spray. Although expensive, it was used freely at Wansborough because the drugs they used there tended to cause a dry mouth. He showed him how to use it.

'That's better,' Carter said, moving his tongue around his mouth. He looked shrewdly at Fraser. 'Your name's Callan, isn't it?'

'That's what it says here.' Fraser indicated his badge.

'From Glasgow?'

'Aye, can't you tell?'

'I knew a bloke in the war called Callan. Jamie Callan.'

Fraser smiled, 'My grandfather was called Jamie. Callan's a common name, though. So's Jamie.'

'Yeah, it was probably two other blokes.' He yawned. 'I think I'd like to rest now, if you don't mind.'

Fraser wondered briefly whether Carter could have known his grandfather, why he'd shut off so abruptly – then he was called to see another patient and forgot about it.

But that evening, over his pint, he found himself thinking about Jamie, the grandfather he'd never met, whose death, he was sure, had ramifications in his own life.

Fraser's father, John, had been a restless man, never able to hold a job for long and had eventually become an alcoholic. Fraser couldn't remember much about him, since he'd died when he was ten, but one thing he did remember was what he'd said at Grannie's one afternoon. Fraser was eight at the time and had asked who the man in the photo on Grannie's sideboard was.

'That's your Granddad, laddie. He was a hero. He flew in bombers in the war and got a medal for saving a man's life.'

'Can I see it?'

Grannie had taken a row of medals out of a drawer and Dad had shown him.

'Can I have them one day?'

Dad laughed. 'They ought to go to Rob, since he's older than you.'

'What happened to Granddad?'

'He was killed in 1944. Shot down.' John's eyes had slid away. 'When I was the same age as you. . . .'

Which probably answered for a great deal, Fraser thought now. In the end, none of the brothers had got any of the medals because John sold them a couple of years later when Grannie died. He'd died himself shortly afterwards, run over by a bus while he was drunk.

'Got a few minutes, Doc?' Harold Carter asked the next day.

He was looking better, Fraser thought, there was even a little colour in his face against the crisp white sheets. For several seconds, he didn't say anything, then, abruptly, he looked up – his eyes were a washed-out brown, but fever bright.

'The Jamie Callan I knew came from Rutherglen in Glasgow, he had a wife called Jeanie and was shot down over Germany in 1944. That's your grandfather, isn't it?'

'It could be,' Fraser said slowly.

'It is. I've been thinking about it since yesterday and it all fits.' He paused. 'Not only that, but you look like him and sound like him.'

Fraser sat down in the chair by the bed. 'It's a hell of a coincidence,' he said, trying to take it in. 'Did you know him well?'

'Put it this way – he saved my life.'

A machine bleeped and a phone rang somewhere. Fraser said at last, 'I knew that he saved someone's life, Mr Carter. He got a medal for it.'

'Well, it was me, an' he deserved it. We were in bombers, he was the dorsal gunner, I was the tail gunner.'

'Lancasters?'

'Halifaxes. Not so well known, but I preferred 'em.' He looked at Fraser long and hard, weighing things up in his mind, then he said, 'I don't believe in coincidence, so I'm going to do something I should've done years ago and tell you exactly what happened to him.' Another pause while he took a breath.

'We were coming back from Germany and got hit by flak. The skipper thought he could get us home, but he was wrong and we came down in the North Sea. The plane sank, but everyone got in the dinghy, everyone except me, that is. I'd been knocked out and was still in the tail. Jamie came back for me, even though the plane was sinking.'

He chuckled. 'They thought we were drowned, 'cos the plane had gone down, but then Jamie suddenly popped up in the water with me. We were picked up next day.' He sighed reflectively. 'Christ, it was cold! They gave us a week off, generous bastards, then it was back into another Halifax and back off to Germany. . . .'

They'd dropped their bombs, turned and were headed for home. Harold worked the hydraulic levers in the rear turret, searching the sky for night-fighters – then the whole plane shuddered as though hit by a pneumatic drill.

There was a scream of agony in his earphones, then nothing. He flipped the switch on the mouthpiece. 'Skipper, you OK?'

No answer.

'Jamie?'

Nothing, except the note of the four engines rising as the plane slid into a dive.

He could guess what had happened – a nightfighter, probably a JU 88, had come up underneath them and raked the bomber along its length with explosive shells – its length except the tail, that is. . . .

He banged the release button at his belly and stumbled through the hatch into the plane. Nothing was recognizable; the shells had reduced the inside of the bomber to a smoking refuse tip.

'Jamie! Jamie!'

He struggled along the walkway and looked up into the dorsal turret – Jamie's hand hung motionless, blood running down it and splashing into his eyes. He started climbing the ladder but a rung gave way and he fell back to the floor. The angle of the plane steepened and the engines began to howl.

He got to his feet and was about to try again when a ball of flame whooshed at him, burning his eyebrows and hair – without thinking, he turned and ran.

His parachute lay just outside the turret hatch. He reached it and in slow motion, threaded his arms through the harness, pulled the belt up between his legs and snapped the tongue into place – another fireball licked at him, then another – the plane was at forty degrees now, engines screaming their guts out.

He turned, tried to pull himself through the hatch but the chute caught the top and he was stuck.

Breathe out, he told himself, get lower, pull, pull . . . and he squeezed himself through.

He sat, flicked the hydraulic lever and incredibly, the turret turned . . . and turned – then a freezing gale tore at him and he somersaulted into space. . . .

'Just in time, I hit the ground just after the plane did. I was a POW for a year.'

Fraser looked at the ordinary, insignificant little man, thought about the thousands of other ordinary little men who'd had to do extraordinary things.

'Was it bad?' he asked. 'POW camp.'

'Not really, 'cept there was never enough food. We sat tight and in the end we were released by the Ruskis of all people.' He looked up at Fraser. 'I meant to go and see your Grannie, tell her what happened, but time went by and after a while, I couldn't. I was too ashamed.'

'Why, for God's sake?'

' 'Cos I didn't save his life after he'd saved mine. 'Cos I ran away instead of helping him.'

'Harold . . .' Fraser found himself calling him by his given name without thinking about it. 'He was dead. There was nothing you could have done for him.'

'But I didn't know that at the time, did I? I just ran.'

'If you'd hung round thinkin' about it, you'd have been dead yourself.'

'Maybe.' He gave a twisted smile. 'But I'll be dead soon anyway. All comes down to dust in the end, dunnit?'

'What was he like, Harold? Would you tell me about him? I don't know much, you see. . . .'

It was as though his life had grown another dimension; all he'd known about his grandfather was that he'd been in the RAF and won a medal, and before that had been a dockie. Now he knew why he'd won it, whose life he'd saved – suddenly, he'd acquired some history.

'He had to fight to get out of the docks,' Harold told him. 'Reserved occupation, y'see, and they didn't want to lose him.'

They'd met when they'd been assigned to the same crew and one of those strange friendships between a big man and a small man began.

'He was larger than life, always fooling around, and yet you had the feeling it was all a bit of a front. Always on about his wife and kids, especially when he'd had a few . . . kept a photo of them in his wallet . . . I know he didn't want to go back to the docks after the war. We had all kinds of plans – we were going to go to Australia and start an engineering firm, or a car sales business in the smoke, or a sheep farm in the north . . . that was the thing about the war, once you'd done a job like we had as aircrew and been respected for it, there was no way you were going back to forelock pulling. . . .'

This had been Harold's problem when he'd eventually de-mobbed and gone back to the brewery where he'd worked before. They *had* expected him to go back to forelock pulling, and when he argued the point, he was sacked.

He'd gone to Australia, intending to settle there; become a rep, got engaged, got jilted, come home again. He soon found another job and within a year, he was married and settled down.

'It was a mistake,' he said. 'The rebound.'

He and Janet had one child, a daughter they called Christine. The birth was difficult, and afterwards, so was sex, for Janet.

'She'd never liked it much anyway, an' being a rep, I could get it elsewhere. So I did.'

It was Christine who'd held the marriage together. Then, when she was seventeen, she'd become pregnant. She'd wanted to have the baby, but they'd persuaded her to have an abortion on medical grounds.

'Another mistake – she became impossible after that and left home. We didn't try to stop her and she vanished.'

And vanished completely, so far as Harold was concerned. He knew Janet was still in touch with her, because she told him Christine was married and had a son. He and Janet had divorced, and when she'd later died, he hadn't been able to tell Christine about the funeral because he'd had no idea where she was. He'd never heard from her since.

'That's why I want this radiotherapy, Fraser. I hired a private dick when I knew I'd got cancer, to find her an' beg her to come an' see me before I died. He's traced her to America and says he'll find her soon.'

He looked up. 'I haven't been a good man, Fraser. I've been a rotten husband and father. But I want to see her and my grandson before I die; I want to tell her I'm sorry. That's why I need a couple more months. Thing is Fraser, am I going to get them?'

Fraser cleared his throat. 'Aye, I think so, given a bit of luck, and you're due that, Harold. You're starting the radiotherapy tomorrow, aren't you?'

A nod.

'Well, Dr Armitage wouldn't have okayed it if he didn't think it would work.' He paused. 'There's also the will to live. If you want to enough, you can do it.'

'I do want to, Fraser. Thanks.'

After a pause, Fraser said, 'Have you told Dr Armitage or Dr Tate about your daughter?'

'No,' he said. 'And I don't want to. It's no one else's business. I only told you because of Jamie.'

Fraser seriously thought about telling Philip or Edwina, or even Helen, but decided in the end to respect Harold's wishes. He realized anyway as he brooded over his pint that evening that he didn't want to tell Helen anything that might seem to increase the intimacy between them. He knew he wanted to finish the affair, regretted now ever having started it. Why? Guilt so soon after Frances?

Aye, and it was getting worse, but that wasn't all there was to it. After her initial coolness, he'd been surprised how quickly Helen had changed towards him. He found her cloying, claustrophobic even – the girlie way she spoke to him sometimes, the way she made too much of things, pressurized him. Every time he went to her house, she tried to make him to stay the night, which was something he simply couldn't do. And then there was the sex itself, she oozed sexuality and couldn't get him into bed fast enough, and yet it always seemed to be so ... perfunctory, over so quickly.

He'd already started drawing away from her and now decided he'd break it to her before the weekend. Then, the next day, his brother Rob phoned him from Glasgow and told him their mother had broken her leg and was in hospital.

'When did this happen?'

'Couple of days ago. Thought you'd want to know.'

'Aye, I would that. How is she?'

'She's no' in pain now they've set the leg.'

'Give her my love and . . .' He hesitated. 'Tell her I'll be up to see her.'

'Aye,' Rob said sceptically. 'I'll believe that when I see it.'

'Just tell her – OK?'

Fraser couldn't really blame him for his attitude. He'd grown apart from his brothers from the moment he'd started doing better at school and was now almost estranged from them.

Edwina gave him the rest of the week off and he drove straight up to Glasgow. Part of him, he realized, was glad of the excuse to put off speaking to Helen.

The surprise and pleasure on his mother's face when she saw him brought a lump to his throat. Rob and his other brother Eddie were there too. They solemnly shook him by the hand and Fraser began to think that maybe his family weren't so bad after all.

On Saturday night, the three of them went out and he told them about Harold and their grandfather.

He'd driven back to Bristol on Sunday to check on his house, then returned to Wansborough on Monday to discover that Harold had died early that morning of pneumonia.

CHAPTER 9

Fraser looked from Tom back to Marcus as he finished his story.

'It hit me when I was standing there looking at his body,' he said. 'He shouldn't have died. None of them should.'

'People do, though,' said Tom. 'All the time.'

'Not this many.' He took some sheets from his briefcase and handed them to Marcus.

'That's the death rate in Wansborough over the last year, and those are comparable death rates in ten other community hospitals across the country. The death rate in Wansborough is significantly higher – look. . . .'

Marcus put on his glasses and cast his eyes down the figures, then handed the sheets to Tom. 'Is it statistically significant?'

Tom studied them a moment before producing a calculator and tapping at the keys. 'For these figures, yes,' he said at last. 'Although ten isn't anything like a large enough sample.'

'It was hard enough getting *that* many,' Fraser protested.

'And I'm not sure that you've used the best method,' Tom continued. 'But yes, these figures do look significant.'

Marcus turned back to Fraser. 'Do you have anything else?'

He shook his head. 'Like I said, it was hard enough getting that much.'

'You told us earlier that you don't know who's doing this,' said Tom. 'Can't you narrow it down a bit? I mean, it's got to be someone with patient contact, hasn't it?'

'Sure, but that still leaves you with seven doctors and at least three dozen nurses and health care assistants.'

'What about the method being used?' said Marcus. 'The ones you saw died of pneumonia – is it possible to give it to someone artificially?'

'I can't see how—'

'You've told us about Dr Singh and his obvious dislike of you – what about him?'

'He'd be at the top of my list,' Fraser agreed.

'Of course, his dislike of you could just as easily be down to your relationship with Sister St John,' Tom observed.

'It could.'

'You told us earlier you were intending to finish that,' Marcus said. 'Have you actually done so yet?'

'No. Why?'

'No reason, just wondering whether it had any effect on anything.' He moved on. 'You've done very well to put these figures together in so short a time, but before we take it any further, we must check them out for ourselves. Can you come back here on Monday morning?'

'You can do it that quickly?'

'We've got access to all that kind of information here on computer,' said Tom.

'And contrary to popular opinion,' Marcus said, 'civil servants do occasionally work over the weekend.'

Fraser thought for a moment. 'They're expecting me back Monday morning,' he said.

'You told them you were seeing your mother, didn't you, so why don't you do that? I'm sure she'll be pleased to see you. Go by train from here, phone them from Glasgow, tell them there's a problem and that you'll be back Monday afternoon – that'll give you time to see us first. We'll pay all your travel, of course,' he added.

'Well, what do you think?' Marcus asked Tom after Fraser had gone.

'If his figures check out, and my gut instinct is they will, we should look into it.'

'I agree. The question is,' Marcus continued after a pause, 'how are we going to do it? 1 can't see an easy way of shoehorning you in there.'

'We're going to have to use Haggis, aren't we, Marcus?' he added to Marcus's enquiring look.

'What if he won't play? He might not – especially when I tell him it means carrying on with his girlfriend.'

Tom thought for a moment. 'He did say he was hard up.'

Marcus grinned. It might work,' he said. 'He wouldn't be able to do it on his own, though.'

'No,' Tom said. 'There is always Jo.'

'Yes, there is, isn't there. But is she going to even speak to us after last time?'

'Use your charm on her – it's always worked before. Besides,' Tom continued reflectively. 'I wouldn't be surprised if she was a bit short of the readies, too.'

★

Fraser's mother was pleased to see him again so soon. As it happened, she was about to be discharged, so he was able to make sure she had the right nursing care and everything she needed in her flat. He rang Edwina who said he could come back Monday afternoon, although something in her tone warned him not to expect any more favours from her.

On Sunday, he went back to Bristol, having decided to take Marcus at his word about train fares. He went through his post, slept in his own bed on Sunday night and caught another train to London on Monday morning.

'Well,' said Marcus when he'd sat down. 'We've repeated your exercise on a larger sample. So far as we're concerned, Wansborough Community Hospital has an unacceptably high death rate and we want to look into it.'

'Good,' Fraser said softly.

'We're going to need some help from you.'

'Sure. Although since I'm going to have to go on working there, I'd prefer it if my colleagues didn't know.'

Marcus said carefully, 'For what we have in mind, it's absolutely essential your colleagues don't know.'

'How d'you mean?'

'How did you think we were going to go about this?'

Fraser shrugged. 'By interviewing everyone concerned, I suppose, gathering all the information you can – it's what you did in Bristol, isn't it?'

'Yes, but we were dealing there with a fait accompli. Here, we're looking at something far more nebulous. We may be sure in our own minds that a crime is being committed, but we have no proof. If we interviewed everyone, then I imagine the killing would stop – for a time, maybe even for good – but we probably wouldn't be able to catch the – er – malefactor. We might strongly suspect someone, but we'd have no proof.'

There was a short silence.

'So what are you going to do?' Fraser asked.

'What we've done in the past is to infiltrate someone who can watch from within, so to speak. It's usually been Tom, although I can't see any opening for him here. Sometimes we've had to enlist inside help.'

Fraser laughed uneasily. 'If you're thinking about me, forget it.'

Marcus looked at him. 'How would you go about it if it were your problem? I'd be interested to hear.'

'I've no idea.'

Marcus didn't say anything, just kept looking at him, and after a moment Fraser went on: 'If you questioned all the staff, surely someone would have noticed something suspicious. If you then compared what everyone said, you'd be able to work it out.'

'But suppose nobody *has* noticed anything – and believe me, that's quite possible – then all we'll have achieved is to alert the killer.'

Fraser didn't reply to this and Marcus went on. 'Could you give me an example of the sort of suspicious something you had in mind?'

'Well . . . the same person always being around when someone dies, someone doing something to a patient they shouldn't be. . . .'

'Who better than a doctor for that?'

'But I'm no' suitable for this kind of thing.'

'You didn't do so badly last year, I seem to recall,' Tom murmured.

'Aye, but that was because I *had* to, because of Frances.'

'All we want for the moment,' said Marcus, 'is someone who'll keep their eyes and ears open. You'd be remunerated, of course.'

Fraser blinked, he hadn't thought of that.

Marcus continued carelessly. 'We thought £2000 a week with a guaranteed minimum of £10,000. I seem to remember you saying you were having difficulty with your mortgage – well, that might help, especially tax free.' Pause. 'Just for keeping your eyes open.'

Fraser laughed weakly. 'I think we both know there'd be more to it than that. The person responsible, the – er – malefactor, might take unkindly to being spied on.'

'Indeed they might, should they become aware of it. Our aim is to ensure they don't. Tom can help you there.'

'I'm only one person, I couldn't cover everything.'

'We've got some back-up in mind.'

'What kind of back-up?'

'We'll go into that if you agree.'

'I'll . . . need to think about it,' Fraser said at last.

'You can have till tomorrow morning, we must know by then.'

He thought about it on the train.

The money would come in handy, and it might not mean much more than keeping his eyes open – then he remembered something: Marcus asking him if he'd finished with Helen.

They wanted him to go on seeing her.

You canny bastard, Marcus, he thought. Seduce me with the money, then give me the bad news after I've agreed.

No. Absolutely not. He'd done his bit, it was up to them to do the rest.

He got back to the hospital at three and went to find Edwina. She was in her room.

'Ah, Fraser,' she said coolly. 'Come in and shut the door, please. Mother better now?'

'Yes, she is. Thanks, Edwina.'

'I'm very glad to hear it,' she said. Then, after a pause: 'We've cut you a lot of slack in this, Fraser, and enough is enough. Is that understood?'

'Perfectly,' he said. There was no point in arguing, let alone telling her she was mixing her clichés.

'Good,' she said. 'We've got a Mrs Ferrers waiting to see you. She's come about her father, Mr Carter who died last week. She was completely hysterical earlier, but we managed to calm her down. You had more to do with him than anyone, so perhaps you could talk to her.'

Fraser slunk off, smarting. Oh, sure, she was within her rights to cuss him off, but what was it about her that gritted every joint in his body?

Mrs Ferrrers was in a side room, red-eyed and looking every one of her forty-something years. She got to her feet as he introduced himself and took his hand. Hers were damp and limp.

She said, 'They told me you spoke with him a lot before he died.' Her voice was an irritating mix of London and New York.

'That's right,' Fraser said. She was overweight and wearing too much make-up and jewellery. 'I came to know him quite well before he died, Mrs Ferrers. I liked him a lot.'

'I have his letter here, the one the PI gave me.' She pulled it out of her handbag. 'It's so sweet, if only he'd contacted me earlier.'

Thinking, You could have contacted him . . . Fraser said carefully, 'He wasn't sure what kind of reception he'd get, which is why he didn't try until he was ill.'

As though she could read his thoughts, she said, 'Pride's a stupid thing, isn't it? I blamed him for everything that went wrong in my life without giving him any credit for the things that went right.'

'All he wanted to do was make his peace with you.'

He told her everything Harold had said to him and her mascara ran as she began crying again, but he felt that the tears were cathartic this time. She said she wanted to stay on to organize his funeral and asked him if he'd come.

It was nearly four by the time he got back to Edwina and told her what had happened.

'He didn't say anything to me about a daughter,' she said, looking at him. 'I wonder why he told you.'

Fraser explained about his relationship with Harold. 'He made me promise not to tell anyone else about it.'

'I see,' she said after a pause. She seemed about to say something else, then gave a wry smile instead. 'Pride is,' she said, 'indeed, a stupid thing.'

Maybe it is, Fraser thought later over his pint in the social club, but it hadn't been pride that had killed Harold before he could see his daughter and grandson.

He thought about Alice Steel and Olive Spencer and the others who might have had their reasons for wanting another two or three months of life. He thought about the last months with Frances.

The idea of carrying on with Helen made him squirm, but if that's what it took.

He phoned Marcus in the morning and told him he'd do it.

'Good,' Marcus said. 'Can you come up here on Saturday to sort all the details out?'

'Sure.'

'Oh, and meanwhile, don't finish your relationship with Sister St John.'

Fraser smiled grimly to himself. 'Why not?' he asked innocently.

'Partly because she's already been very useful in giving you all the gossip and muck raking, but also, of course, because she might be involved.'

CHAPTER 10

Well, Agent Callan, he thought as he put the phone down, better go find her and make up. Not that they'd actually fallen out, he reflected, but she must have noticed how he'd cooled lately, maybe even realized he was about to dump her. She wasn't stupid. He went to look for her in the canteen at lunchtime.

He spotted her at exactly the same time she spotted him. She waved and beckoned him over. Ranjid was with her.

'Going to join us, Fraser?' she asked.

He couldn't refuse, not after he'd been so obviously looking for her. He bought some shepherd's pie and took it back to their table.

'Mother any better?' she asked brightly.

'Yes – thank you.' He told her about it in stilted sentences.

Ranjid stared at him, his face expressionless but his eyes boring into him as though trying to see into his mind.

'Well, that's good news,' said Helen.

'Yes.'

Ranjid, still staring, said, 'So how much longer now is it you're with us, Fraser?'

'Until Clare Simpson comes back from maternity leave. You'd know the date of that better than me, Ranjid,' he said, staring back at him.

'Two months, I believe,' said Helen, still bright.

'Ah, yes,' said Ranjid. 'Two months.'

There was a silence. Fraser ate some Shepherd's pie. Helen said, 'Any idea yet what you'll do after that, Fraser?'

'Not really, no.' He looked at her – she was smiling and he suddenly realised she was enjoying the situation.

Ranjid said, 'Shall we go now, Helen?'

'Yes, let's.' She stood up. 'See you later, Fraser.'

They left.

Ah, shit. Was he too late? He must have done a better job of putting her off than he'd realized. He gave up on the shepherd's pie and went back himself.

After he'd finished the afternoon clinic, he took a deep breath and went along to her office. The door was open and she was at her desk.

'Oh, hello, Fraser.'

He went in and closed the door. 'I'm afraid I've been rather neglecting you lately,' he said. He could hear his voice in his ears.

'That is your prerogative,' she said, prim and cool now. 'You have no duty to attend on me.'

'No, not a duty,' he said slowly. 'I have had a lot on my mind this last week or so.'

'Yes, of course, your mother.'

He said, 'It's not the only thing that's been worrying me.'

She didn't reply.

He went on. 'Perhaps we could go out for a drink tonight?'

'I can't, not tonight.'

'Tomorrow, then?'

'All right,' she said after a pause.

Almost exactly a hundred miles to the north, in the city of Latchvale, Sister Josephine Farewell was attending a health and safety meeting. To say she was annoyed would be an understatement: two livid red spots stained her face as she stared back at Mr David Petterman, the official from the local health and safety office.

'Sister Farewell,' he was saying. 'I clearly remember telling you on my last inspection that the position of the vent in your office is in contravention of section 5, paragraph 23 relating to air conditioning. Why haven't you done anything about it?' He was a small man with glasses and a voice that was always quiet, always even.

Jo swallowed before replying. 'Because at the time, when we pointed out to you how difficult it would be to move it, you said that since the position was only a foot from where it should be, you accepted that it didn't present any actual hazard.'

'Thirty centimetres.'

'I beg your pardon?'

'The vent is thirty centimetres out of place, Sister, and if you remember, I wrote to you the following day saying that having reflected on the matter, I felt that after all, the legislation should be complied with in full.'

'Yes, I remember receiving your letter,' Jo replied, trying to keep her own voice level. 'However, I then discovered that in having the vent moved, we would be in contravention of section 8, paragraph 15, relating to building works in the vicinity of patient care.'

There was a rustle of paper as everyone round the table found the relevant paragraph.

'Ah yes, I see,' said Petterman. He looked up. 'Why didn't you inform me of this?'

'I am informing you now.'

'But surely, you should have informed me as soon as you realized there was a problem.'

'But surely,' said Jo, openly mimicking him, 'a matter of this importance requires discussion at a meeting such as this – I mean, what are we going to do? Shut down ITU in order to move a vent one foot – *sor-ry*, thirty centimetres – to the left?'

'If necessary, Sister Farewell, that is exactly what you will do,' said Petterman, the barely perceptible tightening of his voice betraying his own anger.

Jane Goodall, Jo's immediate superior, quickly intervened. 'I'm sure a way can be found round the problem without closing ITU. Why don't we form a committee, including the building works department and any other interested parties, to discuss this.'

'That, at least, is a constructive suggestion,' said Petterman. He thought about it. 'Yes,' he said at last. 'I will agree to that. Can I leave it with you, Ms Goodall, to arrange?'

'Of course.'

When the meeting had finished, she summoned Jo to her office. 'Why do you go out of your way to antagonize Mr Petterman?' she demanded.

'Because he makes it impossible for us to do our jobs,' Jo blazed back. 'He's a health hazard in himself – shutting down ITU because a vent's one foot out of place, for God's sake.'

'Thirty centimetres,' said Jane, with the ghost of a smile. 'I accept that he's difficult, but we both know that ITU will not be shut down. We can, and will, find a way of placating him.'

'*Appeasing* him, you mean. I didn't become a nurse in order to massage the egos of inadequate little pronks like him.'

'Whether we like it or not, Jo, he does have the power to shut us down. We have to work with him as best we can, even if it does mean massaging his ego. He has the law on his side.'

'Then the law is an ass.'

'That will do, Sister.'

Jo went into the courtyard behind ITU, gobbled a cigarette to calm her nerves, then went back to her office. Perhaps because she was glancing up at the offending vent in the ceiling as she went in, she failed to notice the dark figure sitting in the corner at first – then let out a yelp of surprise when she did.

'Hello, Jo,' said Marcus. 'Sorry if I startled you.'

'Whatever it is,' she said, her heart still pounding. 'The answer's no.'

'That's rather sweeping, isn't it?'

'I remember the last time.'

'Ah, but this is this time,' said Marcus. 'Not the same thing at all.' She smiled despite herself.

'Can we talk now?' he asked

She sighed. 'Come back in an hour.'

'We need a nurse to work in a community hospital for about a month,' he said an hour later.

'Why?' she asked. They were in her office with the door closed.

'Because a doctor working there has come to us with rather a strange story.'

As he outlined it, Jo's mind worked busily. Although she knew it was stupid, her soul revolted at the thought of having to work closely with David Petterman – he'd be quietly crowing over her every minute of every day – and from the sound of it, this assignment wasn't likely to be anything like so dangerous as last time . . . and the money would come in handy.

Jo's widowed mother still lived in the marital home and Jo helped her with the expenses. They could have lived together, but Jo had her own house and, for the sake of their relationship, she wanted to keep it that way. But it was expensive.

'We're offering two thousand a week with a minimum of £10,000, if that's any help,' said Marcus.

'That's all it was last time,' she said, referring to the occasion she and Tom had infiltrated a fertility clinic pretending to be a childless couple. 'What about inflation?'

'As I'm sure you've already worked out, this task isn't anything like so onerous.'

'I'd still like a raise,' she said.

They settled on £2,250 a week.

'When d'you want me to start?' she asked.

'As soon as possible. I'll sort it out with your bosses tomorrow and you can come up to London the day after.'

★

That night in Wansborough Community Hospital, Mary Bailey, aged seventy-four, died of pneumonia. Like Harold, she'd had advanced cancer but hadn't been ready to die yet. Also like Harold, she'd been put on ampicillin, and it hadn't worked.

Fraser dropped the hood of the car when he picked up Helen, then drove up into the downs. After its slow start, spring was in full sap now; the hedgerows pulsed green where they weren't laden with the white of May blossom and the young corn in the fields waved gently in the breeze. They found a pub in one of the villages that served beer straight from the wood and drank it under an apple tree in the garden. It should have been idyllic, but Fraser had work on his mind.

'Listen to those birds,' Helen said. 'They take life as it comes, maybe we should try and learn from them.' Her coolness of the day before had quite gone.

'They don't live long, though, do they?' Fraser said.

'All right misery guts, tell me what ails thee.'

When he didn't reply, she said, 'Sorry, patronizing.' After a pause: 'You said there was something else besides your mother?'

'Yes,' he said. He took a breath, then told her about Harold and his grandfather. 'It was like discovering a part of my family I knew nothing about, so when he died so suddenly,' he said, watching her, 'well, it gave me a bit of a knock.' *God, that sounds unnatural.* He ploughed on. 'Especially since it happened just before he could be reconciled with his daughter.'

'That is really sad.' The low sun caught her face as she spoke, shadowing its bone structure. 'But at least she realizes now what she meant to him.'

'It would have been better if he could've told her himself.'

'Yes, it would,' she said. 'I'm afraid it's another of life's *if onlys*.' She looked up at him. 'You must have seen plenty of them before.'

He forced a smile. 'Meaning that doctors shouldn't become too involved with their patients?'

'Oh, I think that would have been hard in this case with the family connection – but yes, I suppose I do mean that.' Her eyes loomed large. 'I wonder if your own history makes you more vulnerable.'

'Maybe,' he said, not wanting to go there. He thought quickly – *Bring up the fact that he died of pneumonia? No, not yet.*

He tried turning the conversation to her own family, but she no more wanted to talk about that than he did about Frances, so they ended up chatting companionably enough about not very much while the light faded around them, then drove back to Wansborough through the gloaming.

'D'you want to come in?' she said softly.

As he undressed her, he found himself marvelling anew at the freshness of her skin, the firmness of her body.

That was the strange thing, he thought as he drove away afterwards. He still found her sexy, which was why he was able to perform (there was no other word for it) and he still rather liked her, but the two simply didn't connect in the way that makes a relationship. Why not? he wondered. She didn't seem to notice anything. As usual, she'd asked him to stay and he'd made the usual excuses.

Walking down Whitehall with its massive buildings and rows of stately plane trees on Thursday morning, Jo felt the strangest sense of déjà vu. How long was it? Five years? To think she'd sworn never to come back.

The sight of Tom made her heart skip a little, but not quite so much as before, she noticed.

'How are Holly and Hal?' she asked him.

'They're well, thank you,' he replied politely, only the faintest smile betraying his own feelings.

They went over Fraser's story again, only in more detail, then showed her the statistical data.

'This might as well be quantum physics so far as I'm concerned,' Jo said. 'The point is, you're both sure that someone's killing off these patients?'

'Yes,' Tom said. 'Statistics don't lie when they're used properly. People are dying when they shouldn't be and it's got to be either gross incompetence or murder.'

'Shades of Latchvale?' she said. 'Another nutter?'

'We don't know.'

'Whichever,' said Marcus. 'The only way we can prove it is to catch them actually doing it. A nurse and a doctor would seem the best combination for that.'

'Do they have any sister vacancies at the moment?' Jo asked.

'No. There's a senior staff nurse vacancy, though.'

'Then why am I moving? I'd need a pretty good reason to go down from sister to staff nurse.'

'We thought about that – your fiancé has just got a job in Wansborough and you're going to move with him.'

'Must be a pretty good job.'

'It is,' said Tom. He glanced down at the sheet of paper in front of him. 'He's just become – er – management systems analyst with Shroeder Research.' He looked up again. 'Worth fifty K, that is.'

She stared at him. 'Did you just make that up?'

'Certainly not!' said Tom indignantly. 'I used Job Genesis. Look.' He handed the sheet over.

She saw three columns of words:

Management	Systems	Analyst
Policy	Capability	Coordinator
Conceptual	Strategy	Specialist etc.

'You just pick one word from each column,' said Tom. 'And lo! You've created the modern young professional to suit your needs.'

'You cynical bastard – is this your idea?'

'I wish . . . No, I'm afraid it was my boss here.'

Marcus shrugged and managed to look both embarrassed and smug at the same time. 'I've always enjoyed playing with words,' he said.

Jo handed it back. 'Does Schroeder Research exist?'

'Certainly,' said Tom. 'And yes, in the unlikely event of someone phoning and asking for Douggie Pratt, they'd—'

'You *haven't*?'

'No.' Tom grinned. 'We thought you might prefer to choose the name of your fiancé. Anyway, they'd be told he was unavailable at the moment and asked if they'd like to leave a message.'

Jo gave him a look, then turned back to Marcus. 'I take it I'm going as myself?'

'I think so, better to avoid false names and references and so on. Keep as near to the truth as you can.'

'Then there might be another problem – have you checked whether there are any other sister vacancies in Wansborough?'

'Tom?'

Tom went to the computer terminal and tapped at the keyboard for a few moments. 'There is actually, in ENT.'

'So why am I going for a senior staff nurse post in the community hospital instead of a sister in ENT?'

'Are they likely to ask you that?' said Marcus.

'They might well, so I ought to have an answer ready.'

'I take your point' He sighed. 'I was going to suggest you give them a ring now, but we'd better get this sorted out first.' He thought for a moment, then said, 'I wonder if Fraser could help us.'

CHAPTER 11

The next day, Friday, Fraser drove home and on Saturday, caught an early train up to London. The others were already there and Marcus introduced him to Jo.

He'd noticed her as soon as he'd come in, his eyes drawn to the elfin face and long chestnut hair. She stood up and held out her hand. As he took it, he realized that she wasn't quite so young as she'd seemed at first – something in her clear hazel eyes said they'd seen a lot. He aged her at a tactful twenty-nine.

'Do call me Jo.' Her voice was the essence of middle England, he thought – low, musical, well spoken without being plummy. She was wearing jeans and a dark green top with a white T-shirt underneath.

'Fraser,' he said.

Marcus found him a seat and poured him some coffee. 'I'm sorry I had to ring you at work yesterday,' he said. 'But we had to get Jo's interview organized as soon as possible.'

Not a problem, Fraser assured him, then turned back to Jo. 'I've brought you some articles by Philip Armitage – you can say they impressed you so much it made you want to work in the field.'

'Thanks,' she said as he handed them over.

'Did you manage to fix an interview?'

'Monday, with Sister St John, although in theory it's a look-around rather than an interview.'

'I'd be surprised if she didn't offer you a job on the spot.'

'Can she do that? What about employment regulations?'

Fraser shrugged. 'Well, they've advertised and not had any takers, so why not?'

'Talking of Sister St John, Fraser,' Marcus interposed smoothly. 'Have you re-established your relationship with her?'

'Yes,' he said shortly.

'Good. Any other developments?'

'Aye, there's been another death I'm not happy about.' He told them about Mary Bailey.

'Pneumonia again,' said Tom, speaking for the first time. 'Are there any of these suspicious deaths that *haven't* been pneumonia?'

'Not that I've noticed,' he said cautiously. 'Doesn't mean there aren't any, though.'

'But it does bring us back to the question of whether someone's deliberately infecting them.'

'As I said before, it's very unlikely.'

'Why?'

He thought for a moment. 'Apart from the problem of getting a suitable culture of the bacteria, it would be very difficult to administer. You'd have to make an aerosol and somehow get the patient to inhale it. Sooner or later, you'd be seen doing it.'

'Mm,' Tom said. 'It's just that I'm finding the pneumonia coincidence a bit hard to swallow. Could they be using it as a mask for killing them some other way?'

'How d'you mean?'

'Well, waiting until someone gets pneumonia, then killing them by whatever method they're using.'

'I'll need to think about that.'

Marcus suggested they had a look at some of these other methods. 'How would you go about it, Jo?'

'Drugs, I suppose. An overdose of insulin, as we know, mimics heart failure pretty closely.'

'But as we also know, it shows up on PM.'

'What about potassium chloride.' said Tom

'Same problem,' said Marcus. 'Shows up on PM.'

'But are they going to bother with post-mortems on these people? Do they, Fraser?'

'I haven't heard of any,' he said.

'But they *could*,' said Marcus. 'If our killer's doing this on a regular basis, they'll be using something that can't be detected.'

'What about diamorphine?' said Tom. 'I know it's detectable, but so what? A lot of these patients are on diamorphine anyway.'

'The fact that it's an overdose would be detectable,' said Fraser.

'Yeah, but how do you define an overdose? The doctor who administered it could say, "Sure, I was doing it to suppress the terrible pain the patient was in." No one's going to argue with that.'

'Didn't help Shipman in the end,' said Jo. 'Couldn't we check one of these dead people for drugs?'

'How?' Marcus wanted to know.

'Blood sample?'

'Difficult,' said Fraser. 'Getting it from a corpse isn't much easier than the proverbial stone.'

'Yeah, we know,' Jo murmured, exchanging a glance with Tom.

Fraser felt, not for the first time, the past history between them. 'How important is it?' he asked.

'Well, it might just give us the answer,' said Marcus. 'And even if it didn't, it'd probably eliminate some of the possibilities.'

'Pretty important, then,' Fraser said. 'I'll see what I can do with the next one.' He grimaced. 'Assuming there is a next one.'

'Oh, I think we can safely assume that,' Tom said softly.

There was a silence as they ran out of homicidal inspiration, then Tom looked up at Fraser. 'This latest death you've told us about, Mary Bailey, would you say she was typical of them?'

'Very much so,' he repleid. 'She was over seventy, not long to live and with what some would say was a debatable quality of life.'

'What exactly d'you mean by that?' Jo asked.

'Terminal, but neither vegetative nor in acute discomfort.'

'What I'm getting at,' said Tom impatiently, 'is do you think you could predict the likeliest victims in advance, make a list of them?'

Yes, Fraser thought he might be able to manage that.

'Then, once Jo started, you and she could concentrate on watching them.'

Jo, who'd been looking pensive, said suddenly, 'Fraser, these pneumonia cases, you said they were all treated with ampicillin?'

'Aye, it's the standard treatment.'

'But what if they're not? Being treated with ampicillin, I mean – what if they're being given a bogus antibiotic?'

There was another silence, then Marcus said, 'Would that be possible, Fraser?'

He thought about it and nodded. 'And it might explain one or two things. D'you want me to look into it?'

'Don't make it too obvious,' Tom said. 'In fact, it might be better to wait until Jo's there.'

They decided that Fraser would find out how the drug administration system worked generally, then Jo would look at it for loopholes.

Jo asked where she was going to be living.

'Nurses' home?' Marcus suggested. 'We want you near the hospital.'

'Wouldn't I be living with my fiancé?'

'Not if he hadn't moved yet. Let's say he's not due to start till the end of next month. He's working out his notice.'

'So where do Fraser and I meet to talk? We're not supposed to know each other so we don't want to be seen together, do we?'

Tom said he'd be taking a hotel room they could all use.

'But what if I need to talk to him urgently?'

'You'll have to work out something: *Dr Callan, can we discuss this patient a moment, please?*'

Marcus said, 'And you'll both have your mobiles.'

They tossed the logistics around for a while longer, then Marcus took them out to lunch.

The restaurant was crowded but he'd reserved a table, so they were served quite quickly. Jo and Marcus had fish while Tom and Fraser had rack of lamb and Fraser found himself wondering why this was exactly what he'd have expected them to choose. His lamb was excellent. Jo asked him about Helen and the other staff she'd be likely to meet and he did his best to give her a balanced view.

As soon as they'd finished, Jo got up to go, saying she had a train to catch. Fraser would have liked to have gone with her, but Tom had said he wanted him to come back to his office with him, so he couldn't.

They left not long afterwards.

'So, d'you think you can work with Jo?' Tom asked him as they walked back along the wide pavement with its rustling plane trees.

'Sure. D'you think she can work with me?'

Tom said softly, 'I think you'll find she can.'

In his office (which was a lot more basic than Marcus's) Tom rummaged in a drawer and handed him a set of keys, both mortise and yale.

'Skeleton keys?' he asked in surprise.

'We call them universal keys. You never know when they're going to come in handy, so keep them on you.'

He showed him how to use them and gave him a pencil torch to go with them.

'Doesn't Jo get to use the toys as well?' Fraser asked.

'She's still got hers from last time. I forgot to ask for them back. Remiss of me.' He showed him out.

On the train back to Bristol, Fraser wasn't feeling anything like so confident as he'd tried to make out – it was obvious the others were all used to working together and he felt completely out of his depth. Think ten grand, he told himself.

On the ward round on Monday, he spotted a patient that seemed to fit Tom's 'at risk' category: Rose Parker, seventy-five, who had breast cancer with secondaries. She was a retired teacher and probably only had a few months to live, but the look in her eye suggested she was going to make a fight of it. She'd come in for pain and vomiting control and Edwina had put her on morphine and domperidone.

Jo, meanwhile, had arrived for her interview.

'Do sit down, Miss Farewell,' Helen said when they got to her office. 'Good journey?'

'Fine, thanks.' Actually, with two changes, it had been a bit of a pain.

'Would you like some coffee now, or shall we look round first?'

'I'd love to look round,' said Jo, taking the hint – besides, she'd had coffee on the train.

Like Fraser two months earlier, she couldn't help but be impressed by the bright pastel colours, the cleanliness, calmness and efficiency that pervaded the place – surely, nobody could deliberately kill anyone here?

She asked what she hoped were intelligent questions and made what she hoped were pertinent comments before arriving back at Helen's office half an hour later.

'To tell you the truth, Miss Farewell,' Helen said over coffee. 'I can't help being a little surprised that someone with your qualifications and experience should be interested, I'm sure you could have found a sister's post in the area if you'd waited.' She raised her eyebrows quizzically.

'As a matter of fact,' Jo said easily, 'there's one advertised in your ENT department at the moment.'

'Exactly. I'd have thought with your forthcoming marriage the extra money would have been useful.'

Jo was ready for this. 'I am right in thinking Dr Philip Armitage is the consultant here, aren't I?'

'Yes?'

Jo explained how she'd been thinking about a change of direction and had been very impressed by an article of his in *Community Medicine*. 'So when I saw your advert after Mark telling me about this new job here, I decided to apply for it.'

'I see.' Helen continued looking at her for a few more moments, then made up her mind. 'In that case, subject to references of course, I'd like to offer you the post.'

'And I'd like to accept,' Jo said with a smile that was quite genuine. 'When d'you want me to start?'

'When can you start?' Helen asked.

'A week today?'

'That'd be fine – but don't you have to give more notice than that?'

'I gave provisional notice as soon as I knew about Mark's job,' Jo said, and told her how he wasn't moving for a month. 'It'll give me a chance to look at the housing situation.'

When Helen saw her off a few minutes later, Jo was feeling so pleased with the way things had gone that she had to stop herself joining in Helen's greeting to Fraser when he passed them in the corridor.

Ten minutes later, Fraser stuck his head round Helen's door. 'Busy?'

'Do I look busy?'

'I can never tell with you,' he said, smiling. 'I've been thinking – let's eat out tonight, shall we?'

'But I was going to make a lasagne, I've got all the ingredients.'

'I thought it might make a change, that's all.' The truth was that eating out made it easier to avoid sleeping with her – not that he had done any actual sleeping yet.

'Oh, all right,' she said. 'So long as it's not curry.'

'I'll pick you up at eight, then.' He made to go, then said, 'Who was that you were with just now? New rep?'

'I might have known you'd notice her,' Helen said. 'No, as a matter of fact, she's our new senior staff, starting next week.'

'That's good news.' He looked at her more closely. 'Isn't it?'

'Ye-es. It's just that she's almost too good to be true.'

'Oh?' He tried to sound casual. 'In what way?'

'Oh, it's probably just me. I'll be checking on her references, though.'

'I'll see you at eight, then,' he said, deciding to leave it there, although he was itching to know more.

Half an hour later, he went to his room and phoned Jo's mobile. She answered after three rings.

'It's Fraser,' he said. 'Can you talk?'

'So long as you don't expect intricate answers, I'm on the train.'

He could hear the rhythm of the wheels and background chatter. He told her quickly what Helen had said.

'Oh, Lord' she said. 'I wonder what I did.'

'She's probably just not used to such enthusiasm. I take it your references are OK?'

'Of course they are.' She lowered her voice. 'I wonder whether I ought to produce my fiancé, Tom would probably stand in.'

'Won't he seem a bit old?'

She laughed. 'I won't tell him you said that.' She continued more seriously. 'You'd better tell him what you've just told me, though.'

'What can he do?'

'He'll want to know, he's very good at assessing risks.'

Fraser rang Tom's number and told him what had happened.

'Probably doesn't mean anything,' Tom said after thinking about it a moment. 'Just natural cynicism, a lot of nursing sisters seem to have that now.'

'I'm seeing her tonight, d'you want me to try and find out some more?'

'No, for God's sake don't do that,' he said quickly. 'It's just the sort of thing that might start her wondering.'

'What if she brings it up?'

'Oh well, you could express mild interest then, I suppose. But *be careful.*'

Mildly nettled, Fraser rang off.

CHAPTER 12

But Helen didn't say anything more about it, so neither did he.

He'd been worried he'd find it difficult talking to her now that his relationship with her was so false, but to his surprise, he didn't – it was almost as though she, too, realized that something had changed and had adapted herself to it. She'd always been interested in his past life, especially regarding Frances (morbidly so, he thought sometimes), but tonight, he managed to get her to talk about herself and some of the places she'd worked in: London, Reading, Southampton, Coventry.

'You've certainly been around,' he said, watching her face in the candle-light, aware of her beauty, aware that it no longer moved him. 'Where would you say you came from?'

She smiled. 'I wouldn't say I came from anywhere.'

'Where were you born?'

'London. Although we moved around quite a bit.'

'We being you and your mother?'

She nodded, concentrating on her food for a moment.

'What about school, didn't it make that difficult?'

'Oh, I went to a succession of private schools until I was eleven, then she sent me to boarding school – her father had set up some sort of fund for me to do that.'

A bell rang in his head – hadn't she said a couple of weeks earlier that her mother had died when she was six?

'Was it better or worse than all the moving around?' he asked.

She took another mouthful of food, taking her time to answer and he wondered if she'd realized her mistake. 'Neither, really,' she said at last. 'Some of it was good, some not so. A bit like life. I got three decent A levels out of it, so I'm not complaining.'

Sodding awful then, he thought. 'What made you choose nursing?'

'What made you choose medicine?' she shot back.

75

'The nurses? The money? Because it was there? I don't know.'

Her face dimpled as she smiled again. 'Because it was there,' she said. 'That's as good an answer as any.'

Session over, he thought.

The next day, Tuesday, he got chatting to the pair of nurses on the drug round and casually asked whether there always had to be two of them.

The senior of them, a buxom hussy called Carrie with big red hair and blue eyes was only too eager to help.

'If it's only oral drugs, then one SRN can do it on her own,' she told him. 'Or *his* own, of course,' she added archly. 'Mustn't be sexist, must we?' She grinned. 'But if there's anything intravenous, there has to be two.' She shrugged. 'There nearly always is, so there's nearly always two of us.'

'So you sort of check each other out?'

'Yeah,' She said, standing very close as she showed him. One of them read from the list and took the drug from the trolley, while the other gave the drug to the patient and signed the chart. 'That's me, today,' she said, her sexuality, like her scent, hanging around her like a cloud.

'But it could be either of you?'

'Sure. As it comes, really. Anything else I can do for you?' she asked coquettishly.

'I'll let you know,' he said, grinning inanely back at her.

He fled to his office to recover.

Later, in the evening, while he was sitting in his usual corner in the social club, nursing his usual pint and watching the darts match, one of the home team was suddenly called away. The rest of them looked at each other, then round the room and one of them made eye contact with him. He came over and asked Fraser if he'd stand in.

He won the game for them with a shanghai. They cheered, clapped his back, called him Jock and asked him to be a permanent member. He told them it was a fluke (only partly true), but left in a better frame of mind than he'd arrived.

Here we go....

He got in the next morning and found that one of his patients, Roger Trainer, had developed a chest infection in the night and been put on ampicillin. He went to see him. His temperature, heart rate and blood pressure were all up.

'How are you feeling, Mr Trainer?'

'A bit shivery, bit wheezy, you know ... otherwise, not too bad.'

Fraser nodded slowly. What to do?

The thing was, Roger Trainer wasn't what he thought of as an 'at risk' patient; he was seventy-two and had come in with a fractured pelvis which was mending nicely. Other than that, he'd been healthy. There was no reason (officially) for him to interfere with the treatment, so he decided not to.

By late afternoon, he realized Roger was getting better.

In the evening, he went over to Helen's for the postponed lasagne. It was perfect, as was the syllabub to follow, and the wine, and the way she dressed, everything.

They chatted comfortably over the wine, then went to bed, where ironically, he found that by not making so much effort himself, the sex seemed to be better for her.

'Mm,' she said, snuggling into him afterwards. 'That was nice.' Then, pulling her head away, she looked at him, her eyes like lamps in the dark. 'Stay with me Fraser, please.'

'I haven't brought my toothbrush,' he said, trying to make light of it.

'You can borrow mine.'

Perhaps he ought to at least try. 'All right.'

She used the bathroom before him. Waiting for her, he found himself looking at the locked junk room. As she came out, he said, 'Why d'you keep it locked?' He nodded at it. 'Valuable junk?'

'Oh, I've got some personal stuff in there.'

He thought a locked room would be more likely to attract a burglar than otherwise, but didn't say so. He thought about the keys Tom had given him.

He knew the moment she turned the lights out he couldn't stay. He decided to wait until she was sound asleep, then leave without waking her. Her arms were around him. When her breathing deepened, he gently disengaged himself and turned over. She mewed a little in protest, then settled again with her hand round his waist.

He waited. The electric clock by her bed ticked. A car drove away, its lights making patterns across the ceiling. He lay there, wide awake, itching to be gone.

After about twenty minutes, her breathing was deep and regular and he began easing himself away. Her hand flopped on to the mattress. He slithered out of bed and over to his clothes. A floorboard creaked. She mumbled in her sleep. To put them on here or out in the landing? He crept out and had started pulling them on when her door opened.

'You're going?' She looked like a hurt child.

'I can't sleep. I'm sorry, Helen.'

Her expression changed to something thinner, meaner. 'Didn't try very hard, did you?' She picked his clothes up from the floor and threw them at him. 'You'd better get out, then,' she shouted, went back into the bedroom and slammed the door.

He quickly finished dressing and went in after her. She was in bed, turned away from him but he could see the glint of tears on her cheeks in the light from the streetlamp outside.

He said, 'I'm really sorry, Helen.'

'Just go, will you.'

He went. As he drove away, the relief and guilt curdled in his stomach. Oh, you bastard, Marcus, he thought. Ten thousand quid was beginning to seem like not so very much.

The next day, he bought some flowers and, feeling rather cheap, left them on her desk with a note saying sorry.

On the ward round, there was another chest infection that had been put on ampicillin. Edwina left the treatment as it was. Fraser watched all day, but by evening, it was obvious that this one was getting better too.

'Fraser.'

He looked round as Helen caught up with him in the corridor – it was the day after that, Friday.

'Thanks for the flowers.'

'Apology accepted?' he asked.

'Of course it is, and I'm sorry I was so . . . non-understanding.'

'That's all right,' he said. 'I'm sorry, too.'

'Are you going back to Bristol tonight?'

He nodded. 'Yes.'

'One of these days I'm going to persuade you to stay the weekend. You never know, it might help.' He didn't say anything and she went on. 'See you tonight before you go?'

'Sorry, I've arranged to meet someone when I get back. My mother-in-law,' he added. 'We could lunch if you like.'

'I can't, not today,' she said.

Back in his office, he started putting together a list of the 'at risk' patients. Rose Parker from Monday, and another he'd spotted the day before: Cedric White, seventy-seven, with heart disease.

Then he turned on the computer and looked over Ranjid's patients – there was one possible: Daniel Pope, seventy-four, with MS and a broken neck of femur. He was mentally alert, but the MS had got a lot worse since he'd been in hospital. Fraser added him to the list.

A couple of hours later, he found out why Helen couldn't lunch with him – he'd gone back to his flat to get something and saw her with Ranjid, driving away in his car. They didn't see him. What *was* it with them? Fraser wondered about following them . . . then realized the MG was a bit too recognizable.

During the afternoon he thought about the three patients on his list and it occurred to him that most of the suspicious deaths had happened over the weekend. He was going up to London in the morning, so why not stay here tonight and keep an eye on them? There was a patient in a side room, Mollie Perkins, with C. difficile, the hospital diarrhoea bug that can cause anything between a mild case of the runs and death. He'd put her on antibiotics and she'd make a perfect excuse for calling in (God, you're becoming a cynic, he thought. . . .).

He checked them all at half past five before he left. They were fine. He went to his room, showered, had a meal in the canteen. The hospital library was open until eight, so he went there and looked up all he could find on the transmission of pneumococcal pneumonia. The only thing of interest he found was confirmation of what Stones had told him – that it used to be known as 'the old man's friend', because of the painless death it brought about.

When the library closed, he went back to the unit. The sister, who was called Terri, looked at him curiously. 'Hello, Dr Callan.'

'I've been a wee bit worried about Mrs Perkins,' he said. 'How is she now?'

She shrugged. 'Fine when I last saw her.'

'Good. I'll just take a keek while I'm here.'

Mrs P, or at least her insides, were settling down nicely and the three 'at risk' were all still fine as well.

Terri was on the phone as he left. 'No,' she was saying. 'I told you, I've looked there – Dr Callan,' she called after him, 'You haven't seen the on-call bleep anywhere, have you?'

'Sorry, no.'

Rolling her eyes in exasperation at him, she returned to her caller.

When should he check on them again? he wondered as he walked back to the flat. Certainly not while Terri was still there, maybe after the shift changed at midnight.

Back in his room, he tried reading for a while, but couldn't get into it. He was wondering about a drink at the social club when it suddenly occurred to him that now he had Tom's keys, he'd never have a better chance for a snoop in Ranjid's office – Edwina's and Philip's too, for that matter . . . The more he thought about it, the more it seemed to be criminally negligent not to.

CHAPTER 13

Fraser found the keys and went out. It was dusk and no one was around. He slipped through the main door of the unit – the lobby was lit but there was no sign of the orderly. He crossed quickly to the office wing, the down stroke of the T; unlike the wards, the door didn't have a combination lock on it.

He went silently along the corridor to Ranjid's room. Although it wasn't dark outside yet, there was hardly any light and he had to peer at the keys to find one the right size. With the third, the lock turned with a satisfying snick. He went in and relocked the door behind him.

To use the light or not? He had to if he wanted to see properly, and the window faced away from the wards. Better pull the blinds, though.

He surveyed the room. Ranjid's medical degree hung framed on one wall, a picture of an Indian temple on the other. A spider plant descended like a waterfall from the window sill – now that he was here, he realized he had no idea what he was looking for. Well, he'd know if he saw it.

There was a box of vinyl gloves on the side bench. He pulled a pair on. He tried the desk drawers. Locked, but one of the keys soon opened them. The top ones held pens, a stopwatch, a spare stethoscope and a diary. He flicked through the diary, but found nothing of interest. He recognized one or two names – 'Lunch with Patrick' presumably meant Fitzpatrick and 'Helen' spoke for itself.

In the bottom drawers, there were some patient files. Was this it? His heart beat harder as he went through them, but they all seemed to be 'fallers', patients with broken bones, maybe a special interest of Ranjid's. He noted down all the names nevertheless.

Underneath the files, he did find something unexpected – a girlie mag. It was depressingly similar to the ones he remembered seeing as a boy, and somehow pathetic in a medic of Ranjid's standing.

He replaced everything and then went through the filing cabinet and cupboards, but didn't find anything of interest.

The computer? No – anything incriminating would be covered by a password. He relocked everything and let himself out. There was no sound, other than a phone ringing somewhere in the distance. Feeling slightly foolish, he wiped the door handle before going to Edwina's room.

He locked it behind him, closed the blinds and began as before with the desk drawers.

Nothing in the top ones, but again, the bottom one held a surprise, this time a bottle of vodka. He gingerly lifted it out and set it on the desk. It was half full – or half empty, depending on your state of mind. So maybe Edwina needed help in keeping up her easy going image.

He checked the rest of the drawers and made a quick search of the room, but as before, found nothing.

Philip's office, to his surprise, wasn't even locked. Unlike the others, maybe he had nothing to hide – in his office, anyway. Fraser nevertheless locked the door behind him once inside.

The windows of this room faced the wards, but would anyone be looking? He couldn't search without light, and in the unlikely event anyone did notice, they'd assume Philip had come in for something.

The bookcase on the wall was locked and glancing at the titles, he thought he could understand why: there was the first edition of an old friend, *Dacie and Lewis*, an ancient *Topley and Wilson* and an equally venerable *David*. He would have loved to look through them, but didn't dare.

The desk drawers were locked as well and he was sorting out which key to use when there was a knock on the door. 'Philip? Philip, are you there?'

Several things happened at once: Fraser jumped as he recognized the voice – Ranjid's – and dropped the keys, which made a loud rattle on the desk.

'Philip?' The door handle rattled. 'Who is in there?'

Fraser had grabbed the keys and was halfway to the window when he heard another kind of rattle, the one of a key going into a lock. *Christ!* Did Ranjid have one to Philip's room as well?

The blind made screeching noises as he fought his way underneath and scrabbled at the handle of the window ... it squeaked open and he tumbled through and on to a rose bed, picked himself up and ran into the darkness between the unit and the next building. He heard a shout from the window but kept running. He then stopped. He hadn't been seen by

anyone yet, but if he was seen running, they'd remember, so he walked –
fast, but not too fast – back towards the flats, his heart beating sickeningly.
He felt dizzy, drew deep breaths, remembered the gloves and pulled them
off. They'd been shredded by the rose bushes and he hadn't even noticed.
He stuffed them into a pocket. He looked at his watch, half past nine, and
his hands were bleeding.

Ranjid was probably already calling the police – would he be
suspected? Possibly, by Ranjid – what the hell was *he* doing here?

Never mind that now, think. He'd been seen at just after eight by Terri
but not since. If he got to Bristol, he could establish an alibi. Yeah – drive
there now, straight to Mary's. Pick up a few things first, wash his hands?
No, straight there.

He found the car, unzipped the tonneau and drove off – fortunately,
there was a back way out, so he didn't have to drive past the unit. He drove
gently, not making too much noise.

He'd been sweating earlier, but was shivering after a mile. He stopped
and put up the hood.

On the motorway, he kept under eighty – wouldn't do his alibi a lot
of good to be caught speeding – and reached Mary's at a quarter past
ten.

'Fraser! Is something the matter? What have you done to your
hands?'

Inside, the more he tried to explain, the more bemused she looked. At
last she said tiredly: 'All right, Fraser. I don't know what you've got yourself into this time, but I'll say you were here at nine.'

He cleaned up his hands, then phoned Tom.

The silence at the other end as he told him about it was more eloquent
than any amount of swearing could have been. Then Tom said wearily,
'What possessed you, Fraser?'

'It seemed. . . .' He swallowed.

'Like a good idea at the time?'

'Just too good an opportunity to miss. I thought I might find something useful.'

'And did you?'

'No.'

'Two rules, Fraser – no, three. Never search peoples' offices unless
you've got a specific object in mind. Never do so unless you've got either
an escape route or an explanation for being there. And never, *never* forget
that Sod's law will invariably operate. Got that?'

Fraser nodded miserably. 'Aye.' He swallowed again. 'Sorry.'

'All right.' A sigh drifted down the line (possibly because Tom could remember doing much the same sort of thing himself when he'd started).

'You did right to get back to Bristol. Is your mother-in-law OK about giving you an alibi?'

'I think so.'

'Better let me speak to her.'

Fraser handed her the receiver. Yes, she did remember Mr Jones, and yes, she thought she realized the importance of what Fraser was doing. She handed the phone back.

'Should I still come up tomorrow?' Fraser asked him. 'I mean, what if the police come looking for me here?'

Tom thought for a moment, then said, 'No, stick to what you were going to do – we've got a lot of stuff to talk about. See you tomorrow.'

Fraser got his story straight with Mary, then went home.

He caught the nine o'clock train in the morning. He was the last to arrive again.

'Ah, Fraser,' Marcus said. 'You'd better sit down and tell us about it.'

He spoke, Fraser thought, more in sorrow than in anger – Shakespeare? He put it out of his mind as Marcus poured him some coffee. Neither of the other two said anything.

'Thanks.' He took a gulp of the coffee, burned his mouth, and began telling them, feeling his face burning as well.

When he'd finished, Tom said, 'You heard a shout as you ran away – could he have recognized you?'

Fraser shook his head. 'Unlikely. I was into the shadows before I heard it.'

'OK. You're certain no one saw you going into the hospital?'

'Aye. I wouldn't have gone through with it otherwise.'

'So no one saw you there after eight?'

'No.'

'And you're sure you didn't leave any prints?'

'I am.'

Tom let out a breath. 'Well, thanks to a mix of luck and serendipity, I think we may have got away with it.'

Jo said, 'But whoever's doing the killing is going to hear about this – won't it put them on their guard?'

Thanks, Jo, Fraser thought.

'No, I don't think so,' said Tom. 'That's what I meant by we. Hospitals get broken into all the time. Since none of the doors they *know* the intruder got through were locked, there's no mystery as to how it was done. Fraser had a perfectly good reason for being there at eight, and thanks to his alibi, couldn't have been there at nine. I think we're OK.'

'Won't they wonder why Armitage's door was locked if he usually leaves it unlocked?' Jo again.

'I'm not too worried about that, either,' Tom said. 'The intruder might have locked it with the key inside, or if there wasn't one, maybe Singh got confused about whether it really was locked or not.'

Marcus asked whether they'd got anything positive out of it. 'For instance, those names you took down, Fraser?'

Fraser said he'd look them up when he got back. 'I don't think they'll tell us anything though, they just didn't seem right.'

'We've learned a bit about their peccadilloes though, haven't we?' Jo observed. 'The bosses, I mean – I wonder what Fraser would've found if he'd made it into Armitage's desk.'

Marcus smiled faintly, then turned back to Fraser. 'It wasn't a bad idea keeping an eye on the patients, although it'll be a lot easier when you can both do it.' He paused. 'I imagine Tom's already said all that's needed about the other.'

Fraser nodded. He could feel his cheeks glowing again and hoped that his beard hid it.

'Did you bring the other list? The at risk patients.'

He found it and handed it over. Marcus glanced down it, then handed it on to Tom, who did the same before passing it to Jo.

Tom said, 'But they're all well at the moment?'

'They were at eight last night. There have been two others, though.' He told them about the false alarms.

'But these weren't people you'd thought of as at risk?' Tom said.

Fraser shook his head. 'And they got better.' He drew a breath. 'After last night,' he said, 'I hope to God I'm right about all this.'

'Well, now would certainly be a great time to tell us you'd got doubts,' Jo murmured into the silence.

'A week's nothing,' Tom said after shooting her a look. 'Forget it.'

After another short silence, Marcus asked him if he'd been able to look at the drug system and he told him what he'd found out from the two nurses.

'Sounds like standard practise,' said Jo. 'I'll take a closer look at it when I get there.'

'There is another problem,' said Fraser. 'I should've thought of it before, but it only occurred to me during the false alarms.' He looked round. 'What do we do if one of these patients does get resistant pneumonia before we work out how it's being done?'

'I'd wondered about that,' said Jo.

'How d'you mean?' said Tom.

'Well, I couldn't just stand by and watch them die, but if we did anything to prevent it, then we risk whoever's doing it realizing we know.'

Marcus said, 'Couldn't you, as a doctor, simply put them on a different antibiotic?'

'*I* probably could, although I'd likely be asked to explain why later. Jo couldn't. She'd have to suggest it to a doctor and she'd almost certainly be told to give the ampicillin more time to work.'

'And by the time I did manage to persuade someone,' said Jo, 'it'd probably be too late. I don't like it either.'

'Tom?' said Marcus.

'It's a problem.' Tom thought for a moment. 'If – when – it happens,' he said, 'could you, Jo, give them some antibiotic we knew was OK without anyone knowing?'

'I won't know that until I've seen the set-up. Then, maybe, so long as they were on my patch.'

'And if they weren't?'

'Then I'd have no business going anywhere near them.' She continued quickly. 'But if I was caught giving unauthorised drugs to *anyone*, I could be struck off. I want a written guarantee that that won't happen, Marcus.'

'You can both have that,' Marcus said.

'Fraser, could you do it?' Tom said.

'Aye, so long as they were on Edwina's list. But there's still the other problem – if they got better, won't the person responsible wonder why?'

'Couldn't we use that to our advantage?' asked Jo.

'How?' said Marcus.

She leaned forward. 'Say we have a patient, Mrs Smith – she gets pneumonia and is put on ampicillin. Either I do the drugs round myself and make sure she gets the real thing, or I give her some on the side later – extra ampicillin won't hurt her.'

'But how will *you* know you're giving her the real thing?'

'I'll break open a new pack, then keep some back and have it tested. Then, when she *doesn't* die, the person who gave them the dummy might give themselves away.'

'It's worth a try,' said Tom. 'What d'you think, Fraser?'

He nodded. 'It's probably the best we can do. But if we're going to do that, Jo and I have got to be able to meet and talk, in my room, if necessary.'

'You can't afford to be seen together,' said Tom. 'You'll have to use the hotel room.'

'There might not be time for that.'

They eventually agreed that if one of them found a case, they would immediately phone the other's mobile.

'Which means mobiles on at all times,' Marcus said, looking from one to the other.

'What if they're not allowed?' asked Jo.

'Leave it on and say you forgot,' replied Tom.

After a pause, Marcus continued, 'There's one more thing before we go to lunch – death certificates. Fraser, what actually goes on the victims' certificatess for cause of death?'

Fraser shrugged. 'Pneumonia, I suppose.'

'But you don't know for a fact?'

He shook his head.

'What I'm getting at is that you could argue that they wouldn't have got pneumonia if they hadn't had cancer in the first place. So what's put on them – pneumonia or cancer? Can you find out? It does strike me there's scope for hiding dodgy deaths there.'

They went for lunch in the same place. Jo said she had to leave early again and this time, Fraser went with her.

It was a fine day and even the stately plane trees seemed to be enjoying the sun. The breeze rustled in their leaves and caught Jo's chestnut hair as she walked. Fraser had a job keeping up with her. For something to say, he asked her how long it took her to get home.

'An hour and a half,' she said. 'So long as I catch the next train.' She looked at her watch. 'There isn't another direct one today.'

'When is it?'

'Half an hour.'

'Ach, that's loads of time.'

She smiled unwillingly. 'I have a phobia about missing trains.'

They walked on in silence for a few moments, then he said, 'Are you worried about Monday?'

'A bit, although I just want to get on with it now. Don't you?'

'Yeah. I just hope I'm right about it.'

She looked at him curiously. 'Are you really worried about that?'

He gave her a lopsided grin. 'I'm worried about what Marcus'd say if I was wrong. Wouldn't you be? Especially after Friday's cock-up.'

'I wouldn't worry too much about *that* if I were you – I assure you Tom's done worse things.' She paused. 'As for the other, Marcus would never have agreed to set this up if he wasn't convinced. Here's the station.'

They bought tickets from the machine. Fraser said, 'I'll see you to your train.'

'We're on different lines, aren't we? You want Paddington, that's Bakerloo.'

They stood awkwardly for a moment, then he thrust out his hand. 'I'll probably see you Monday, then. From afar, that is.'

She grinned at him as she took it, then waved as she vanished down the escalator.

CHAPTER 14

The police called round an hour after he got home.

'Dr Callan?' There were two of them, Sergeant Griffiths and Constable Davey of the Wiltshire police. 'Can we come in, please sir?'

He took them to the living room. Offer them tea? No, he wouldn't have done normally, not until he'd known what they wanted. They sat down and Davey pulled a notebook from his pocket.

'I believe you work as a locum staff grade at Wansborough Community Hospital, Dr Callan?'

'Aye, I do. Why?'

'Could you tell us where you were at nine o'clock last night please, sir?'

'At my mother-in-law's at Horfield – why d'you want to know this?'

Davey looked at Griffiths, who nodded.

'An intruder got into the hospital last night, sir. We understand you were there yourself at eight o'clock.'

'An intruder?' *Don't overdo it.* 'When?'

'About nine.'

'What for? Drugs?'

'Not so far as we know, sir. It was the director's. . . .' He consulted the notebook again. 'Dr Armitage's office that was broken into.'

'Was anything taken?'

Not so far as they could make out, no. 'Sister Stokes says you were there at just after eight – is that so?'

'It is,' he agreed.

Had he noticed anything suspicious, anyone hanging around?

He thought about it, then shook his head. 'Sorry, but no, I didn't.'

'What time did you leave the hospital?'

'Just after Sister Stokes saw me. Say five past or thereabouts.'

'Where did you go then?'

Back to his flat, he told them, where he'd picked up a few things and then driven to his mother-in-law's.

What time had he arrived there?

Oh, a bit before nine. Five to, ten to. . . .'

'And she'd confirm that, would she, sir?'

'Of course she would.' He looked from one to the other of them. 'Are you trying to suggest *I* did it?'

'No sir, we're not,' Griffiths said blandly. 'At this stage, we're just eliminating people from our inquiries. Could I have your mother-in-law's address, please?'

Davey noted it down. They got to their feet and Griffiths handed him a card. 'If you do remember anything else, sir. . . .'

'I'll tell you straight away.'

As soon as they'd gone, he phoned Tom's mobile. 'Should I warn Mary?'

'Has she got a mobile?'

'I don't know.'

'Then don't, not if it means using a landline. I think you should ring Armitage, though. Maybe Helen as well. Let me know what they say.'

Fraser called Philip at home.

'No, nothing was either stolen or broken,' Philip told him. 'Look, if you don't mind, Fraser, we'll talk about it on Monday.'

He rang off. He sensed, although he didn't know why, that Philip had someone with him.

He called Helen, but there was no answer, so he left a message.

'D'you think she's with him?' Tom asked when he phoned him back.

'I've no idea.'

'What *is* their relationship? I know you've said they're close, but how close?'

'Close, but platonic,' Fraser said after a pause.

'How d'you know that?' Tom persisted.

'Close because of the way they're completely at ease with each other. Platonic because if she was two timing me with anyone, it'd be Ranjid.'

'Mm. All right,' Tom said, still dubious.

Fraser had intended going to see Philip first thing on Monday, but Philip pre-empted him by calling a meeting of all the medics and heads of departments. He told them briefly what had happened. 'We might never have known about it at all,' he said, 'If it wasn't for the fact that Ranjid had to go in with the on-call bleep.'

Ranjid, who'd been staring at Fraser since he'd come in, said. 'What I'd like to know is what Dr Callan was doing here at eight o'clock.' He turned back to Fraser. 'You weren't on call, were you?'

'You know perfectly well I wasn't, Ranjid. As I told the police, I stayed to do some work in the library, then looked in on a patient before going home.'

'What patient?'

Fraser explained about Mrs Perkins and her infection. 'I've not had much experience with C diff, so I was worried about her.'

'What were you doing in the library that was so important?'

'Ranjid, I think that's enough,' Philip said sharply.

'I was looking up C diff, if you must know,' Fraser said, staring straight back at him. 'And I have to say I'm getting a tad tired of your attitude, Ranjid.' His anger was quite unfeigned.

'My room was broken—' Ranjid began furiously, but Philip cut him off.

'I said that's enough, both of you.' He let the silence hang a moment before continuing: 'Ranjid thinks his office was broken into as well, despite the fact that, unlike mine, it was locked. I'll obviously have to follow suit in future,' he added. He looked round. 'Does anyone else think their office was broken into? Edwina? Helen? Janet?' This last was Janet Towers, who was in charge of admin.

They all shook their heads.

'All right. The police think it was probably an opportunist looking for anything he could lay his hands on, and I see no reason to disagree with them. What it means for us is that we're going to have to upgrade our security.'

They discussed this for half an hour, then broke up.

Fraser, aware that Ranjid was still watching him, caught up with Helen. 'See you tonight?' he said.

'Sorry, I can't,' she said. 'Wednesday?'

He nodded. 'OK.'

Ranjid joined them. 'You've cut your hand, Fraser,' he said.

'Yes.' He held it up. 'Rose bush in my garden.'

Ranjid nodded. 'I thought somehow it might be a rose bush,' he said, and moved on.

Jo, who was starting that morning, probably wouldn't have known there'd been an intruder if she hadn't already known, so low key was the general reaction.

She spent the first hour sorting out administrative details, then was left with Jackie Lee, one of the senior sisters.

It was over ten years since Jo had nursed any older patients, or geriatrics, as she'd known them then, and if Wansborough Community Hospital was anything to go by, things had changed. She knew that most of the old ex-workhouse hospitals had gone now, but even ten years before, geriatric hospitals had tended to be in old buildings for which no one could think of a better use.

Jackie Lee was a cheerful black woman of about forty with a comfortable figure and hair sprinkled with grey. She told Jo in passing about the intruder.

'Has it ever happened before?' Jo asked.

'Not to my knowledge. I've always thought the security a bit lax. They'll have to do somethin' now.' She spoke with a slight Caribbean lilt. 'Anyway, let's get started, shall we?'

She showed Jo round.

'Yes, we do,' she said in answer to Jo's observation that they used a lot of health care assistants rather than qualified nurses. 'Most of the nursing here is routine. Also . . .' she lowered her voice. 'We're on a very tight budget.'

Much of the basic nursing was routine, but Jo was pleasantly surprised by the standards of the HCA's. The patients were turned regularly to prevent bedsores, their bodily needs were attended to more or less when required (and there were one or two very difficult patients), and an effort was made to see that all those who were able to ate at least some of the food that was brought to them.

'What on earth made you want to work with the wrinklies instead of ITU?' Jackie asked over a companionable cigarette in the courtyard. ('If they do ban it even out here, I shall bloody well go out on the street if I want one,' she'd said mutinously when Jo raised the question.)

Jo explained about her fiancé and also about being enthused by Philip Armitage's article.

'Have you met him yet?' Jackie asked.

Jo shook her head.

'You will tomorrow on Ranjid Singh's ward round. He's a sweetie – Philip, that is.'

'What about the rest?'

Jackie made a face. 'The usual mix.' She lowered her voice again – 'Singh's screwy, Edwina Tate floats around on a cloud and Saint Helen – well, you've met her, haven't you?'

Jo laughed. 'Does everyone call her that?'

'Not to her face. Oh, she's all right, jus' takes everythin' too seriously, especially herself.'

'What about the staff grades and housemen?'

'None of them are really nasty – although you need to watch Becca Lake, she can be a cow. We've got a locum staff grade who's quite tasty, although rumour has it that he's got a thing going with Saint Helen.'

'I'd have thought, from what you said, that she'd have taken herself too seriously for that.'

'None of us here take ourselves too seriously for that,' Jackie intoned.

They cackled briefly before stubbing out their fags and going back in, where Jackie went over a few more things with her before turning her loose.

It was, Jo thought, the opposite end of the spectrum from ITU. It was nursing in a lower key: no monitors, no jump leads for restarting stalled hearts, no adrenalin churning emergencies – and yet the time didn't drag, far from it, because not only were there less nurses, but less staff per patient, so she was on the move throughout the day.

When she came off duty at four, she drove to the hotel where Tom had booked a room and reported that she hadn't got much to report.

Tom said, 'Better not tell Fraser what Sister Jackie said about him.'

'Why not?'

'Don't want him getting ideas above his station, do we?'

Jo smiled, said, 'There's not much likelihood of that. I don't think he's a happy man.'

'No, I suppose not,' said Tom after a pause.

They had an early dinner together in the hotel.

'In the unlikely event of anyone seeing us,' Tom said. 'I'm your fiancé.'

She decided not to tell him about Fraser's comment concerning his age.

They chatted comfortably and Jo found herself thinking, He's still the sexiest man I know, but if he were to make a pass at me now, I'd turn him down.

It was Ranjid Singh's ward round the next morning. Jackie introduced her to both him and Philip, who gravely shook her hand. When she mentioned the article of his she'd read, he smiled rather self-consciously.

'Thank you,' he said. Then, ironically: 'Well, I suppose your presence here would indicate that it's done *some* good.'

She instinctively liked him and was impressed by the professionalism of the team as they moved from bed to bed. She watched carefully, but every patient, she thought, was recommended treatment appropriate to their condition.

She did spot one she thought fitted Tom's 'at risk' category: Shirley Norman, aged seventy-one, admitted with acute phase MS. She'd lost a lot of body movement and found it difficult even to speak clearly, but Jo could see the glint of intelligence behind her eyes. She'd been prescribed methyl prednisolone, but it didn't seem to be helping as much as it had. Singh opted to leave the treatment as it was for a while longer in the hope of improvement.

After he'd finished the morning clinic, Fraser closed the door of his office and started searching the computer for the information Marcus wanted. First, he called up Mary Bailey's record – 'Cause of death: Cancer.' No mention of pneumonia. Well, well. . . .

He found some of the others. Harold Carter – Cause of death: Cancer. John Bickenhall – Cause of death: Pulmonary embolus.

Alice Steel, however, who'd had MS, was down as dying from pneumonia, as was Mavis Perrins. The trend seemed to be that where the patient had had a known killing disease, like cancer or heart disease, this was put down as the cause of death, not pneumonia. But if they'd had a chronic condition, such as MS, Parkinson's or Alzheimer's, pneumonia was entered.

So what were the proportions? He called up and printed out the figures from the computer and tried to work them out for a six-month period. As taken from the records, deaths from pneumonia were around 30 per cent of the total, from cancer 24 per cent, from heart conditions 15 per cent.

He then rang his contacts in Glasgow and Bristol again and asked if they could do the same for their areas. They groaned aloud on hearing his voice, but said they'd try. He was still speaking to one of them when the door opened and Edwina came in.

'I'd better go,' he said into the phone. 'Thanks for your help, Gavin – speak to you later.'

Edwina had sat down by the desk with the computer terminal and there was no way she could miss the printouts he'd been working on.

'My, you have been busy,' she said, looking at the screen and the figures he'd written down. 'What's all this in aid of?'

His mind raced – no point in trying to lie, she'd spot it immediately. 'I'm trying to work out roughly the causes of death here over a period of time. Seasonal changes, things like that.'

'Why?' she said sharply. 'It's not still the pneumonia business, is it? You were told to drop that.'

'No, of course not, just the general trends and seasonal changes . . .' He could feel himself floundering. 'It occurred to me that a comparison with other hospitals might be interesting, might even be worth publishing.'

'*Publishing*! Not really within your remit, I'd have thought, Fraser.'

Counter attack. 'No, but since being here, Edwina, I've been wondering about specializing in community medicine, making a career of it.'

'Well . . .' She stared back at him, lost for words. 'Well, I'm glad we've inspired you so much. Perhaps we should have a talk about it.'

'I'd really like that, Edwina,' he said as sincerely as he could.

'Good. We'll do that.' She took a breath. 'Anyway, I only came to say I'm away some of next week – you weren't thinking of visiting your mother again, were you?'

He said he thought she was stable now.

'Good. I know you can handle the ward round and clinics, but there's a departmental meeting at the trust on Monday. There have to be at least two medics from here, so you'll have to go in my place.'

'Wouldn't Ranjid be better?' he asked.

'No, as deputy, Ranjid has to stay. Besides,' she added pointedly, 'bearing in mind what you've just told me, you should be interested.'

'Yes, I would, now that you mention it.'

After she'd gone, he slumped in his chair and expelled a breath. Bloody sodding typical – in future, he'd have to have a story ready for anything that wasn't strictly part of the job.

It occurred to him then that Edwina obviously didn't feel it necessary to follow the rules she'd set down for him concerning closed office doors.

In the evening, he drove down to Tom's hotel. They went down to the bar and Fraser described the meeting about the intruder.

'Singh's attitude's interesting, isn't it?' Tom said. 'Does he really think it was you, or is it just part of his general campaign against you?'

Fraser shrugged. 'God knows. I'm just glad the others don't take him seriously.'

'Sounds to me as though they don't take the intruder too seriously, either.'

'No. Something else happened, though.' He told him how Edwina had caught him looking up the causes of death on the computer.

Tom took a mouthful of beer while he thought about it. 'Was *her* attitude reasonable?' he said at last. 'Or could there be another motive?'

It was Fraser's turn to think. 'Well, she's generally pissed off with me at the moment,' he said. 'What with the time I've had off and the previous pneumonia business, so in her mind, it could have been reasonable.'

'All right.' Tom nodded. 'But try not to let her catch you like that again.'

Fraser felt himself bristling, but all he said was, 'OK.'

'Did you get anything useful on the death certificates?'

Fraser told him what he'd found and how he'd rung his contacts for figures to compare it with.

'It's a good idea,' Tom said. 'But did you think to ask them to check how their areas record pneumonia deaths? They might be doing the same as you and recording them as cancer.'

'Ah, shit,' Fraser groaned.

'Well, it's only just occurred to me. Can you ask them tomorrow?'

Maybe it *had* only just occurred to Tom, Fraser thought as he drove back to his flat, but Tom hadn't had all day to think about it. And he could already imagine the reactions of Gavin and Peter when he asked them.

CHAPTER 15

He was right, they swore at him keen and hard when he rang them the next morning, using almost exactly the same words, although in different accents. Then they resignedly said they'd try.

Jo, meanwhile, had decided it was time she started earning her baksheesh and accompanied the two SRN's on the drug round. It was as Fraser had said: one nurse read from the list while the other dispensed the drugs and signed the patient's drug chart. The drug trolley itself was kept locked, as was the drug cabinet when not in use and there was only one set of keys, usually held by the senior nurse on duty.

Next, she waited until Jackie had gone to lunch, then went to the office and asked the clerk where the notes of patients who had recently died were kept.

'Cabinet in the corner, third drawer down. But we only keep them a month, they go to Medical Records after that.'

Jo thanked her, then extracted the files of the six patients on Fraser's list who'd died of pneumonia. She found the drug chart for each one and noted which nurse had given the patients their antibiotics in the final few days.

With two of the patients, the same signature, C. Tucker, appeared throughout. With two of the others, C. Tucker had given some of the ampicillin doses, but not all, and with the last two, she didn't figure at all. There was no discernible pattern with any other signature.

Two out of six – four, if you counted the times C. Tucker had administered just some of the antibiotic. She looked through them again. In two of the six cases, the first dose of ampicillin had been given intravenously; in the others, it was all in tablet form, but C. Tucker had given both the injected doses.

Significant?

She said to the clerk, 'D'you know offhand where I could find nurse – er – C. Tucker?'

'Oh, that's Carrie Tucker, she's on late shift this week.'

'Oh, right. I'll catch her some other time.'

She quickly scanned the notes again to see if there was anything else, but there wasn't, so she returned the folders, thanked the clerk and left.

Did it amount to a pattern? She'd have to talk to Fraser about it.

An hour later, she saw him in the main corridor. She was holding a set of patient's notes, so she went over to him.

'Excuse me . . . Dr Callan?'

He turned. 'Hello – you're new here, aren't you?'

'Yes, I started this week. Staff Nurse Jo Farewell.'

'How can I help, Jo?'

She pointed out something in the notes, said in an undertone, 'I need to see you.'

'This evening?'

'If possible.'

'Can you find my flat?'

'I think so.'

'Come round at six. I'll be waiting by the outer door. If you see anyone you recognize, keep walking.'

'All right. Thanks,' she said more loudly. She turned to go, then something made her glance up – Saint Helen had just come out of her office and was standing there staring at them.

'Well, she certainly didn't waste any time sorting out the eligible male,' Helen said to Fraser in her room a few minutes later.

'Ach, don't be daft,' he said, genuinely irritated. 'She was asking me about the drug dose of one of the patients.'

'Why you?'

'It's one of my patients. Besides, she's married.'

'What makes you think that?'

'The ring on the third finger of her left hand.'

'She's engaged, actually, although trust you to look—' She broke off, closed her eyes and compressed her lips for a moment. 'I'm sorry, Fraser,' she said. 'I'm sorry, I'm just a bit stressed at the moment.'

'Sure.' He squeezed her shoulders, acutely aware that a truly affectionate lover would do more.

She said, 'I know it's short notice, but can you come round tomorrow instead of tonight?'

'No, I'm sorry, but I can't.'

'Pressing social engagement?'

'Not exactly. As a matter of fact, I'm playing in a darts match.'

'A *darts* match?'

He explained how he'd been enrolled into the darts team. 'I did promise, so I can't really let them down. I'm sorry.'

'Oh, that's all right – if a darts match is really more important than me, then OK, fine.'

'Can you not manage tonight?'

'Oh, I expect so. Assume I can unless I let you know otherwise.' He kissed her cheek, squeezed her shoulder again and then left, feeling foolish, inadequate, self-conscious, wishing the whole ghastly charade was over. Wondered how much longer he could keep it up.

Later, when he got back to his room, he phoned Jo. 'It's Fraser,' he said. 'Helen saw us talking.'

'I know.'

'Well, she cross-examined me about it afterwards, so I think, to be on the safe side, you'd better not come.'

'Why? D'you think she might be watching or something?'

'I know it sounds daft, but I don't want to take any chances. Can you tell me what it's about now?'

'I'll try,' she said, and told him what she'd found out about Carrie Tucker.

'I know her,' he said. 'She was the one I spoke to on the drug round.'

'What's she like?'

'Big, pushy lassie, red hair – we do need to talk about this, don't we? How about tomorrow lunchtime?'

But Jo couldn't manage that and they decided to leave it until Marcus came down on Friday.

At Helen's that evening, the moodiness of the morning had gone; she was bright, chatty and good company.

Why, Fraser wondered? Was it the wine? She'd had quite a bit. Or was it just part of the artificiality of their relationship? He'd thought she'd bring up the break-in, or Ranjid's behaviour, but to his surprise, she didn't.

She said suddenly, 'Fraser, is it true that you're thinking of specializing in care of older people?'

He laughed in disbelief. 'Who told you that?'

'Philip. Why, wasn't I supposed to know?'

'It's not that, it's just the way things get round here. I mentioned it to Edwina, and I suppose she must have told him. I only said it to her as a passing thought.'

'So it's not true, then?'

'Ah, I don't know, Helen ... I *do* find it interesting, much more than I thought I would, but I still don't really know what I want to do.'

She said quietly, 'I think you'd be very good at it.'

'Why?' he asked, curious.

She drank some more wine before replying. 'Because you're compassionate with the patients, but clear-sighted at the same time, not sentimental.'

'How d'you mean?'

'You care about them – ghastly word – but you haven't let that blind you to the fact that it's sometimes kinder to let them go.'

'I thought most people accepted that.'

'Oh, you'd be surprised – we've had locums before who've insisted on the patient's right to life no matter what. Never mind how much they're suffering, never mind what the relatives think. The right to pain and indignity. . . .' she tailed off.

'I didn't realize you felt so strongly,' he said, looking at her.

She shrugged, refilled her glass and drank. 'You can't *not* feel strongly,' she said more calmly. 'Can you imagine suffering, but at the same time being utterly powerless, without meaning, totally in the control of others? Sorry – forgot, you probably *can*, can't you?' She stared across the table at him, her eyes huge in the candlelight. 'Wasn't there ever a time, Fraser, when you thought about ending Frances' life?'

He stared at her, astonished. 'No,' he said.

'Sorry, perhaps I shouldn't have asked,' she said, and turned easily to lighter things.

Driving back, he asked himself whether her attitude made her a suspect. Probably not, he thought; her attitude wasn't so different from his – except for the *suffering without meaning* part of it, Frances' life had *never* been without meaning.

That was what really surprised him – the fact she could ask such a question of him.

The next day at lunchtime he was again going over to his flat for something and again saw Ranjid and Helen driving off together. He looked over at his own car, then noticed a taxi disgorging a couple of passengers at the main entrance, and on impulse, ran over to it.

'Could you follow that car, please?' he said, pointing to Ranjid's Mazda as it disappeared down the hill.

The driver looked back at him incredulously. 'You want me to follow that car?'

'Yes.'

The driver continued staring at him.

'My girlfriend's in it,' he added, realizing he had to say more. 'With someone else.' He shrugged helplessly, pathetically.

Grumbling, the driver started the meter and set off. Fortunately, Ranjid wasn't a fast driver and they caught up quite quickly.

'OK, so I'm following him, so now what?' the driver said.

'Well, carry on. Not too close, though.'

With a sigh, the driver complied. They were never like this on the telly, Fraser thought. It was already evident they were going to Helen's house and five minutes later, Ranjid drew up in her drive.

The taxi driver pulled up fifty yards short as Helen found her key and unlocked the house. Ranjid followed her inside and the door shut.

'You gonna stay and watch?' the driver enquired.

'I'd like to give it five minutes,' Fraser replied levelly.

'Well, you can do it on your own, then.'

Fraser thought quickly – he wouldn't get another taxi easily from here and he didn't fancy walking back, so, much as he hated giving in – 'No, back to the hospital, please.'

They drove in silence.

As Fraser paid him, the driver looked at him with complete contempt. Fraser suddenly realized he didn't care – which, he supposed, must be a good thing in a secret agent.

Back in his flat, he made some coffee and thought about it. There *could* be an innocent explanation. He smiled grimly as another thought struck him – innocent or not, he'd only too gladly hand Helen over to Ranjid.

Walking back from the social club in the dark that evening, having won the game for them again, he'd just reached the trees when two figures materialized in front of him. He knew instantly what it meant and ran, not realizing there was a third until a well-placed foot sent him sprawling on to the playing field. He tried to get up but a sandbag to the back of his head nose-dived him into the grass again. Then two of them grabbed his arms and hauled him upright. He wasn't knocked out, only dazed.

The other one closed in. 'So, here's the guy who won't take a hint,' he said, staring him in the eyes. Fraser was quite unprepared for the fist that sank deep into his guts . . . he heaved, retched, tried to double over.

'Hold him.' The leader grabbed his hair, yanked his head back and looked him in the eyes again. 'You're not wanted here, see. Got that?'

Fraser, knowing he was about to be punched in exactly the same place again, lashed out with a foot and caught his ankle.

The man let out a yell. 'Hold him up,' he snarled and went for him, windmilling with both fists. Fraser clenched his stomach muscles, tried to hunch over and most of it landed round his head and shoulders.

'*Hey!*'

They looked round – the darts team had emerged from the club.

'It's Jock,' one of them said and they started running.

'Hold him,' the leader said again. He stepped back and took a measured kick at Fraser's balls but Fraser saw it coming and managed to twist slightly so that his thigh took some of the blow, but it was bad enough and he let out a screech. They dropped him and ran for it and he sank to the ground clutching his groin. He was dimly aware of their footsteps as they ran, then the darts team clustered around.

'You all right, Jock?'

'D'you need a doctor?'

'Ah *am* a feckin' doctor,' he managed between his teeth. He took a deep breath and blew it out slowly. *Stimulate endorphins and ease the pain – at least, that's the theory.* 'Be all right in a minute. . . .' He took another deep breath.

'D'you want the police?'

'Don't think that'll do much good now.'

' 'Oo were they?'

Fraser shook his head.

'Bring him inside and I'll give him some brandy.' The barman had joined them.

They eased him up and helped him walk to the bar; the barman produced a shot that was at least a triple and Fraser gratefully took a pull. 'Ahh. . . .' he said, then tossed back the rest.

'Better?'

'Yeah. Thanks.'

'What happened?'

He told them, leaving out the warning they'd given him.

'Muggers, I suppose,' said the team's spokesman, who was called Ron. 'Did they take anything?'

Fraser shook his head again.

The barman was looking at him curiously. 'Sounds more like bully boys to me. You been getting up anyone's nose lately?'

'I don't even live round here, I'm a locum. You probably stopped them before they could take anything.'

They pushed it around a bit more, then Ron and one of the others said they'd walk with Fraser back to his flat. At the stairs, he thanked them, sincerely. 'I owe you, gents.'

'Forget it,' said Ron.

'No, don't forget it,' said the other. 'We want you in the team.'

Fraser laughed, then winced. 'See you,' he said.

In his room, he took some paracetamol, then gingerly stripped off and stepped into the shower. The hot water flowed over his body, soothing his aches. Back in his room, he pulled on his boxers and bundled up his dirty clothes. Found his whisky and poured – it was only then he thought to ring Tom.

'I'm coming up,' Tom said.

'No, wait. . . .' But he'd already rung off.

He slowly drank the whisky. Tom was with him ten minutes later. He made Fraser describe the men and what they'd said.

'You're sure about that?' *Here's the guy who won't take a hint.* 'Nothing about leaving Helen St John alone?'

'No. There's something else about her, though.' He told Tom how he'd followed her and Ranjid.

'D'you think they're. . . ?' Tom left the sentence unfinished.

'Tonkin'?' Fraser shrugged. 'No idea. What d'you think?'

'How should I know?' Then, 'I wonder what her game is.'

'At this exact moment in time, Tom, I don't give a – a tonk.'

Tom smiled. 'All right. Get some sleep and we'll talk about it tomorrow,' he said, and left.

Fraser made himself drink some water, switched off the light and manoeuvred himself into bed, trying not to pull his stomach muscles. His head swirled, but for a long time, sleep wouldn't come. The pain nagged at him – his belly, his balls, even the back of his head. He lay there, thanking God, or providence, that the leader hadn't got his second punch in.

CHAPTER 16

On Friday morning he could hardly move and the livid red bruise on his belly stabbed as he squirmed out of bed. His head didn't feel much better, though whether from the sandbag or the booze, he couldn't be sure. He took more paracetamol, had another hot shower, then a strong coffee and off to work.

By the time he got there, the aches had eased a bit and his body was more or less responding to his brain so long as he didn't move too quickly.

He was on his way from his office to the wards to check the at risk patients on his list when he saw two familiar figures at the reception desk – Nigel Fleming and Patricia Matlock MP. The latter looked up and saw him, and her eyes gleamed in recognition. 'Dr Callan, isn't it? Fraser?'

He stopped as she came over to him. 'That's right, er . . .' he hesitated, unsure whether to call her Miss or Mrs or Ms.

'Patricia Matlock,' she enunciated clearly. 'We met at Patrick's party.'

'Aye, I'm sorry, I do remember. I was surprised you should remember me.'

'Oh, you caused quite a stir,' she said.

'I did?'

'Oh yes. That nice Dr Singh was rushing round quite foaming at the mouth after you decamped with his girlfriend.'

'I hadn't realized it was as bad as that.'

'Oh yes,' she repeated. 'He even accused Patrick of being in league with you. Most embarrassing.' She didn't look in the least embarrassed. 'But I dare say it all ended up happily ever after?'

'That would depend on your point of view.'

She gave a silvery laugh. 'I dare say it would.' Her smile faded like a light on a dimmer switch. 'I trust you haven't also forgotten what I said about muddy waters.'

'The blues singer, you mean?'

This time her smile was more of a grimace. 'No Fraser, not the blues singer.'

Fleming came over. 'Oh hello, it's Dr Callan, isn't it?'

'That's right,' he said again. 'How're you, Mr Fleming?'

'Well, thank you. You too, I hope?' He didn't give a tonk, either.

As Fraser nevertheless assured him he was, Philip came out. He looked tired and strained. He nodded to Fraser and asked the others through.

The image of the MP's face remained with Fraser as he continued on his way. Fleming's face merely repelled, but hers both repelled and attracted in equal measure. Why was that? he wondered; Well, she was an alpha female, of course – Fleming would merely dominate, but she probably liked to mix her methods where males were concerned.

Rose Parker and Cedric White both had visitors and both looked fine. Rose especially – her visitor was a young man, not much more than a boy. He was talking animatedly, she was smiling broadly.

Fraser went back to his office and looked up the others on the computer. They were all fine as well.

But were they fine because the perpetrator had suspended operations? Or because – dread thought – he was wrong about the whole thing?

His headache had come back and he rubbed at his eyes with his fingers.

At about the same time, Jo and Jackie were having their fag break in the courtyard. Jackie said suddenly, 'Sharon tells me you were going through some of the notes of dead patients yesterday.'

'Yes, I was.' *Never say any more than you have to.*

'Any particular reason?'

'I was interested in what the most common killers are here. Why, did I do something wrong?'

'No . . . Besides, you don't have to look through the actual notes, we do keep statistics of that sort of thing.'

'I'd be interested to see them – although of course, they don't give the depth of information that notes do.'

Jackie was still looking at her. 'Sharon also said you were asking about one of the nurses.'

'Yes, Carrie Tucker, I thought I'd have a word with her. It struck me that you seem to have a lot of pneumonia here and I was going to ask her about those particular patients.' It sounded weak in Jo's ears as she said it, but Jackie didn't pick up on it.

Instead, she said defensively, 'I don't think we have any more pneumonia here than anywhere else. It is a common cause of death in older people, you know.'

Press home the advantage. 'Yes, but haven't you ever wondered why, Jackie?'

'Well, there are lots of reasons: decreased lung efficiency, the fact that supine patients can't clear all the rubbish in them. . . . Anyway, all I was going to say was that I'd appreciate your mentioning it to me another time.'

'Of course – and I'm sorry if I've offended,' Jo said with a smile.

'Fine, let's forget it.' Jackie stubbed out her fag and they went back in.

Bloody hell, Jo thought as she followed her, Fraser wasn't kidding about everyone knowing what everyone else did here.

On Singh's ward round, she noted another 'at risk' patient: Lily Stokes, aged seventy-five with cancer of the thyroid that had metastasized. She probably only had a few months to live, but was neither senile nor vegetative. Singh prescribed doxamethadone and radiotherapy to ease her symptoms.

When the ward round was over, she checked the others on her list: Shirley Norman in room one and Rose Parker in three.

Shirley was fine, but Rose beckoned her over. 'I'm sorry to trouble you, nurse,' she began, her voice little more than a hoarse whisper. She broke off, swallowed. 'Dry mouth, been talking too much. . . .'

'I'll get you something for it.'

She shook her head. 'Already got one, in there. . . .' She indicated her cabinet.

Jo found the glandosalve dispenser and handed it to her.

'That's better,' said Rose when she'd used it. 'You know, it makes me feel very uncomfortable, not being able to speak.' She smiled. 'Although I can think of more than a few who might have been glad of it when I was teaching. Anyway, I only wanted to ask you if you'd put this in the post for me, please.' She held out a letter.

'Of course,' said Jo, taking it. 'Where did you teach?'

'In the same primary school in Wansborough all my life.' She smiled again. 'That probably sounds a bit sad to you – that's the expression these days, isn't it? But some of them do still remember me. They come and see me, you know. That's why I get so hoarse.'

'What a lovely compliment,' Jo said sincerely.

Rose nodded complacently. 'Yes, it is, isn't it? Makes me feel that my life wasn't completely wasted.'

'Not if they do that, it wasn't.'

They chatted for a few more minutes before Jo left, still smiling. She rather liked Rose.

'Is it connected with the other attack, the first?' Marcus asked.

They were all in Tom's hotel room that evening and Fraser had been telling them about the latest offence on his person.

'Got to be,' said Tom. 'What with the reference to the guy who won't take a hint. The first was a warning, the second was meant to seriously hurt.'

'We don't want a third, then,' said Marcus.

'No, we don't,' Fraser agreed feelingly – the effects had caught up with him now, he ached all over and pain jabbed behind his eyes.

'I've got some ideas that might help you there, Fraser,' Tom said. 'We'll talk about it afterwards. The thing is, who's behind it?'

'Well, it's either Ranjid or whoever's behind the killings.'

'I hope to God it is him,' Tom said. 'Because otherwise it means someone's on to you.'

'Couldn't it be both?' said Jo.

They looked at her and she continued. 'Ranjid could be both behind the killings *and* jealous of Fraser. Unless Saint Helen's in it with him.'

'I don't think so,' said Fraser.

'Why not?'

'I just don't,' he said irritably.

'Then why is she stringing you along the way she is?' said Tom.

'If anybody's doing any stringing along at the moment, it's me,' Fraser said. He told them about Helen's moods, the way she'd got so upset when he wouldn't stay the night with her. 'She wasn't putting that on,' he said. 'It was real. And you know something? It was worse than the beating.'

'I sympathize,' said Marcus. 'But you've got to carry on with it – for now, anyway.' He turned to Jo. 'Have you had a chance to look at the drug system yet?'

Jo described what she'd seen. 'It would be easy enough for someone to substitute bogus ampicillin beforehand,' she said. 'Although it would mean that *all* the patients were getting it.'

Fraser shook his head. 'That can't be right, it worked perfectly well with the two false alarms.'

Marcus said, 'Which leaves us with someone somehow targeting them.'

Jo told them about Carrie Tucker's signatures on the drug chart. 'And you've seen her on the drug round too, haven't you, Fraser?'

He nodded.

Tom said, 'She certainly does seem to be around the drug trolley a lot, doesn't she? But how would she do it?'

'It would be easy for the nurse actually giving the drug to substitute a dummy,' Jo said. 'But there'd be a pattern, wouldn't there? It would be the same nurse's signature on the chart with every death.'

'But didn't you say there're always two nurses on the drug round?

Carrie could have been the *other* one.'

'But that would mean there were two nurses in on it, wouldn't it?'

'No, I don't think so,' said Tom. He jumped up and paced around a moment before turning back to them. 'Case one: Nurse X gives the proper drug to Carrie, who does a quick switch and gives the dummy to the patient and signs the chart – OK?'

They nodded.

'Case two: Carrie makes the switch when she takes the drug from the trolley and gives it to Nurse X, who then gives it to the patient and signs the chart.' He looked at Jo. 'You're going to have to find out if Carrie was on the rounds with the dead patients where her signature *doesn't* appear.'

Jo let out a groan. 'I've already had one sister giving me a third degree.' She told them about Jackie's interrogation.

'All right,' said Tom. 'Do what you can without arousing suspicion.' He asked how many at risk patients they'd noticed now. 'So that's five,' he said when they'd finished, but Fraser couldn't hold back any longer.

'It's five *supposedly* at risk patients who've had absolutely nothing wrong with them,' he said. 'We've also had two not at risk patients who've had pneumonia and got better. Either they've suspended operations, or I've got it all wrong.'

Marcus said quietly, 'The reason we're here, Fraser, is because when we checked your figures, they indicated that you were right.'

'But it's been two weeks and there's been nothing.'

'And we're going to give it another two weeks at least.'

Tom said, 'Fraser, it's not really surprising there's been a lull. Everyone knew about your row with Singh over pneumonia deaths and then Edwina found you looking at causes of death.'

After a moment, Fraser nodded.

Marcus said, 'These five patients, can you cover them all between you?'

They could, except for Daniel Pope, who was Singh's patient and not on Jo's list.

'What about the weekend?' said Fraser.

'You can't afford to hang around with no good reason,' said Tom. 'You especially, Fraser.'

'But it's when they tend to go down with it.'

There was a silence, then Jo said, 'I'm due back at four on Sunday, if that's any help.'

Fraser said, 'I told Helen I'd see her tonight. That means I can stay over, pick up something in my office tomorrow and look them up on the computer.'

'That's the best we can do for now. You'll be working some of the next weekends, won't you, Jo?'

She nodded.

'That'll make it easier.'

The meeting broke up and Jo left. Fraser was about to go too when Tom stopped him. 'We were going to have a word, weren't we?' He took him aside, opened his case and brought out a torch combined with a screamer.

'You'll be amazed at just how much noise it makes,' he said at Fraser's look of disdain. 'Enough to put anyone off their stroke.'

'What if they grab me before I can use it?'

'Always keep it in your hand when you're walking in the dark, but if you are grabbed, try and stamp on their instep – it's as good as a kick in the goolies and not so predictable.'

Fraser smiled as Tom showed him how to do it, remembering for some reason what he'd said to Helen about ghoulies on another evening.

'And Fraser,' Tom said quietly. 'Marcus and I wouldn't be doing this if we didn't think there was something to it. OK?'

'OK.'

Jo, driving back to Latchvale, thought about Fraser's doubts and wondered if she was beginning to get them too. Oh sure, the place was a bit claustrophobic and incestuous, but so were a lot of self-contained hospital departments. And, as Fraser had said, nothing was happening.

Oh well, she thought philosophically, ten grand, plus getting away from David Petterman, who's complaining?

But when she got back to the ward at four on Sunday afternoon, it was to find that Rose Parker had developed pneumonia on Saturday and was being treated with ampicillin.

CHAPTER 17

'When did it start?' she asked, trying to curb the urgency in her voice.

'I'm not sure. Yesterday morning, I think.' Sarah, the staff nurse she was taking over from, stared back at her strangely.'

'Have you got the notes?'

'Here.' Sarah handed them to her and she flicked through them: *'Restless with coughing Friday night, examined by Dr Oakley Saturday 08.30 and put on oral ampicillin.'*

She looked up. 'Let's go and have a look at her.'

Rose was not well. Her face was flushed, her pulse and respiration up. Her skin was hot and dry and her temperature 39°C, but she didn't appear to be in any pain.

'Was she like this yesterday?' Jo asked.

'Not quite so bad.'

'When's her next dose of ampicillin due?'

Sarah consulted the drug chart. 'Two hours.'

'Are there any other patients showing the same symptoms?'

'Well, there's Mr Tabor with bronchopneumonia.'

'I know about him, I mean new cases.'

Sarah shook her head. 'No.'

Jo went back to the sisters' office, thought for a few moments, then, after making sure no one was near enough to overhear, phoned Fraser's mobile number and explained what had happened.

'What's she like?' he asked.

She told him. 'The ampicillin should be working by now, surely?'

'It can take a while – I don't like the sound of this, though.'

'Should I give her some more out of a new pack?'

'You're the one on the spot, what do you think?'

'I think she should have more now, intravenously, and two further doses over the next eight hours.'

'Can you do that without being seen?'

'I think so, yes.'

He thought for a second, then said, 'Do it. Too much ampicillin's better than none in her case. Tell me if there are any developments.'

'When are you coming back?'

'I could come now, but there wouldn't be much point – I'll stick to tomorrow morning. Can you come to my flat at lunchtime?'

'What time's that?'

'One. I'll let you know if I can't make it. You'd better go and give the first dose now. Oh, and keep some of the ampicillin for analysis.'

'Yes, doctor.'

She found the key to the drug store and went over to the door. Two nurses were talking at the station while an HCA was turning a patient over. She walked out of the room and down the corridor. Sarah was in one of the other rooms, chatting to Mrs Grove. She reached the store and let herself in.

There was no one there. No reason why there should be.

Ignoring the drugs trolley, she went over to the glass-fronted cupboard, unlocked it and pushed the glass to one side . . . . broke open a new box of ampicillin vials and slipped one into her pocket.

How to do this? Openly, or surreptitiously?

Openly – if you're seen acting surreptitiously, people remember. They don't remember normality.

She found a small trolley and put on it a sharps bin, kidney dish, mediswabs, syringe and needle and more ampicillin from the new pack. She found some water for the injection and made it up, put the loaded syringe into the kidney dish and covered it with a cloth. She relocked the cabinet, then, as an afterthought, unlocked the trolley and put some of the oral ampicillin into her other pocket. Then, she relocked it and set off.

A nurse pushing a squeaky trolley up the corridor, what could be more normal? And yet she felt as though the walls had grown eyes in addition to the ears they'd always had, and were following her every inch of the way.

Into Rose's room and over to her bed. No nurses or HCAs, but one of the other patients was watching her – she smiled back. 'Everything all right, Mrs Johnson?'

'Yes, thank you, dear.'

She quickly drew the curtains round Rose's bed. Rose was barely conscious.

'Just going to give you some more medicine, Mrs Parker,' she whispered into her ear. 'OK?'

She squeezed the flaccid warm flesh of her upper arm, feeling for a vein with the fingers of her other hand. There! A quick wipe with the medis-wab and in with the needle – Rose didn't even jump.

Ease back the plunger till a wisp of blood shows you're in the vein, then quickly push it home. Withdraw and press down with swab to seal the puncture wound.

When she was sure it wasn't bleeding any more, she discarded every-thing into the sharps bin, pulled the curtains back and wheeled the trol-ley over to a corner. Not a soul in sight, other than the patients.

When she got back to the office, she realized she was trembling slightly. Reaction. And she was going to have to do it twice more.

C'mon Jo, she told herself. There's nothing to it.

Maybe not, but for her, it was unknown territory – she'd never given an unauthorized drug before.

There was plenty to do and the four hours to the next dose passed quickly enough. Rose even seemed a little better, enough to mumble sleepily, 'What are you doing, nurse?'

'Just giving you some more medicine.' She used the other arm to avoid bruising.

By the time the third dose was due, she was feeling more relaxed; it was nearly midnight, the patients were all asleep and there were less staff about. She made up the injection as before and carried the loaded syringe to the trolley in the kidney dish.

The first thing she noticed was that the site of the second injection had bled slightly, staining the sheets. Cursing, she cleaned it up as best she could without starting the bleeding again. Rose was breathing noisily, certainly no better, maybe even a little worse.

She found another site in the first arm and injected. It was while she was holding the swab against the wound to make sure it didn't bleed that she heard Tessa, another of the staff nurses, come in with one of the HCAs. 'I saw her come in here – Jo,' she called. 'Jo, where are you?'

Shit! If they found her here with the trolley, she'd have no explanation. She swallowed, then hoping for the best, she bent Rose's arm over the swab and tucked it inside the sheet. She manoeuvred the trolley round to the other side of the bed, quietly parted the curtain and eased it through into the no man's land the other side . . . then she noisily drew the curtain on Tessa's side. 'Hello?'

Tessa came over. 'Ah, there you are, Jo,' she said 'Katie's a bit worried about Mrs Drew.'

It took her five minutes to sort the problem out and go back to Rose to check on her arm. It had bled a little, but seemed to have stopped now. She tidied it up, then quickly wheeled the trolley back to its corner, just before Geraldine, her replacement, arrived.

Jo handed over, asking her to keep an eye on Rose, then walked slowly back to her room. She needed a stiff whisky and a couple of cigarettes before she'd wound down enough to sleep.

When Fraser got in Monday morning, he was told by one of the nurses that Rose had taken a turn for the worse and that Tim Oakley had added erythromycin.

They went to look at her. Pulse, respiration and temperature were all up again although, as before, she didn't seem to be in any pain or discomfort.

'When did she start the erythromycin?' Fraser asked.

'Two hours ago.'

Not enough time for it to have worked yet.

But if it *didn't* work, Rose was going to die. What to do?

If he changed the antibiotic again now, and *that* didn't work, he'd have to produce a pretty good explanation. And even if it *did* work, for that matter.... Better leave it for now.

An hour later, she was worse.

He found Edwina. She told him to put her on oxygen, but give the erythromycin more time to work. He was almost certain now that Rose was going to die whatever they did. There was nothing more he could do for her, but there was, perhaps, something he could do for subsequent victims.

It was morbid, maybe even gruesome, but the more he thought about it, the more he knew he had to.

He found a couple of swabs and a vacutainer set and went to Rose's room. The curtains were drawn around her bed. No other staff around, so he stepped through. She was still alive.

First, the swabs. He removed the oxygen mask and, placing his hand under her neck, gently tilted her head back. Mentally begging her pardon, he pushed one of the swabs into her mouth and down the side of her throat. She gagged, he simply wasn't as good at it as the nurses – he'd had less practice.... The other side and out. He put the swab back into its tube, then used the second swab on her nose before replacing the oxygen mask.

He swallowed – now the blood.

He listened, couldn't hear anything. Took the vacutainer set out, fitted the needle, slotted a tube into the sheath. No time for a tourniquet – he squeezed her upper arm and felt for a vein with his other hand ... there! He picked up the sheath and pushed in the needle.

Missed, feck it!

He drew it back, pushed again, then felt the faint pop as it punctured the vein. He pushed the end of the tube – a quick hiss and it filled with blood. Withdraw and press cotton wool to stop bleeding.

Footsteps. . . .

'She's over here, doctor.'

He stuffed the sheath, needle and all, into his pocket, whipped away the cotton wool and put her arm back under the sheet. He stepped back just as the curtain opened and the nurse came in, followed by Edwina.

'Fraser, what are you doing here?'

'Oh, hello, Edwina. I was just wondering if there was any more we could do here.'

'Mm.' She picked up the chart and studied it for a moment, felt Rose's forehead and then pulled back the sheet to take her wrist. 'She's been bleeding – hadn't you noticed, Fraser?'

He shook his head. 'I only got here just before you. The erythromycin injection, presumably.'

'Mm. D'you have any ideas?'

'Add another antibiotic?'

'Which?'

'Cefataxin?'

'That presupposes we're dealing with pneumococcus.'

'I think it must be, don't you?'

'Mm.' She looked at him, then nodded slowly. 'All right.' She turned to the nurse. 'But make it tetracycline.'

'Yes, doctor.'

As they turned to go, something stabbed into Fraser's side and he let out a grunt.

'Are you all right, Fraser?'

'Sure. Just a twinge in my back.' *Just the bloody vacutainer needle.*

Should be all right, he thought. Don't suppose she's got hepatitis or HIV.

She died an hour later.

CHAPTER 18

A couple of hours and a ward round later, Fraser hustled Jo through the main entrance of his block and up the stairs to his flat.

'She's dead,' he said as soon as they were inside.

She sat down quickly on his bed. 'She can't be, she wasn't that bad when I left her.'

'Well, she deteriorated pretty quickly after that. They called Tim and he added another antibiotic, but it was too late. She died two hours ago.'

She was looking at him curiously as though not quite sure what to say, and before she could, he said, 'Yes, I was wrong to doubt – she was killed like the others.'

Jo let it out as a sigh. 'Poor Rose,' she said. 'Well, there's no point in going through that again. What shall we do next time?'

'How easy was it?' he asked. 'Giving the ampicillin?'

'All right, except for the last dose – I nearly got caught then.' She told him what had happened, 'If I'd been seen, I wouldn't have had any excuse. What's so funny?'

'Nothing. Nothing's funny, really.' He described how he'd acquired his needlestick injury.

'Bloody hell,' she said.

'Exactly.' He paused. 'You've still no idea how it's being done?'

She shook her head. 'None. Either *all* the ampicillin's no good, or the bug's resistant to it.'

He sighed. 'Neither have I.' He looked at her. 'Could you do it again, if you had to?'

'Jesus, Fraser – after what happened to *you*? Sooner or later one of us is going to be caught – sooner, probably.'

'Just once more?'

'Why? What's the point?'

'I'll get hold of some cefataxin for next time, there can't be many pneumos resistant to that.'

'Haemophilus is though, isn't it?'

'This has got to be pneumococcus to kill so quickly – and I may be able to prove it this time.'

'How?'

He smiled. 'With these . . .' He showed her the swabs and the blood he'd taken. 'They might not grow anything,' he said. 'But then again, they might. Did you get the ampicillin samples?'

She nodded and showed him. He said, 'You'd better get them all down to Tom, the sooner he can—'

There was a knock at the door.

They looked at each other.

'Who is it?' he called.

'It's me, Helen.'

He motioned Jo to the loo. 'Just coming,' he said loudly to cover any sound.

The loo door silently closed and the handle moved slowly up. He went over to the door and, arranging his features into a smile, opened it. 'Helen . . .' He kissed her, 'How did you get in – downstairs, I mean?'

She came inside. 'Someone was coming out – Fraser, I've been trying to ring you, Philip's looking all over for you, you're supposed to be going to a meeting with him.'

'Ah, *shit*.' He didn't have to pretend. 'I'd forgotten all about it.'

She looked at her watch. 'If you hurry, you'll catch him.'

'Let me get my jacket.'

As he turned, he saw Jo's handbag on his bed beside the samples. He snatched up his jacket and virtually manhandled Helen out of the room and pulled the door shut behind him. *Had she seen it?*

'Where is your mobile?' she said as they clattered down the stairs.

'In my office.' *Perhaps she hadn't.* 'Thanks for coming to get me, Helen,' he said.

'If you'd had your mobile. . . .'

'Yeah, I know.' He held the door downstairs open for her. 'Is Philip really mad?'

'Well, he isn't pleased.'

He swore again. They half walked, half ran across the road and round the corner of the unit to see Philip waiting at the entrance, looking at his watch.

'Fraser!' he called out. 'Where the hell have you been?' Extreme language, for Philip.

'I'm so sorry, Philip. I clean forgot.'

'So it would appear – haven't you got your bleeper, or your mobile?'

'In my white coat, in there . . .' He indicated the unit.

'Well, thank God Helen found you – come on, we've got five minutes.'

With a quick, grateful glance at Helen, Fraser followed Philip over to the playing field and round its perimeter.

His stomach rumbled; he hadn't had time for breakfast and had been counting on a quick dash to the canteen for lunch after he'd seen Jo. They walked in silence past the social club and up the steps to the Georgian portico of the trust.

The boardroom was on the ground floor. Places were set round the polished oak table, but only two or three people were seated; most still mingled round the tea and coffee trolley where George Woodvine was being mother.

'Philip,' he called as they made their way through. 'And will ye take a biscuit?' he said to Fraser as he served them.

'I'll take two please – I missed lunch.'

Patrick, dapper as ever, came over and said hello, then the meeting was called to order. Woodvine formally opened it, then more or less handed over to Fleming.

Today, the chief executive was wearing a black pinstripe suit which made Woodvine's tweeds look slightly shabby, and his black hair was brushed back so carefully that the widow's peak looked as though it had been painted on to his pale forehead. His voice wouldn't have been out of place in Christie's and Fraser found himself disliking him even more than he had at the orgy. He took them through the minutes of the last meeting, and then matters arising from the minutes.

Fraser glanced round at some of the others. The middle-aged lady opposite him was making notes, paying careful attention to everything that was being said, while the younger, rather attractive woman next to her seemed about as interested as Fraser. She caught him looking and her mouth turned down slightly at the corners.

Woodvine drooped at the head of the table, as though he might drop off at any moment, and if it wasn't for the gathering discomfort in his stomach, Fraser thought he might join him. It (his stomach) obviously regarded the two biscuits it had been offered an insult and was threatening to make its protest audible. Fraser heaved it in, aware of the pain still lurking in his muscles. The strategy seemed to work and after a few moments, he relaxed slightly – and just as Fleming's modulated voice paused, it (his stomach) rumbled like an ill-tempered geyser.

Fleming's eyes flicked at him in irritation over his half-moon spectacles, then he continued his drone. Fraser felt himself flush and his eyes went involuntarily to the younger woman, who was trying not to smile.

Another rumble, louder this time, which everyone studiously ignored. He grimly hauled his guts in and held them there.

Then the middle-aged woman started speaking and Fraser tuned into her. 'How ever did we get into this state, Nigel?' she was saying. 'Twenty million pounds in debt. . . .'

'I'm assuming that's a rhetorical question, Maddy,' Fleming said in a tired voice. 'We have been over this before, on many occasions.'

'Maybe we have, Nigel, but *I* still don't understand it – and I'm sure I'm not the only one here who doesn't.' She looked deliberately round, then back at Fleming. 'How *did* it happen?'

Fleming, who knew perfectly well that she was doing it just to rub his nose in it again, spoke quickly. 'It was a combination of the building of the new community hospital which, I'm sure we all agree, was imperative in the circumstances, and the euro conversion. Thanks to Philip here, we managed to save some money on the hospital, but the costs of the euro conversion took us by surprise.'

'How much was that again, Nigel?' enquired his tormentor.

'Five million. A memorable figure as I'm sure you recollect, Maddy.'

The younger woman obviously felt that this was the cue for her to contribute. 'Why *did* we go on spending so much on it when it was obvious that a referendum in this country would kick it out?'

'Ah,' said Maddy. 'Now that's something I *can* recall – I do clearly remember suggesting on several occasions that we should drop it before all the money was spent.'

'As you know perfectly well, Maddy,' Fleming said, his anger barely under control now. 'Our political masters wouldn't hear of it. They were sure – they still are sure for that matter – that our joining is inevitable in the end, and wanted it done as quickly as possible.'

'Five million,' mused Maddy, lingering over the figure. 'I wonder how many hip replacements that represents.'

'Or doctors,' said the younger woman. 'Or nurses. . . .'

'I couldn't say,' Fleming said. 'How many more times, Maddy, are you going to insist on looking backwards to this, rather than forward?'

'As many times as it needs to ensure this can't happen again,' she retorted. 'On which note—'

Fleming seemed to make up his mind about something and firmly overrode her. 'As it happens, I do have some good news for the meeting, although it must remain confidential at this stage.' He looked round the table, sure of their attention now. 'My sources inform me that the grade two listing of St James's is to be lifted, so we shall be able to go ahead with the demolition of the building and the sale of the land shortly. That should enable us to recoup a good deal of the money.'

'Well, thank God for that,' said Woodvine, who seemed to have woken up, and there were murmurs of agreement around the table, although not from the two ladies.

'Thank God indeed,' said Fleming. 'Or at least, thank the good sense of the architectural listing committee. But I must emphasize that it is confidential at this time. The official announcement will be made next month.'

Looking at him, Fraser had the sudden conviction that he'd had no intention – and maybe no authority – to make the announcement just then, but had been forced to in order to deflect attention from the money spent on the euro preparation.

Five million! Had they really spent that that much on it? He knew that all the trusts had been ordered to prepare for it, and to find the money from their existing budgets, but he hadn't realized how much had been involved.

He glanced over at Philip, who was staring down at the pad in front of him, and realized that the news had come as no surprise to him . . . then he remembered Fleming's visit to the hospital the previous Friday with Patricia Matlock – they must have told him then.

But why wasn't he happier about it?

The rest of the business was dealt with quite briskly and about forty minutes later, Fraser and Philip started back to the unit. At first, Philip didn't say anything and Fraser thought he was going to remain as silent as he had on the way.

Suddenly, he turned to him. 'Having sat through all that, Fraser, d'you still think you want a career in community medicine? Edwina told me what you said,' he added.

'Surely, most of that wasn't directly concerned with it?'

'No, I suppose not.' He thought for a moment. 'It was mostly concerned with money, wasn't it? So I suppose I meant. . . .' He paused again. 'How do we balance the care of human beings against pure economics? As doctors, we have a duty to do our best for our patients – however we construe that – but how far are we constrained, *adulterated*, by economics?'

'A fair bit, I dare say,' Fraser murmured.

'A fair bit, as you say.' He sighed. 'I've spent my career trying not to be corrupted by money, but maybe we're all doomed to failure in the end.'

Fraser looked at him. 'You really think you've failed?'

'Yes – as I said, to the extent that we all fail.' He paused, then. 'The thing is not to allow yourself to be corrupted beyond that extent.'

'How do we know when we've reached it?'

Another pause. 'I suppose we have to use our individual judgement.'

'Isn't that the same thing as having principles?'

'Having principles should go without saying. Maybe I'm thinking more about being on your guard against manipulation – by government, or anyone.'

Fraser would have liked to pump him a bit more, but Philip smiled suddenly, brilliantly, and clapped him on the shoulder. 'The thoughts of Philip Armitage – forgive me for burdening you with them. But think carefully about your career, Fraser. Give it time.'

Fraser said, 'Doesn't what you say apply to all areas of medicine?'

Philip thought for a moment, then slowly shook his head. 'I'm not sure that it does,' he said, and wouldn't be drawn any more.

CHAPTER 19

Jo had waited in the loo until she was sure Fraser and Helen had gone, then gathered up the samples from the bed and taken them to Tom. She told him about Rose Parker.

'Who gave her the first doses of antibiotic?' Tom asked. 'Was it Carrie Tucker?'

'According to the chart it was Sophie Rogers, but I don't know who was with her.'

'Can you find out?'

'I'll try,' she said. 'But Tom, there's another problem – if it *is* Carrie doing it, she's only on duty eight hours a day, so the rest of the time, Rose would have been getting the real thing.'

'Unless these are all bogus as well.' He nodded at the drug samples she'd brought. 'And they look all right to me.'

'And as Fraser said, it would've been noticed if none of it was working.'

'Mm.' He got up and walked over to the window before turning back to her. 'Is it possible,' he said slowly, 'that if Rose was given bogus antibiotic, say for the first three doses, that the real one would fail to work later?'

'I *think* so,' she said. 'You'll have to ask Fraser. Although the way Rose was, I'd have thought the ampicillin I gave her would've worked.'

'All right, I'll talk to him.' He paused. 'Is he over his wobbly now?'

'Yeah – I think Rose's death shook him as much as me.'

He nodded. 'I'll get all these samples off to the lab – maybe they'll be able to tell us something.' He sighed. 'It's a bugger, isn't it?'

'Yes,' she agreed sadly, thinking of Rose. 'It is.'

Later, when she was back on duty, she engineered a chat with Sophie Rogers, and on the pretext of asking her about the onset of Rose's pneumonia, discovered that Carrie hadn't been with her when she'd given her the first two doses of ampicillin.

★

Taking Helen out was a chore that Fraser didn't look forward to, and yet it was hardly ever as bad as he thought it was going to be.

It wasn't this Monday. They went to a pub and she laughed when he described the trust meeting and his wayward guts. Then he told her about the trust's debts and the money spent on the euro preparations.

'Yes, it's appalling,' she said, referring to the euro. 'When you think of all the misery that money could relieve. I'm surprised someone hasn't gone to the papers about it.'

'Why don't you, if you feel so strongly?'

'I couldn't,' she said, shaking her head. 'I know it sounds stupid, but if you've been trusted with confidential information, you can't somehow. I can't, anyway.'

It was then that he decided she probably had nothing to do with the killings. He told her about Armitage's reaction, or lack of it, to the news of the lifting of the grade two listing of St James', and his strange mood afterwards.

'He's got a lot on his mind at the moment,' she said.

He asked her what.

She said vaguely, 'Oh, Ranjid. . . .'

'Why Ranjid?'

'Well, you've seen what he's been like lately – and there's also Fleming, whom he cares for no more than you do.'

'Why is that?' he probed. 'He can't have much effect on Philip, can he?'

'He holds the purse strings. It's what administrators do, why they can make life difficult for those under them.' She obviously didn't want to talk about it any more, so he didn't press her.

She didn't ask him in when he dropped her off, either, and he drove away feeling guilty that he was so relieved. In a pally platonic sort of way, he'd rather enjoyed her company, but he couldn't feel any more for her than that. Exactly what *did* she feel for him, he wondered? She seemed to want to go on seeing him, and yet she was two-timing him with Ranjid.

The next morning, Tuesday, Gavin in Glasgow came back to him with his figures: deaths there were 28 per cent from pneumonia, 25 per cent cancer, 18 per cent heart conditions, and the pneumonia deaths were recorded as such. Not much different from Wansborough's.

With an eye on the door, Fraser worked out what he thought were the numbers of pneumonia deaths recorded at Wansborough as something else, then adjusted the figures to take account of it. Now the figure for pneumonia came out at over 40 per cent of the total. Far too high.

The figures from Bristol came an hour later. They were much the same as Glasgow's. He went down to Tom's hotel at lunchtime and showed him.

'Does this put your mind at rest?' Tom asked.

He nodded. 'Aye. It was anyway, after Rose – if you can call it that.'

Tom asked him whether the real antibiotic could have failed if she'd been given a dummy one first. 'Jo seemed to think it was possible,' he said.

'She's right, any infection can get to a point of no return where it's too late for any antibiotic, however good.'

'Could that be how it's being done?'

Fraser hesitate. 'If it were, we'd see some of them getting better.'

'Yeah, Jo said that as well.' He sighed. 'Maybe the results from the lab'll tell us something. Anything else?'

Fraser told him about the trust meeting, the euro and the lifting of the grade two listing of St James'.

'Hang on,' said Tom, reaching for his notebook. 'Let me try and get this into some sort of context.'

So Fraser described the St James' scandal and how the grade two listing held up the sale of the site and exacerbated their money problems.

Over the next few days, Fraser and Jo kept watch on the patients at risk as best as they could. Of the five, they thought Shirley Norman was the most likely, because of her immobility – she wasn't responding to treatment and was getting depressed about it.

Tom acquired some cefataxin for them and on Wednesday, Fraser thought he was going to have to use it when Stanley Forbes, who wasn't on the list, went down with a chest infection, then he realized it was another false alarm.

Jo, meanwhile, had a couple of domestic problems to deal with.

On Wednesday, Debbie, one of the HCAs, came looking for her. 'Jo, Mrs B's at it again. . . .'

Jo strode determinedly into room four. 'What is it this time, Mrs Bailey?'

'This food, it isn't fit for pigs.' Mrs B was a scrawny, vinegary woman who'd come in with a broken arm. 'It in't just me, you know.' She looked round. 'We all feel the same, don't we girls?'

Mrs Sherlock, whom Jo thought weak in the head, nodded in agreement. One or two of the others mumbled.

Then Lily Stokes said, 'Don't you go including me, Daisy Bailey, I think it's fine.'

Mrs B shot her a look of pure poison.

Jo said, 'It's exactly the same food that we all have, Mrs Bailey. All the patients, all the staff.' Mrs B snorted. Jo went on: 'If you really don't like it, you can always ask a friend to bring you some in.' If you've got any friends, she added silently.

She looked round. 'Anyone else have anything they wish to say?'

They didn't. One or two were clearly having difficulty in hiding their *schadenfreude*.

Then on Thursday, she was accosted in the corridor by a big, red-haired nurse.

'I hear you've been asking about me,' she said. 'Carrie Tucker.' Which meant something like: *What's your caper then, missus?*

'That's right,' said Jo, who'd recognized her from Fraser's description. She explained her interest in the pneumonia cases and how she simply wanted to talk to someone who'd seen them.

Carrie heard her out impatiently. 'Yeah, so what is it with you and pneumonia, then? Jackie said you had a thing about it.'

Gee, thanks, Jackie. 'It's an interest of mine, always has—'

'So why didn't you ask me to my face about it?' she interrupted.

'I am, now.'

They eyeballed each other a bit longer, then Carrie backed down. 'So what d'you want to know, then?' she asked sulkily.

Yes, she agreed, after Jo told her, both cases had developed very quickly and by the time anyone had thought of adding another antibiotic, it had been too late. 'It does happen, you know,' she said defensively.

Jo reported this to Tom. 'The trouble is,' she said. 'I can't ask any of the others now if she was with them on the drug round – it'd be bound to get back to her.'

Tom thought for a moment. 'What's your gut feeling?' he asked. 'Is she involved?'

'I disliked her intensely,' Jo said slowly. 'But I don't think she'd have been so in your face at me if she was.'

'Then leave it,' said Tom. 'In fact it might be an idea to keep your head down for a while before anyone else starts wondering about you.'

Bit late for that, she thought.

So she and Fraser kept watching, like good shepherds both, but nothing happened. She had, she realized, begun to feel a bit like a shepherd in the responsibility and, yes, the fondness she was feeling for these particularly vulnerable members of her flock. Especially Lily Stokes.

On Friday, Mrs Bailey, whose bed was next to Lily's, called Jo over. 'Can't you do something about them kids?' she demanded, pointing at Lily's grandchildren.

Payback time for Lily. However, the children were being rather noisy, so Jo asked them to calm down. They immediately looked mutinous and Jo was drawing breath to get heavy when Lily intervened.

'Now look what you've done,' she said to them. 'The nurse'll have to make you go away, which means I won't see you so often. If that happens, I won't get better so quickly, and if *that* happens, you won't be able to come and stay at my house, will you?'

It wasn't so much the words themselves, Jo realized, but the way she used them. Anyway, it worked, much to the annoyance of Mrs B.

'So *now* what do we do?' Marcus demanded irritably.

It was Saturday morning at the hotel, a beautiful day, which was maybe part of the reason they were all feeling so jaded. They'd held over the meeting from Friday evening so that they could see the results from the forensic lab, which had just been faxed through.

There was nothing wrong with any of the ampicillin. The blood Fraser had taken from Rose Parker showed no sign of any poison or drug over-dose, other than a high level of ampicillin, and the swabs he'd taken had grown virulent pneumococci that were completely resistant to it.

'Can I see it, please?' Fraser said, and Tom passed it over.

'With all due respect, Fraser,' Tom said, not sounding particularly respectful. 'This does rather suggest to me that these patients are some-how being deliberately infected.'

'Maybe it does – to you,' Fraser murmured, not taking his eyes from the report. 'But I thought you'd taken me on for my medical expertise and I'm telling you . . .' Now he looked up. 'That it can't be done.'

'Yes, you've told us that several times,' Marcus said, his voice acid smooth. 'Do you think you might see your way to explaining why not?'

Realizing that Marcus was a tick away from ignition, Fraser concen-trated his thoughts. 'If this organism was somehow being used to give people pneumonia, it would have to be subcultured, and that would destroy its virulence.'

'That doesn't leave me any the wiser.'

Fraser tried again: 'To isolate the organism, you have to grow it on an agar plate from an infected patient, then keep it alive by passing it to further plates, subculturing it. And that's the problem – sub-cultured pneumococci very quickly lose their virulence, their ability to cause pneu-monia.'

There was a brief silence, then Tom said, 'How quickly is *very*?'

'*Very* very. One, maybe two subcultures at the most.'

'But exactly how does it lose its virulence?' Marcus asked. 'I mean, it's the same bug, isn't it?'

'Aye, but with one important difference. On agar, it loses its capsule, and its capsule is essential for it to remain virulent.'

'All right, what's its capsule?'

Just that, Fraser explained, a capsule made of a jelly-like substance which surrounded each individual bacterium and protected it from being engulfed by white cells. 'You can squirt as many cultured, non-capsulated pneumococci into someone's lungs as you like, but they won't get pneumonia. The white cells get them first.'

'And if they *are* capsulated?'

'Then that person will probably get pneumonia and die. But as I said, you can only get capsulated pneumococci by taking them straight from someone who's already infected.'

'Could they be doing that?' asked Tom. 'I mean, growing them up from the last infected person – like you've just done.'

'You'd still have to subculture it into a liquid medium to infect the next person.'

Jo, who'd been quiet until now, said, 'Isn't there some way of stimulating cultured bugs to grow capsules?'

'If there is, I haven't heard of it.'

'Can you check on it?' Tom said, then turned back to Marcus. 'In answer to your earlier question, I think the only thing we *can* do now is make sure we treat the next case with the cefataxin and hope they get better. As Jo said, there's a good chance whoever's doing it'll give themselves away.'

Marcus nodded his acceptance, then turned to Jo. 'Were the patients all right this morning?'

'They were fine – at least, mine were. . . .' She looked at Fraser.

'Mine too,' he said. 'I saw them last night and looked them up this morning on the computer.'

'When are you on duty again?' Marcus asked Jo.

'Midnight tomorrow.'

'OK. Both of you do what you can to keep watching them. If it comes to it, phone the ward and say you're just checking.'

There wasn't much else to talk about and shortly afterwards, Jo and Fraser were relieved to find themselves on the pavement outside. Fraser let out a sigh. 'What's got into Marcus?'

She shrugged. 'Bad hair day?'

'*Marcus?*' he said, picturing the shiny bald head. They both laughed, then he said, 'What are you doing now?'

She looked up at the sky. 'It's a nice day, I think I'll go for a walk.'

'A *walk?*'

She laughed at his surprise, then explained how she'd been doing an evening course in archaeology. 'There's a place near here called the

Wansdyke I thought I'd go and see.'

'Wansdyke as in Wansborough, I suppose.' He looked at her a moment. 'Can I come with you?'

She looked almost as surprised as he had. 'I suppose so. . . .'

'Ach, if you're that keen, forget it.'

'No, it's not that – I was thinking about us not being seen together.'

They arranged to meet outside the town an hour later after Fraser had checked the patients again.

CHAPTER 20

They met in a car park on the outskirts of town. She'd brought some lunch and a map, and showed him where she wanted to go.

'I know that road,' he said, smiling. It was the narrow road over the downs that led to Fitzpatrick's place and he gave her a censored account of the party as he drove away.

Although it was only three weeks since he'd been there, the downs felt completely different; they'd filled out with greenery that still seemed to be growing as they floated through it. Sheep speckled the fields.

They stopped in a small car park at the top, just before the scarp. He zipped up the tonneau and they set off along the Wansdyke, an earthen bank about four feet high with a ditch to one side that ran atop the ridge. He asked her who'd built it.

'The theory I like best,' she said, 'is that the British warlord we call Arthur had seen Hadrian's Wall and decided to build his own version down here, to keep the Saxons out.'

'Ah, you're a romantic,' he said. 'Probably just a gang of dark age hoodies with nothing better to do.'

She stuck her tongue out at him. 'Have you ever seen Hadrian's Wall?'

'Aye. And I have to say it's more impressive than this.'

'Oh, this would have been bigger when it was built. Imagine having to climb out of that.' She pointed down into the ditch. 'And then up here with a row of angry Britons waiting to chuck spears at you.'

'Certainly a deterrent,' agreed Fraser.

They walked on. Larks hung in the blue above them, almost invisible, showering them with tinselled song. Insects hurried about their business.

She was slightly ahead of him, dressed in jeans and patterned blouse and he watched as she walked with that swaying motion that is entirely the preserve of women, her free arm inclined away from her body. She wasn't beautiful like Helen, he thought, but she was somehow more female.

To their left, the scarp fell away to the valley below, while in the distance, a dark blue plateau underlined the lighter blue of the sky.

'What are those hills over there?' he asked for something to say.

'Salisbury Plain.'

'You know your geography round here, don't you?'

She said, 'I have reason to remember Salisbury Plain.'

'Not altogether a pleasant memory, from your tone?'

'Not altogether, no,' She agreed. After a pause, she related how she and Tom had infiltrated a dodgy fertility clinic there, posing as a childless couple.

Fraser looked at her anew – he'd wondered about her past relationship with Tom, but hadn't realized it had been so dangerous.

'I'm surprised you came back for more,' he said.

'So am I, to tell you the truth,' she said with a grin. 'This isn't anything like so bad, of course, and I had my reasons.' She told him about her mother, the safety committee and David Petterman. By now, they'd walked two or three miles and she suggested they stop for lunch. They sat atop the ridge. Everything was balanced just right, he thought, the hot sun on his face tempered by the breeze flowing up the scarp.

She'd bought some mature cheddar that crumbled and fizzed on the tongue, crusty bread, tomatoes and a can of beer.

'Best meal I've had for months,' he mumbled as he finished.

She smiled, but didn't reply; returned to gazing down at the section of hill they'd just passed. After a few moments, she said, 'Look down there, it's so perfect, it's almost as though it were man-made.' The scarp dropped away in regular terraces to the plain below, where it ended abruptly. 'And down there, it's like a sea,' she said.

She was right, he thought. The fields below were dead flat and the corn planted there came right up to the base of the hill. The wind caught the tops of the stalks, moulded them into waves that marched across the plain and broke on the shore of the scarp – he half closed his eyes and the illusion was complete: he was looking at a green sea breaking on a lee shore. It occurred to him that for perhaps the first time since Frances died, he felt happy.

He finished his beer, savouring the sharp taste of the hops, the warm fuzziness in his head. He turned to Jo. 'D'you know something? I'm happy.'

'I'm glad,' she said.

On impulse, he leaned towards her and kissed the side of her mouth. She smiled but didn't move and he put an arm round her to draw her to him.

'Uh, uh,' she said, shaking her head and pulling away.

'Why not?'

'Because I don't want to. Anyway, what d'you think I am? You're already involved with someone.'

'Ach, that doesn't count for anything.'

'Maybe not for you, but have you thought about her? Maybe it does for her. It certainly does for me.'

She took her cigarettes from her bag, lit one and it seemed to him as if she was deliberately raising a barrier between them. A voice told him to stop digging, but he couldn't. 'It can't end soon enough for me.'

She blew smoke, said, 'You can say that now, but nobody forced you into her bed in the first place, did they?'

'No,' he admitted. 'I suppose not.' Anyway, who wants to kiss an ashtray, he thought?

You do, a voice inside him answered.

He swallowed. 'You're right,' he said. 'I apologize.'

'No need,' she said. 'Forget it.'

They set off again. He felt conscious of his hot face, of every part of his body, like a schoolboy caught playing with himself. Forget it, he thought, but he knew it would be a while before he did.

She stopped and opened the map. 'If we go down there' – she pointed to a path that led down the shallow slope 'there's another path that should take us back to the car.'

'Fine,' said Fraser, trying not to sulk.

The shrubs thickened as they descended. The wind died and the sun homed in. They walked quickly, brushing away flies. After a while, the hedge was replaced with barbed wire; sheep dotted the fields and tufts of their wool clung to the barbs.

Jo stopped to look at her map again. 'It should be here somewhere.'

Fraser slapped at a horsefly. 'Maybe it's beyond those trees.'

They hurried on into the belt of trees, and as they emerged, they found themselves confronted by a strange sight – a man bent over a sheep, which was on its back waving its legs in the air. A dog lolled beside him.

Jo looked uncertainly at Fraser, then called out, 'Excuse me.'

'*Ahh!*' The man straightened and turned in one movement. 'Cor,' he said. 'You made I jump.' Button brown eyes peered at them from beneath a cloth cap.

'Sorry. We're a bit lost. There's a path here somewhere.'

'Ah. Well. Yers.' He rubbed furtively at his chin. He was dressed in shapeless brown trousers belted at the waist, a shirt that could've been any colour and a jacket whose pockets bulged as though they were full of apples. He could have been any age between fifty and seventy. He said, 'Lemme just finish 'ere an' I'll be with 'ee.' He grabbed the sheep's fleece and hauled it upright. It bleated plaintively.

'Ged on, ban't be nothin' wrong with 'ee,' he said, giving it a shove. It tottered a few paces before reaching down to crop some grass. He picked up an old-fashioned shepherd's crook and came over to them. The dog followed.

'What's wrong with it?' Jo asked.

'Nothin'. They're stupid buggers, sheep – beggin' yer pardon, miss. They falls over on their backs an' can't get up again.' He looked round to where it was still cropping grass. 'She'll be all right now.'

Jo had her map out again. 'Can you tell us where this path is?'

He peered myopically and Fraser guessed he knew perfectly well which path they meant.

'Ah,' he said. 'That one. It ain't used much now.'

'Can we use it?' said Jo. 'Otherwise we've got to walk back to the top of the hill.' She smiled at him winningly.

He sniffed. 'Or right,' he said at last. 'I'll show 'ee.' He put his foot on the lower strand of wire and lifted the upper.

Jo bent and wriggled through. Fraser watched the shepherd's eyes as they were drawn to her bum – he looked up suddenly, caught Fraser watching him and winked. Fraser tried to restrain a grin as Jo straightened and looked from one to the other of them with a puzzled expression. Fraser ducked under the wire.

They followed him along the side of the copse. Sheep ran away from them, bleating to their lambs, which were almost as big as their mothers.

'They're yours?' Fraser asked.

'Ah. I'll be sellin' 'em on soon, not that I'll get much, bloody supermarkets – beggin' yer pardon, miss.'

'That's all right,' said Jo. 'Can't you sell them to a farmer's market or something?'

'I suppose, but I still gotta go through an approved slaughter 'ouse an' the nearest one's sixty mile. . . .' He regaled them with an account of the iniquities of the Common Agricultural Policy ('Beggin' yer pardon, miss') as the path curved into the trees. Ahead of them lay a clearing and in the middle stood a caravan propped up on breezeblocks. Beside it were a shed and a pick-up truck.

'My place,' said the shepherd. Then, to Fraser's surprise: 'Will 'ee stop an' have a cuppa?'

'That'd be nice,' said Jo, to Fraser's even greater surprise. 'Thank you.'

The shepherd fished a key from his pocket and opened the door. They followed him inside. The small kitchen wasn't tidy, but nor was it sordid. Close to, the man emitted a slight earthy smell, not unpleasant. He put a kettle on the gas range.

'How long have you been here?' Fraser asked.

'Twenty year.' He grinned at them. 'Council bin tryin' to get rid o' me ever since, but me landlord sticks up for me.' He paused, then said, 'You won't tell about the path, will 'ee? I know 'tis a right of way, but I'm fed up wi' people's dogs chasin' me sheep.'

The kettle boiled and he made the tea. After he'd handed them theirs, he extracted a half-smoked roll-up from behind his ear.

'Have one of these,' said Jo, holding out her pack.

As she lit up for both of them, his eyes flicked to Fraser.

'He's a doctor,' she said. 'Doesn't believe in it.'

Fraser smiled and took a sip of his tea. It wasn't as foul as it looked. A few minutes later, the shepherd showed them which way to go.

'Thanks,' said Jo. 'We won't split on you.'

He watched them until they were out of sight.

'D'you make a habit of taking tea with strange men?' he asked.

She laughed. 'I only did because he was so sure we wouldn't.'

'I'm not surprised they want to move him,' said Fraser. 'What with no mains and no sanitation.'

'You think he should be moved, then?'

'No, he's not doing anyone any harm.'

They stopped talking as the path steepened through a thick belt of conifers. Twenty minutes later, they emerged from the trees on to the Wansdyke, and five minutes after that, they reached the car.

'Can we drive back that way?' Jo asked, pointing to the scarp.

Even though Fraser had done it before, it still felt like driving over the edge of a cliff. Below them, the sea of corn lay waiting.

He dropped her off at the car park an hour later.

'I'll check the patients again on the computer,' he said. 'Then I might as well go home for the night. I'll phone the ward about mine in the morning and you can do the same for yours.'

'What about Daniel Pope?'

He shrugged helplessly. 'He's Singh's patient and not on your list, so even if he did get ill, we couldn't do anything.'

'All right,' she said. 'I'll phone you tomorrow.'

All right for some, she thought as she drove back to her room. Probably wanted to lick his wounds, she reflected with a smile; she rather liked Fraser, but had no intention of getting involved with him.

Fraser drove home, still feeling stupid. Why had he done it? Did he like her, fancy her? Sure, who wouldn't? But what possessed him of the idea that she'd succumb to his charms just like that? No, he'd made a fool of himself.

The next morning, Sunday, Jo rang the ward from her room.

'Staff Nurse Tucker speaking.'

Oh God, it would be her. 'Hello, Carrie, it's Jo Farewell here.'

'Oh, hello Jo, how can I help you?'

Too late to back out now. 'I was just a bit worried about Mrs Stokes in room four.'

'Oh?'

'She seemed very down when I left. Is she OK now?'

'Mrs Stokes . . . Oh yes, she's fine. You take your job very seriously, don't you, Jo?'

'Yes, I suppose I do. Thanks, Carrie.' She switched the phone off and let out a sigh. She simply couldn't go on doing that.

She pottered around in the afternoon, had a meal in the canteen, then read in her room until midnight – she knew it was no good trying to sleep before her first night on duty.

She took over from Sarah Howe.

'Anyone I should watch out for?'

'Yes, Mrs Stokes in room four – her chest infection's developed into pneumonia and she's very poorly.'

CHAPTER 21

'*What?*'

Startled, Sarah began to repeat herself.

'It's all right,' Jo said. 'I heard you. It's just that I was worried about her and asked Carrie this morning if she was OK and she told me she was.'

Sarah glanced round, then said quietly, 'Strictly between you and I, Jo, I don't think Carrie's the most reliable member of staff we have here.'

'I had the same impression,' Jo murmured. 'How bad is Mrs Stokes?'

'Not good. She's on intravenous ampicillin, although it hasn't really had time to work yet.'

Jo went to look at her as soon as Sarah had gone. Lily wasn't good, her temperature, pulse and respiration were all high and she was barely conscious – it was Rose Parker all over again.

Jo went back to the office. There was no one around, so she phoned Fraser's mobile number. He answered sleepily after four rings.

She quickly told him about it. 'I don't like the look of it, Fraser.'

'Have you got the cefataxin?'

'Yes.'

'Give her' – he thought for a moment – 'give her two grams now intravenously, and repeat twice, four hourly.'

'*Four* hourly?'

'Yes. I'll have a look at her when I come in and decide where to go from there.'

'We need to talk.'

'We will, tomorrow. Go and give her the first dose.'

The graveyard shift had the least number of staff and the patients were nearly all sleeping. This should have been an advantage, but it also meant that every noise she made was magnified: the echo of her footsteps, the rumble of the trolley, the swish of the curtains.

Lily actually seemed to get worse after the first injection and Jo was seriously wondering whether to ventilate her, but she improved slightly after the second. Come on Lily, she silently willed her.

Between times, she had plenty to think about – Carrie Tucker: was she just lazy, or something worse?

By the time she prepared the third injection at 7:30, the patients were waking up. Lily seemed better and was conscious enough to complain.

'Not another injection, please, nurse,' she moaned.

'Shh, it'll make you better,' Jo whispered.

She made sure the bleeding had stopped, then opened the curtains to find herself looking straight into the bright beady eyes of Mrs Bailey.

Oh no. . . . She forced a smile. 'Good morning, Mrs Bailey. How are you feeling?'

'Better'n 'er, that's for sure.' She nodded at Lily. 'Why're you giving 'er 'n injection, then?'

'I wasn't.'

'You was, I 'eard you. An' there's s'posed to be two of you, in't there?'

'You heard wrongly – I was taking her blood pressure.' With another smile, she wheeled the little trolley away.

Oh, shit. Would she tell anyone? She might.

Jo thought about it and when she handed over to Jackie ten minutes later, she tried for some damage limitation. 'Mrs Stokes hasn't been too good during the night, but she seems a bit better now – I've just done her obs and they're all down a little.'

'Thanks, Jo, I'll keep an eye on her.'

Jo went back to her room, waited until she was sure Fraser would have arrived, then bleeped him and told him what had happened.

'Does Jackie know about your relationship with Mrs Bailey?' he asked.

'Yes.'

'If she tells on you, deny it, say it's spite. It'll be your word against hers.'

'We do need to talk about it, Fraser – and Carrie Tucker.'

'Go to Tom at lunchtime and I'll join you as soon as I can.'

A couple of hours later, Fraser walked quietly into the room Lily shared with five others. He looked at the chart of one of Edwina's patients and pretended to note something from it. Then, as he was walking out, he paused and casually picked up Lily's chart. Her obs were all still coming down. He looked up and smiled at her. She tentatively smiled back; she did seem better than Jo had described, he thought.

At one, he drove down to the hotel. Jo was already there with Tom. He told them about Lily.

'The thing is, Fraser,' Jo said. 'Should she have more cefataxin now?

Only I'd hate to see all my good work go to waste.'

'Ideally yes, but I don't see how we can – not until you're back on duty, anyway.'

'Is she going to get better without it?' Tom asked.

'I *think* so. She's had three big doses – that ought to do it.'

'Is *ought* good enough? Could you give her more if it came to it?'

'I can't – she's not my patient, I had no business even looking at her chart.'

Tom drew a breath and nodded. 'All right,' he said. 'Try and keep an eye on her, though.' He paused. 'The next question: is it deliberate, is she another victim?'

'She *must* be,' said Jo. 'We knew she was at risk, it's happened at the weekend, like Rose, and the infection's resistant to ampicillin.'

Fraser nodded his agreement.

'So what about Carrie?' Tom said. 'I know you didn't think so, Jo, but she does always seem to be around, doesn't she?'

'Bit of a coincidence,' agreed Fraser.

'Yes it is,' said Tom. 'So you'd better keep an eye on her as well, Fraser.'

'How the hell'm I supposed to do that?' he demanded. 'I've got no reason to be hanging around her.'

'Oh, I don't know,' Jo said sweetly. 'She'll probably assume you fancy her.'

'Thank you so very much,' Fraser said between his teeth, kicking himself for falling into the trap.

He looked in on Lily again after another three hours. To his relief, she was sitting up, reading a magazine. As he turned to leave, Carrie and another nurse came in with the drug trolley. He went over and talked to one of Edwina's patients, covertly watching the two of them as he did. They stopped at Lily's bed, pulled the curtain round, and Fraser, remembering the film about the man with X-ray eyes, smiled wryly.

After a few moments, they came out again, wheeling the trolley. Carrie looked up and met his eyes. She beamed at him, waggled her fingers and mouthed 'Hello' before going to the next patient.

Thanks, Jo, Fraser thought.

When Jo came on at midnight, Lily was definitely better and slept the night through.

Jackie came in at eight. Jo handed over, noticing as she did that Jackie seemed to have difficulty in meeting her eyes. When she'd finished, Jackie said, 'Jo, we have to go and see Helen.'

'What, now?'

Jackie nodded.

'Why?'

'She'll tell you when we get there.'

It's got to be Mrs Bailey, Jo thought, and as they walked in silence to Helen's office, she went over all the arguments in her head.

'Come in,' said Helen. 'Sit down, please.'

Funny, reflected Jo, how the word please can turn a friendly sentence into a hostile one.

'Staff Nurse Farewell, one of the patients, Mrs Bailey, has made a serious allegation about you, serious enough for it to come to me.' She looked at Jackie. 'Sister?'

'Jo,' Jackie said to her. 'Mrs Bailey says she saw you giving Mrs Stokes an unauthorized injection on your own.'

'Oh, what absolute rubbish!' Jo said with what she hoped was the right mixture of amusement and scorn.

'So why is she saying it?' Helen asked icily.

'I've no idea. What exactly did she say?'

Jackie took over again. 'She told us that yesterday morning you drew the curtains round Mrs Stokes's bed and then she heard her say: "Not another injection, please, nurse." You whispered: "Shh, it'll make you better," and then she saw you coming out with a trolley loaded with injection materials.'

'But you saw me yourself, Jackie, at least, you saw me just afterwards – when I told you that she'd been poorly during the night and that I'd just done her obs. That's what Mrs Bailey saw.'

Helen leaned forward, her clear grey eyes locked on to Jo's. 'So why did Mrs Stokes say "Not another injection, please, nurse?" '

Jo frowned. 'She did say something like that, when I was putting the cuff on her arm. She was still delirious, I suppose that's what she thought I was doing.'

'But you tried to silence her. "Shh, it'll make you better." '

'What I said was: "Shh, you'll soon feel better." '

'There are needle marks on her arms.'

Jo shrugged. 'She's had blood samples taken most days, hasn't she? Plus intravenous ampicillin, so I suppose there would be.'

There was a silence while Helen continued staring at her.

Jo thought: Have they asked Lily? They must have and she couldn't remember, or they'd have said. She made herself say, 'Have you tried asking Mrs Stokes?'

'She couldn't remember,' Helen said shortly. 'So are you saying that

Mrs Bailey made all this up, Staff Nurse?'

Jo said slowly, 'She probably believes it – or at least, some of it.' She turned back to Jackie. 'You remember she and I had a run-in the other day?'

Jackie nodded. 'Yes.'

'Well, that's probably it then, there's a measure of spite in what she's saying.'

Jackie turned to Helen. 'She's certainly difficult, Helen, and I can imagine her being vindictive. And it's true that she had – er – a difference of opinion with Jo last week.'

Helen was still staring at Jo. 'How did that come about, Staff Nurse?'

'She was complaining about the food, telling the other patients in the room that it wasn't fit for pigs. I asked her to desist.'

'Just that?'

'She was trying to get the other patients to complain as well, so I put it quite firmly.'

'In front of the other patients?'

'Yes.'

'Was that wise, d'you think?'

Jo hesitated again. *Time for some humble pie?* 'Perhaps not, Sister.'

Helen said, 'I'm not happy about this, Staff Nurse.' She paused, searching for words. 'I don't like complaints from patients.'

Jo felt herself colouring. 'I'm very sorry it should have happened, Sister.'

'So am I. All right, you can go now. Not you, Jackie.'

Jo walked slowly back to the ward. To wait for Jackie, or not to wait for her? *Wait, it's what she'd have done in normal circumstances.*

Jackie came back five minutes later and Jo pounced. 'Jackie,' she hissed. 'Why couldn't you sort it out with me? Why involve Helen? And why bounce it on me like that?'

Jackie waved her into the office and shut the door. 'Because Helen told me we had to play it that way.'

Jo blew out her cheeks. 'But how did she know about it?'

'Mrs Bailey came out with it on the ward round yesterday morning. We shut her up, then Helen and I questioned her about it afterwards. I'm sorry, Jo, it's obviously a storm in a teacup.'

So why didn't Fraser warn me? Oh, he wouldn't have been there, Mrs B is one of Singh's patients.

Jackie was looking at Jo closely. 'You haven't done something else to upset Saint Helen, have you? She does seem to have it in for you.'

Jo shrugged helplessly. 'I've got the same feeling. The only thing I can think of is that she did seem suspicious of me because I dropped a grade to come here.'

'But it's only natural you should want to move with your fiancé.'

'Does she often take against people like that?'

'Not usually, no.'

Jo let out a sigh. 'Just one of those things, I suppose.' She smiled. 'Thanks for sticking up for me, Jackie.'

'That's all right. I wish I could have done more.'

Jo walked back to her room deep in thought. She lit a fag as soon as she'd shut the door.

It wasn't just one of those things, there had to be a reason for Helen to dislike her so obviously. Did she suspect something between her and Fraser, had she seen her handbag on his bed that time? But how would she have known it was hers? She jerked as though electrified. *Or was it because Helen knew that Mrs B was telling the truth?*

Everything pointed to it, her body language, the way she'd stared at her so relentlessly, the way she'd set the trap. So how did she know?

Because Lily hadn't died as she was supposed to – that's how.

She called Fraser.

CHAPTER 22

'Fraser? It's me, Jo – can you talk?'

'I've got about five minutes.'

'It's Helen – I'm sure of it.'

For a moment, he couldn't speak. 'But how? D'you have evidence?'

She told him about Mrs Bailey and Helen's interrogation. 'It was the way she went for me, the way she looked at me. She knew I'd given those injections.'

Fraser tried to pull his thoughts together. 'So it all comes down to the way she looked at you?'

'You weren't there, Fraser – she knew.'

He said carefully, 'You've told me before how she dislikes you, and I've had the same impression. Are you sure it wasn't just her dislike?'

'Yes, I am sure. We have to go and see Tom about it.'

'Yes. I've got to go for the ward round now. I'll try and get an early lunch – will you be in your room?'

'Yes.'

'I'll ring you in an hour and a half, two hours. OK?' He put the phone down, ran his hands over his face. Could she be right, just when he'd made his mind up that it wasn't Helen? He took a breath, stood up and went to meet the others.

Helen smiled when she saw him. He smiled back.

No, it wasn't her. It was just bad chemistry – Helen and Jo simply didn't like each other.

The ward round went slowly, uneventfully. When it was over, Helen got him on his own. 'Are you still OK for tonight?'

'Sure.'

'No darts matches or other pressing engagements?'

'No,' he said with a smile. 'Eight?'

'I'll look forward to it.'

Edwina made no problems about him taking early lunch. She said, 'I'll do this morning's clinic if you'll do this afternoon's.'

'Thanks, Edwina.'

Actually, he reflected as he went back to his office, she was getting the better deal by some margin – the afternoon clinic was always worse than the morning's. He phoned Jo. 'I'll come over to you,' he told her. 'And we'll go in your car. Less conspicuous.'

She was waiting for him and they went quickly to her Mini. He sat low in the seat with his head down until they were clear of the hospital.

'No second thoughts?' he asked her.

'No. How about you?'

'I find it very difficult to accept.'

'Let's see what Tom says.'

'Oh, I'm sure he'll agree with you,' he said pointedly. 'Have you phoned him?'

'I told him the outline,' she admitted.

He grunted and they didn't say any more until they got there.

Tom ushered them in. Jo went over the events of the morning again while Tom listened carefully.

'Tell me again why you're so sure,' he said.

'The way she set it up and then her outright hostility towards me. There's no doubt in my mind but that she *knows* I gave those injections. And there's only one way she could know – Lily Stokes should have died, she was expecting her to die and the fact that she *didn't* must be due to interference – my interference. I'm the only one who could have done it.'

'Fraser?'

'I can't agree. Helen's comments about Jo, what Jo's told me about Helen's attitude to her all indicate that she doesn't like her. That's the reason for the hostility. It's just that – hostility.'

'Her dislike is based on suspicion,' said Jo. 'She's never really accepted that someone like me would drop a grade for the privilege of working there.'

'Do you like *her*, Jo?' Fraser asked.

'You know I don't, Fraser,' she replied.

'Why not?' Tom asked.

'Because she doesn't like me . . . all right,' she said before either of them could protest. 'Because I think she's cold, self-centred and egotistical.'

'What do you base that on?' Tom again.

'Intuition,' said Fraser with the suspicion of a sneer.

Tom said mildly, 'I have a healthy respect for intuition.' He turned back to Jo. 'Can you back it up with reason?'

'It's rather personal,' Jo said after a pause. She took a cigarette out and lit it. 'I find her attitude to patients, to people in general, cold and impersonal. Oh, I know a nurse has to be to an extent but I can feel no warmth in her towards the patients, or to anyone really – other than Fraser.' She drew on the cigarette. 'And only someone utterly self-centred would press an affair the way she has with a man as recently bereaved as Fraser. Sorry, Fraser,' she added.

Fraser said, 'Doesn't that make my point? They dislike each other and that's why Jo is predisposed against her.'

'I could say the opposite,' Jo said. 'The fact that you've been sleeping with her predisposes you towards her.'

'I can assure you that it doesn't,' Fraser spat.

'That's enough,' Tom said sharply, making it clear he meant both of them. After a pause, he went on, 'I have to take what Jo says seriously, although I accept there's no proof. When are you seeing her again?' he asked Fraser.

'Tonight.'

'Supposing, just for the sake of argument, that Jo's right . . . Helen has no reason for suspecting you, does she?'

'No,' he said slowly. 'Unless she saw Jo's handbag that time in my room.'

'How would she know it was mine?' Jo demanded.

'I don't know, unless she saw you come in.'

'How *could* she have?'

'All right, all right,' said Tom. He took out a cheroot and tapped it thoughtfully against the pack before lighting it. 'We've got to get this sorted. You, Fraser, are going to have to say something about Jo and Mrs Stokes to test her reaction.'

'Then she'd certainly bloody suspect me,' Fraser exploded.

'Depends how you put it. It's a serious business accusing a nurse of tampering with a patient – surely you'd have heard about it on the grapevine?'

Fraser took a breath. 'I don't like it,' he said.

'I understand that,' Tom said. 'But for the moment, the way we are, we're stuck.'

Fraser said nothing.

Jo said, 'I'm not giving any more unauthorized injections. Next time, I'll be caught.'

Fraser pressed his lips together. 'You're ganging up on me,' he said.

Tom said, 'if she's innocent, as you say she is, then she won't notice anything and there's no harm done.'

'And if she isn't?'

'Then she may show it. If she does, there's still no reason for her to suspect you of anything. It depends on how you put it. I'll help you with that.'

Fraser capitulated.

The day went slowly. Jo tried to sleep and Fraser fought his way through the clinic. He was about to leave when he saw George Woodvine come out of Philip's room. George looked up, caught sight of him and came quickly over.

'Fraser,' he said quietly, 'Can I have a word?'

'Sure,' said Fraser. He led him to his office.

'I'm not quite sure how to put this,' George began after they'd sat down? There was none of his usual mimicry, Fraser noticed. 'Is Philip worried about something, d'you know?'

How to play this? 'It has crossed my mind,' he said carefully.

George nodded. 'Mine too. I thought so at the meeting last week, and even more now. In fact, I'm rather worried myself. D'you have any idea of what might be wrong?'

'No, I'm afraid I don't. Have you tried Ranjid or Edwina?'

George gave a half chuckle. 'Ranjid's absorbed in his own troubles and Edwina wouldn't notice till it bit her.' He sighed. 'There's something the matter and I feel a certain responsibility. Would Helen have any idea, d'you think?'

Is he hinting that I should ask her? 'Well, she knows he's got problems, but not, I think, what they are. Have you tried asking him?'

Another smile. 'Yes – just now as a matter of fact. He denied it, quite convincingly . . . but somehow, I remain unconvinced.'

His clear grey eyes looked into Fraser's and Fraser had a sudden, strong urge to confide in him – No. Tom would kill him.

'I'm sorry I can't be any help,' he said.

George nodded again. 'It was a long shot, but thanks anyway.' He got to his feet and so did Fraser. At the door, he said, 'If you do hear anything, or think of anything. . . .'

'I'll let you know.'

George thanked him again and left.

Fraser walked slowly back to his flat, thinking about what Philip had said to him after the meeting: 'The thing is not to allow yourself to be corrupted beyond that extent. . . .'

But *what* extent? Had he realized what was going on? Was he party to it?

He showered and hung around in his flat before going to Helen's house at eight. He made himself eat, left saying anything about Lily until they'd finished and she'd topped up their wine glasses.

He took a sip, then looked up. 'I know what I was meaning to ask you,' he said. 'I heard something odd today – is it true one of the nurses was caught injecting a patient with something they shouldn't?' *Clumsy, clumsy. . . .'*

'Who told you that?'

'Oh . . . the one called Carrie.'

'Carrie Tucker,' Helen said. 'I wonder how *she* found out?'

'Then it's true?'

'Not the way you put it, no. It was your friend, Staff Nurse Farewell.'

'What friend?'

'You'd know which one if you saw her, the new one with the big brown eyes and the fuck me smile.'

Chance'd be a fine thing. . . . 'Oh, the one who's engaged?'

'That's the one.' She gave him a fairly straightforward account.

'Well, it sounds as though it's her word against the patient's,' Fraser said when she's finished.

'And I'd normally take her's,' Helen said. 'It's just that there were needle marks on Mrs Stokes's arms.'

'Well, I suppose she's having blood samples, as well as injections?'

'Pretty much every day, but there were a lot that looked recent.'

'Did you try asking Mrs Stokes?'

Helen nodded. 'She couldn't remember.'

'Was she ill or anything afterwards?' Fraser asked.

'She was ill anyway.'

The phone went and she got up to answer it. Fraser heard her groan, then say, 'All right, I'll be there in a few minutes.'

'Problems?' he said as she came back in.

'I've got to go in. They've lost the key to the controlled drugs cabinet and I've got the only spare one.'

'D'you want me to come with you?'

'No, you stay. I'll be fifteen minutes, if that.'

A moment later, the front door slammed. He took another mouthful of wine, went over in his mind what she'd said. It was all perfectly plausible and natural, except for that comment about Jo's smile.

A thought occurred to him – this was the first, and very likely the last, time he'd be alone in Helen's house, and now that he had Tom's keys, he could open the locked door. He jumped up and almost ran to the stairs. It was spying, prying even. But if he didn't, he'd always wonder.

He tried the door. Locked. Pulled out the keys, selected one and tried it – too big. The next one fit the hole, but wouldn't turn. Feeling foolish, he tried a third and with a loud click, the lock sprang.

How long had she been gone? Five minutes, more? He had another five at the outside, he thought, easing the door open.

It was dim and slightly musty. He fumbled for the light switch – and found himself in a picture gallery.

He realized immediately that the paintings must be her mother's, and this was confirmed by the large framed photo standing on the cabinet at the far end of the room – a semi profile of a woman with the same high cheekbones and sultry mouth, although the discontentment in the down-turned lips was even more marked.

He looked at the first picture. It was of a beach, like the one in the sitting-room, with the same combination of muted colours and intense draughtsmanship, but his eyes were drawn to the cloud formation above it that swirled, Van Gogh-like, and resolved into faces that leered down, mocking the figure that stood alone before the waves. Fraser looked closely – there was no doubt, it was the same girl, only now she was pregnant.

He swallowed and moved on to a beautifully executed study of Edvard Munch's *The Scream*, in the same muted colours as the beach. What made it so much worse than the original was the pram with a baby in it laughing at the woman's torment. He moved on. Here was the same woman, in convict's clothing with a ball and chain attached to her leg, only the ball was the same laughing baby.

The next featured a grave, the freshly dug earth surrounded by wrought-iron railings that became spearheads, while from the earth sprouted obscenely green brambles that became barbed wire as it twisted round and around the railings. . . .

A door banged below.

'You won't believe it but they'd found the bloody thing . . . Fraser?'

He moved to the door, flicked off the light, eased it shut. 'Fraser, where are you?'

'I'm up here.' Lock it? No, not enough time to find the right key.

'Oh. Well, they'd found the bloody thing by the time I'd got there,' she said as he came down the stairs. 'Well, no harm done, I suppose. Why don't you bring the wine into the sitting-room?'

'Sure.'

So Jo was right all the time, he thought as he collected the wine. He didn't know *how* he knew, only that he did. What the hell was he going to do? He took the wine to the sitting-room.

'Are you all right,' she asked, looking at him.

'My guts again,' he said. 'I'm OK now.'

'Probably all the canteen food you eat.' She grinned. 'Now, if you were to move in with me. . . .'

'I'd be too far from the darts team,' he said, making himself grin back at her, thinking: If I go now and she finds the unlocked door. . . . But how the hell was he going to relock it?

'Aren't you going to pour me some wine?'

'Sure.' If I stay a while, maybe I'll get a chance.

He filled the glasses, sat beside her.

'You are a bit pale,' she said.

'I daresay I'll recover.' He drank some wine. 'It seems crazy not to keep a spare key on the ward. What would happen if you were away?'

'Philip's got one, and if the worst came to the worst, admin have a master somewhere. It is ridiculous, but Health and Safety insisted after an incident last year. You *are* recovering, aren't you?'

He was nibbling her ear, running the tip of his tongue down her cheek. He worried for a moment that he wouldn't be able to rise to it although he knew he had to try. Then she unbuttoned his shirt, put in her hand and he felt himself harden.

'Let's go upstairs,' he said.

For once, the fact that she came quickly was a blessing. Afterwards, he lay beside her, willing her to sleep.

In the darkness, she said, 'Do you like me, Fraser?'

' 'Course I do,' he said. 'I wouldn't be here if I didn't.'

She held his arm, touched his shoulder with her forehead. 'I'm glad you're here, Fraser.'

'I'm glad you're glad.'

He lay there, willing himself to be still although his nerves crawled.

After a while, he could bear it no longer. He kissed her cheek and slid out of bed. He quickly dressed. He knew she wasn't asleep, although she didn't say anything. He left, not daring to try and lock the unlocked door.

CHAPTER 23

As soon as he was out of sight of her house, he stopped and rang Tom. 'It's Fraser, I need to see you.'

'I'll be in my room.'

Tom let him in fifteen minutes later. 'You look as though you need a drink,' he said.

'Aye, I do that. I'll get a taxi back.'

Tom poured them both a whisky.

Fraser took a mouthful. 'I did as you asked with Helen tonight and I now agree with Jo – she's in this somewhere.'

'What changed your mind?'

Fraser told him about the picture gallery.

Tom lit a cheroot. 'How does that make her involved?' he asked.

Fraser stared at him. 'Doesn't it make you think she is?'

'Sure, but I'd like to hear it from you.'

Fraser tossed back the whisky and held his glass out for a refill. 'You'll agree with me that Helen's mother must have been unbalanced?'

'I'd say she was barking and I haven't even seen the pictures,' Tom said as he poured.

'Well, Helen's inherited it.'

'And that's it, like mother like daughter, QED?'

'All right, all right. . . .' He drank some more of the whisky while he thought. 'OK, I think we can assume she was never married to the father – I'm thinking of the beach painting.'

Tom inclined his head.

'Well, it screwed her up,' he continued. 'Made her bitter and twisted and she took it out on the baby, Helen.'

'How d'you work that out?'

'She blamed the baby – the Munch study with it laughing at her, then the one with it as a ball and chain – she blamed it for screwing up her life, took it out on it – her, Helen, I mean.'

Tom nodded thoughtfully. 'You could be right,' he said. 'This being before uncool unmarried mothers evolved into trendy single parents. I wonder why she didn't have an abortion.'

'Maybe it was before the change in the law. I'll bet she was obsessed with death, of both the child's and her own. I'd hazard a guess she killed herself in the end.'

Tom looked at him interrogatively.

'That one of the grave,' Fraser said. 'She was foretelling it, subconsciously perhaps. And there's another thing.' He told him about the discrepancy in the ages Helen had said she was when her mother died.

Tom thought for a moment. 'I think you're right,' he said. 'But how does it make Helen a killer? Wouldn't it tend to make her feel the opposite, that life was precious?'

'Yeah, but it could just as easily go the other way. Look at the people who abuse children, their own or others – they almost always turn out to have been abused themselves. You'd think it would make them inclined to be the opposite, but it doesn't always, does it?'

'No,' agreed Tom.

Fraser took another mouthful of whisky. 'She grew up knowing she wasn't wanted. Oh, no expense spared on schooling, but that's not the same thing, is it? So far as her mother was concerned, she was in the way, useless, and in the end, her very existence led to her mother's suicide.'

'But what about the grandparents who put up the money? Wouldn't they have wanted her? Grandparents usually do.'

'Not these necessarily, not if they were upper crust and it fucked their daughter's marriage prospects. They'd have been an embarrassment, mother and daughter both.'

'That's a bit cynical, isn't it?' Tom said with a smile. 'Sure you're not indulging your inverted snobbery?'

Fraser unwillingly smiled back. 'What I'm trying to say is that after an upbringing like that, where unwanted people are beneath notice – disposable – she'd see nothing wrong in getting rid of those whose lives served no purpose, who were in the way.'

Tom drew on his cheroot. 'I think I follow you,' he said. 'Although it's a hell of a jump. I'll try it out on one of our tame shrinks tomorrow.'

'The thing is,' Fraser said slowly. 'I'm wondering if it puts Jo in danger.' He told him how he'd raised the subject of the illicit injections and Helen's reaction to it. 'The way she told me about it was harmless enough, but that crack about Jo's fuck me smile was nasty.' Tom nodded thoughtfully and Fraser continued. 'I think she hates her, and she also regards her as someone in the way . . . I'm thinking about the attacks on me in the hospital grounds.'

'I take your point.' Tom looked at his watch, then keyed a number into his mobile. 'Jo, are you still in your room? Good, stay there until we come and get you.'

Fraser caught the squawk of protest from the other end.

'Please Jo, just do as I say, for once. We'll be with you inside fifteen minutes.' He cut the connection. 'Give me that card, Fraser – the taxi one.'

Fraser handed it to him. 'I need a taxi, very urgently please, County Hotel.'

It arrived a minute after they got down to the lobby.

'Nurses' home, Royal Infirmary please. An extra tenner if you do it in five minutes,' he added.

The driver didn't waste any time talking.

In the back, Tom said quietly to Fraser, 'It's still best if you're not seen with her – wait for me while I take her in.'

They didn't say any more until they saw Jo waiting at the doorway.

'Community Hospital,' Tom said as soon as she got in. 'Why didn't you wait inside?' he asked her.

'Because I'm late – this had better be good, Tom.'

'I'll tell you when we get there. Keep your head down, Fraser.'

The taxi came to a stop again and Jo and Tom half walked, half ran to the entrance. Tom reappeared a few minutes later. 'Where are you going?' he said to Fraser, who was getting out of the taxi.

'Back to my flat.'

'We've still got some talking to do.'

Fraser shrugged. 'OK, we'll do it there.'

'Sure, so long as you don't mind my cheroots.'

Fraser did mind, but felt it was preferable to another trip downtown. Tom paid off the taxi.

'You did it in six,' he said, handing the driver a ten-pound note. 'But I'm feeling generous.'

'The question is,' he said when they were in Fraser's flat. 'Is she doing it on her own?'

'I wouldn't have thought so,' Fraser said slowly. 'If it *is* being done by somehow infecting them with pneumococci, I think she'd need help.'

'From a medic?'

Fraser nodded. 'Almost certainly. Which means either Ranjid or Edwina.'

'Why not Armitage? He's the boss, and he was the one who employed her, wasn't he, because they'd worked together before?'

'But he's worked with Edwina before as well, that's why he employed her.'

'That doesn't exactly absolve him, does it?'

'No, I just don't think – although. . . .'

'Yes?'

'He is worried about something.' He told him what Philip had been saying after the meeting, and also what George Woodvine had said today.

'D'you know what it is he's worried about?'

Fraser shook his head. 'Although I did wonder if he'd begun to suspect what's going on.'

'Mm. Well, I think it puts all three of them in the frame.' He looked up. 'So which of them would you go for?'

'I don't know. Maybe this is the connection between Helen and Ranjid – and yet. . . .'

'Yes?'

'And yet there's the fact that both times I've been beaten up, it's been just after Edwina's found out about my snooping – the second time after she actually caught me at it.'

'Couldn't you say the same for Ranjid? He found out quickly enough the first time.'

'But how would he have known about the second time? Unless Edwina told him, I suppose. Then there's the way she's pumped me about my attitude to hopeless cases . . . and her detachment. . . .'

'Yeah, you've mentioned that before – what exactly d'you mean by it?'

Fraser closed his eyes a moment – the whisky and stress were beginning to get to him. 'Her utter self-containment – she ignores the things that don't concern her, seems unaware of them, and yet focuses like a flash when something does bother her. You never know where you are with her.'

'So your intuition's telling you it's her?' Tom said with the hint of a smirk.

Fraser gave him a sour look. 'And yet it's Ranjid that Helen's got the relationship with,' he said. 'And this isn't the first time he's been involved in the ill treatment of patients, is it?'

Tom's face screwed up in thought. 'Could be any of them, couldn't it? You see, unlike you, I'm not inclined to absolve Armitage. And yet it could just as equally be Tate – she and Helen would have known each other if they'd both worked with Armitage before.' He looked up. 'And where, I wonder, does the ubiquitous Carrie Tucker fit in?'

'God, I'd forgotten her,' said Fraser. 'The thing is, when Helen wanted to know how I'd heard about Jo, I told her that Carrie had told me.'

'So if she is involved, Helen would've known you were lying.'

'Especially if she finds that door unlocked.'

'I'm sorry, I'm sorry,' Jo said as she ran into the sisters' office at ten past midnight.

'I was about to ring you,' Sarah said reprovingly.

'I'll make it up to you.' Jo took a breath. 'Anything I should know about?'

'It's touch and go whether Mrs Castle'll last the night.'

'Have her family been told?'

The nearest was a daughter in London. Sarah said. 'She's going to try and get here tomorrow morning.'

Jo nodded. 'Does she need anything?'

'I shouldn't think so, she's on a diamorphine syringe driver.' Sarah paused. 'I'll be off, then.'

'Sure. I'm sorry, Sarah.'

'It's all right.'

Jo quickly checked all the patients, then went back to the office and sat down. She hated being late, although she appreciated why Tom and Fraser had made her so. She wondered what had changed Fraser's mind about Helen. Doubtless she'd find out.

She realized she was hating this job already and asked herself why. It wasn't the danger, such as it was, or even the graveyard shifts, although she didn't care for those either – it was the overall oppressiveness of the place. She pondered this.

It was the fact that everything was so clean and well ordered on the surface, but underneath all the good manners and platitudes, she could sense something. Not evil exactly, but corrupt – a worse corruption than any of the illnesses the patients had.

She sighed. Tom had admitted that although they were all agreed now that Helen was involved, they knew nothing else. Not how, where, when, why, not even whether anyone else was involved.

She looked in on Mrs Castle, then, on impulse, on Lily Stokes. She was sleeping peacefully. How had Saint Helen infected her? (She agreed with Tom about that.) Some sort of atomizer to spray a suspension of pneumococci up her nose?

But if that was it, she was bound to be seen doing it sooner or later, as Jo had discovered to her cost. Unless it was done as part of something everyday, innocently.

She glanced around, looking at the equipment. The oxygen mask, could that be infected in some way? She picked it up, turned it over, but couldn't see how, especially as it was used after infection had set in, not before.

An idea pricked at the periphery of her mind; she trembled slightly with the effort of holding on to it, then walked quickly out to the courtyard and lit a cigarette to try and develop it. It flickered and caught alight.

Yes. . . .

It wasn't the complete answer, no, but it might be part of it.

Proving it would be the problem.

For a second, the flicker became a flash – Health and Safety, Jo, how could you forget that? She stubbed the fag out and went back to the office.

CHAPTER 24

Wednesday. Fraser woke with a snap – the alarm had gone off an hour ago, but he'd muted it and closed his eyes again, just for a couple of minutes.

He jumped out of bed. He was tired, his head ached and the room smelled of Tom's cheroots. It was a quarter past nine.

He groaned: he'd give anything for a shower. He swallowed some paracetamol, splashed water over face and under pits and dragged on some clothes. Cleaned his teeth and ran out of the flat. 'Good of you to drop by,' Edwina murmured as he arrived.

'I'm sorry, Edwina, I—'

'Let's get started, shall we?'

The ward round was followed by the morning clinic. Fraser watched her throughout – her professionalism was beyond doubt, but was there also a coldness, a callousness even?

'Symptomatic treatment only, I think. . . .'

'Just make him comfortable and let the family know. . . .'

'I think it would be cruel to attempt to treat this condition. . . .'

Jo drove him down to Tom's hotel at lunchtime. She'd brought a large shopping bag with her. He asked what was in it and she said to wait till they got there.

Tom had laid on some sandwiches, half of which Fraser ganneted within five minutes of his arrival.

'Well, has your subconscious come up with anything while you were asleep?' Tom asked him.

He swallowed. 'If it did, the whisky killed it. How about you?'

'Something, maybe.' He drew a breath. 'Let's assume they've got a virulent culture of the bug, never mind how for the moment – they've got to put it into some sort of spray and get it into the victim's lungs, right?'

Fraser gulped some coffee. 'However they're doing it, they'd be seen eventually, like Jo was.' The paracetamol hadn't helped much and his head felt like suet.

Tom leaned forward. 'But what if it was a part of something that happens anyway? Something that's done routinely to patients, maybe even something they do themselves. They use inhalants, don't they?'

'Yeah, but that's after they get pneumonia, not before.'

'There must be some things they have before.' He turned to Jo, who'd been silent until now. 'Any ideas, Jo?'

'Yes, as a matter of fact.'

They looked at her.

'Glandosalve.'

'But that's not an inhalant,' Fraser said after a pause. 'It's just a saliva replacement for a dry mouth.'

'I know, but it's used before patients get ill, isn't it? And if you spray a suspension of bacteria into your mouth, you're going to inhale some of them, aren't you?'

Fraser half lifted a foot to kick himself. *Of course you are. . . .*

'And what could be easier than swapping a Glandosalve dispenser without being noticed?' Jo added, driving the nail home.

'What do you think, Fraser?' Tom asked.

'It's certainly a possibility. But exactly how we go about proving it, I don't know.'

'We need to get hold of one,' Tom said. 'One that's been used by a victim, obviously.'

'That's goin' to be difficult,' said Fraser. 'Since you can bet your life they'll have stopped operations again for the moment.'

'What happens to them when they're used up?'

'Into a sharps bin and off to the incinerator, like everything else. The last one would have been Mrs Stokes, and that'll have gone by now.'

A horrible suspicion occurred to him as Jo said, 'Well, maybe I can help you there.' She opened the shopping bag and took out a sharps bin, wrapped in clear polythene.

'From Mrs Stokes?' Tom asked in wonderment.

She nodded. 'I used it to get rid of the injection materials and wheeled it over to the side of the ward. It was still there.'

'Jo, you're a wonder – I'll get it up to the forensic lab this afternoon.'

'But do we know the Glandosalve dispenser's in there?' Fraser asked. 'You didn't open it, did you?'

'Not on your life. I shone a torch through the hole though, and counted at least three of them.'

Tom put an arm round her and kissed her. Fraser told himself not to sulk.

'Well, I'm glad I didn't find it,' he said.

They looked at him enquiringly.

'Bein' kissed by Tom.'

'Jealous?' Tom enquired.

Fraser shook his head.

Tom continued. 'Well, there's not much more we can do now till we get a result from it.'

'Then what?' asked Fraser.

'Depends on the result – if it shows us how the killings are done, we go to the police, by which I don't mean we stroll down to the nearest nick, we do it through Marcus.' He looked at Fraser. 'When are you seeing Helen again?'

'Tomorrow evening.'

'Not much fun for you, I daresay, but you'd better go through with it. We don't want to spook her.'

Fraser nodded shortly. 'What about Jo, making sure she's not attacked?'

'I'll go back to the nurses' home with her, check over her car and escort her while she's on night duty.'

'There's a limit to how long we can go on like this,' Jo said.

'Well, I'm hoping that once we hear from the lab, we'll be able to start feeling collars.'

'What if we're not?' Fraser said.

'What if you're hit by a meteorite on the way back? Talking of which, shouldn't you be going?'

Fraser looked at his watch, said, 'Oh Christ!' and leaped for the door.

He recovered his car easily enough, but it was ordained that there should be a traffic jam in the town centre and he was twenty minutes late.

'Dr Tate's been looking for you,' her secretary informed him. 'She's doing the afternoon clinic now.'

'Could you tell her I'm here as soon as she's finished with the patient she's with?'

Five minutes later, he went in. She regarded him without expression. 'You can take over now,' she said. 'But I want to see you as soon as you've finished.'

The clinic lasted about an hour and then he went to her office.

'Shut the door and sit down,' she said. 'What has got into you, Fraser? You're treating this place like some sort of convenience, you come and go as you please, you're late twice today and if I hadn't been here, God knows what would have happened. Have you got some sort of personal problem?'

'Yes,' he said.

'Well?'

'I-I need some money, urgently,' he improvised. 'It's keeping me awake at night and this afternoon, I was with the bank manager.'

'Can you tell me why you need this money?'

'It's for my mother.'

Her expression told him he'd used this once too often. She knew he was lying, she knew that he knew, and he had a sudden conviction that it was her behind everything.

She said, 'You cannot allow family problems to affect your medical responsibilities. I hope you succeed in solving your problems, whatever they may be, but this cannot happen again. If it does, you're out. Is that clear?'

'Yes.' It was hard for him not to burst into maniacal laughter – he was late because he was trying to arrange her downfall, and she was disciplining him for it.

'Good. You may now resume your duties.'

The door clicked behind him and he leaned against the wall for a moment.

'Problems?'

He turned to see Helen, who'd just come out of her own room. He motioned her a little way down the corridor. 'I was late back from lunch and Edwina's just given me a bollockin' for it.' He grinned at her. 'I can't stop, I'll see you tomorrow evening if not before.'

That evening, he played darts, but his heart wasn't in it and he left as early as he could. He felt utterly drained and fell into bed, but not to sleep. Images chased through his mind. Was he right about Edwina? What was he going to say to Helen tomorrow? If Edwina was in it, she and Helen must have compared notes. What if the sharps bin showed nothing?

After an hour, he gave up and took a sleeping pill, something he avoided if possible. When at last he slept, it was to dream of Frances.

'It's all right,' she said to him. 'I'm better now – really.' And that was all.

He awoke, wept briefly, then went back to sleep again. And in the morning, he felt completely refreshed.

The day passed. He didn't dare go to Tom at lunchtime, but phoned him. Tom told him that the sharps bin had arrived at the lab yesterday, but there was no news yet.

He'd dreaded seeing Helen all day, but when he went round in the evening, her greeting was no different from usual. She didn't say anything about the picture gallery door. He took her for a drive, some whim making him take the road to the Wansdyke. He stopped at the crest of the escarpment.

The sun, almost red, was balanced like a ball on the rim of the distant hills. The coarse grass of the scarp below seemed to pulsate with green, but lower down, it became dull and down still further, where the scarp met the plain, it was a dull misty blue.

'It's beautiful,' she said.

The red sun lit her face – half nature, half sculpture. *She's beautiful*, he thought. *And a killer. . . . Why? Does she know that I know?*

She caught him looking at her and smiled sadly.

They went to a pub where, incredibly, he found no difficulty in chatting with her. She simply liked being with him, he realized, and because of that, he found no difficulty in being with her. *She knows*, he thought. *She knows everything*.

When he dropped her off, she didn't ask him inside. She kissed the side of his mouth, said, 'Love you, Fraser,' and was gone.

Friday. Tom phoned him in the morning. 'We'll come to you, is one o'clock OK?'

'You've got some news?'

'Some. I'll tell you then.'

Tom and Jo were waiting in Tom's car behind the block. They followed Fraser upstairs and into the flat.

'Well, what is it?' Fraser demanded.

Jo sat in the armchair as Tom began to speak.

'One of the three Glandosalve dispensers in the sharps bin had a small plastic attachment fitted round the jet, so that when it was operated, some of the contents were sucked out.'

Fraser said impatiently, 'What was in the attachment?'

'Not very much by this time – all right, all right. . . .' He held up his hand as Fraser mock-threatened to strangle him.

'The small amount of liquid still there was a maintenance medium containing a heavy suspension of pneumococci. These were cultured and found to be ampicillin resistant.'

Fraser let out a sigh.

'However,' Tom continued deliberately. 'After what you'd said, I asked them to check whether they had capsules. Apparently, they didn't. Are you absolutely sure that pneumococci without capsules can't cause pneumonia?'

'Yes.'

'Then what's going on? This has to be the way they're doing it. Could some of them mutate?'

'Maybe, eventually. But it wouldn't give rise to the kind of rapid, overwhelming infections we've been seeing. It could take weeks.'

Jo said from the armchair, 'Could the patients be given something to make them susceptible, some sort of immunosuppressant?'

'I suppose so,' Fraser said slowly. 'Although I've no notion of what. I'll do some research on it.'

'This afternoon?' Tom asked.

'I'll try.'

After a slight pause, Tom continued, 'This must be the answer, there's no point in setting it up otherwise. I'm going to have to go ahead on what we've got.'

'How d'you mean, go ahead?'

'I'm going to tell Marcus what we've got and recommend that Helen St John, Tate, Singh and Armitage are arrested tomorrow.'

'What we've got isn't proof,' Fraser said.

'We'll search their houses – one of them's got to have facilities for preparing this stuff.'

'What if it's being done by someone else – Stones, for instance?'

'I think we could have him arrested as well. We've no choice, Fraser. We're not going to find any more evidence and the longer we leave it, the more danger there is they'll be able to cover it up.' He sighed. 'My fear is that they already have.'

Fraser nodded slowly. 'All right.' He looked up. 'If I get back now, maybe I'll be able to find something.'

He went to the hospital library and withdrew a weighty tome, but as it turned out, the afternoon clinic was exceptionally heavy and he had no time to read it. He was on his way back to his office at five, meaning to put in an hour when Helen stopped him in the corridor.

'Were you going back to Bristol tonight?'

'Er – yes, I was.'

'Could you come round to my house before you go? It's important.' She seemed unnaturally calm, almost serene. 'I'm not after your body, or even your soul, but I do have to talk to you. Please, Fraser.'

'All right,' he said, suddenly making up his mind. 'What time?'

'Whenever. Seven.'

'OK. Seven.'

She turned and left. Fraser went into his office and phoned Tom.

'You know,' Tom said slowly. 'She might be going to come out with it – confess.'

'I wondered that.'

'Have you got anywhere with your research?'

'No,' he told him.

'Go to your flat now and I'll meet you there as soon as I can.'

Fraser let him in fifteen minutes later. Jo was with him.

Tom said, 'You were right when you said earlier we haven't got proof, not foolproof proof.' He paused. 'If she wants to tell you about it, it's a chance we can't pass up.'

'Then again, she might have something else in mind. She is mad, Tom.'

'Let me finish. I suggest that we wire you up so that we can hear everything and then wait just round the corner.'

Jo said, 'It's not you she hates, Fraser – if it's anyone, it's me. I think Tom's right and she wants to get it off her chest to ... to someone she loves.'

Tom said, 'If she confessed, we could nail the other bastards, and it would go easier for her.'

'All right,' Fraser said.

CHAPTER 25

Nearly half an hour to go, she wished she'd made it earlier now. She had to tell him, that had been obvious from the moment she'd found the unlocked door. But would he understand? Probably not, Helen realized as she topped up her glass, but she had to try.

It was so – blindingly – obvious. Life was filled with pain and suffering enough without the added indignity of protracted death. Why should anyone have to put up with the agonizingly slow slide into oblivion that was the lot of those with terminal illness? Which means most of us in the long run. And why did people have to put up with it? She filled her glass again – better make this the last, don't want to be pissed.

Where was I? Oh yes, why did people have to put up with it? Because of an outmoded convention that insisted it was everybody's right, for God's sake, to go through it. What about their right to be released?

Released from the pain, the indignity, the knowledge that you were in the way – *wastefully* in the way, the knowledge that everybody around was waiting for you to shuffle off your thingy-whatever. Oh, some might protest, but only because convention had taught them to.

Society had to be shown the way forward and she, they, were the ones with the courage to do it, the courage to declare it, be imprisoned for their beliefs if necessary.

But she hadn't reckoned on Fraser. Or rather, she realized as she drank, she hadn't reckoned on her own feelings for him.

She'd started the affair at Patrick's party to deflect his attention from the pneumonia deaths. God, it had been difficult juggling him with Ranjid, but what she hadn't reckoned on was falling in love with him.

Why? She didn't do love, hadn't since she was a teenager, so why with him? Because he was damaged, like her? Although nothing like so much as her, she saw in a rare burst of self-knowledge. And now, she was going to have to tell him.

The doorbell rang.

So soon? Now that the moment had come, she found she was afraid – scared of the look on his face when she told him.

She swallowed the rest of her drink. The bell rang again. Go on – open it, damn you.

Fraser pressed the bellpush, heard it ringing inside, stood fidgeting on the doorstep. Open it, damn you. He rang again.

Nothing, not a sound.

Oh God, she hasn't topped herself? He fumbled with Tom's keys, somehow got one into the lock and turned it.

'Helen? It's Fraser, where are you?'

She was in the sitting room, lying on her back. Her throat had been cut and he thought she'd been stabbed as well. The blood had poured down her top and on to the carpet where it lay in a glassy pool. Her eyes stared accusingly up at him.

He started towards her, then realized there was no point in checking for signs of life. Shouldn't touch anything anyway. . . .

He stood there frozen as the realization hit him that this was Helen, the Helen he'd been to bed with, been talking with barely two hours earlier. What a waste. His throat tightened. Had she done it herself? He looked round for a knife, but couldn't see one. Then his mobile found its way to his hand and he called Tom.

'She's here.' His voice was surprisingly cool. 'She's dead, murdered.'

'Are you sure?'

' 'Course I'm bloody sure, her throat's been cut.'

'I mean, are you sure she didn't do it herself?'

'Not a chance.'

'Fraser,' Tom said clearly. 'He might still be there. Don't look for him, just get out of the house – now!'

Fraser's head snapped round to the doorway – nothing. He swallowed, made his way quietly over, paused, put his head round the door jamb . . . nobody there, no sound. Over to the front door and out.

'I've left the house,' he said.

'No sign of anyone?'

'No. Shall I phone the police?'

'Wait till I'm there – I'll be less than a minute.'

He put the phone away and vomited on to the lawn. Across the road, a curtain twitched.

The police didn't release Fraser until after midnight. Although both he and Tom were vouched for by Marcus and Commander Harris, Marcus's police liaison, the Wansborough police were reluctant to let Fraser go because he'd been the one to find the body, and it's a cherished police theory that the person who finds the body is the most likely killer.

He and Tom told them the whole story, omitting only Jo's part in it.

Edwina and Singh were brought in for questioning and their houses searched, although nothing incriminating was found. They expressed incredulity and then outrage when they realized what they were being questioned for.

Officers were sent to question Stones and Philip Armitage. Stones admitted his friendship with Ranjid Singh, but threatened legal action when he realized what it was about.

There was no answer at Philip's house, although his car was in the garage. The police sergeant broke a pane in the back door in order to unlock it and found Philip sitting in an armchair in his study. His throat had also been cut, but apparently by his own hand, since the knife was still in it. On the desk was a handwritten note on a slip of paper: 'I'm sorry, but there's no other way now. P.A.'

The sergeant radioed for assistance.

The forensic lab released some preliminary results on Monday. The knife found in Philip's hand was the same one that had killed Helen – her blood was on it as well as his, and also on his hands and clothes. There were no fingerprints on the knife other than his own. The note was definitely in his handwriting.

Edwina, Singh and the others at the hospital stated that Philip and Helen had known each other for a long time. Their relationship was known to be very close, although nobody had suspected anything sexual in it. Singh then told them he remembered how Philip had expressed his unease about Fraser and Helen's affair to him.

When Singh and Edwina were told that Helen had been suspected of deliberately infecting patients with pneumonia, they ridiculed the idea – especially when they heard it was Fraser's. Yes, there was a lot of pneumonia among their patients, but no more than in most community hospitals.

'Dr Callan had a bee in his bonnet about this from the moment he started,' Edwina told them. 'I knew about his recent bereavement, of course, and put his erratic behaviour down to that.' Nonetheless, she told them, she'd been seriously thinking of having him dismissed, bereavement notwithstanding. Singh backed all this up.

'You never knew what he was going to do next,' he said, and told them how Fraser had gone behind his back to Dr Stones claiming there was a pneumonia epidemic at the hospital.

Stones told them how he'd thought Fraser excitable and unstable when he'd come to see him.

'I tried to explain to him why his fears were misplaced, but obviously, I didn't get through to him.'

He was shown the doctored Glandosalve dispenser found in the sharps bin, and also the report on the pneumococci cultured from it.

'The attached device is a complete mystery to me,' he said. 'But I can tell you one thing for certain: these bacteria could not have given anyone pneumonia. In this condition, they're completely harmless.' (He was supported in this by two other bacteriologists.) If they wanted to know where it had come from, he added, perhaps they need look no further than the people who said they'd discovered it.

On Tuesday, Tom and Marcus attended a meeting with Harris and Superintendent Burns, who was in charge of the case in Wansborough.

'As things stand,' said Harris. 'If the deceased were still alive, I doubt they'd be charged on the evidence we have at present. And if they were, the Crown Prosecution Service would almost certainly chuck it out.'

'What about the doctored Glandosalve dispenser?' asked Marcus.

'It's certainly odd,' Burns agreed. 'But we have no idea, as Dr Stones pointed out, where it came from. If this ever came to court, the defence would undoubtedly suggest that your – er – temporary employee had planted it.'

'Out of the question,' said Tom.

'So you say.' Burns, while he accepted the necessity of departments such as Marcus's, intensely disliked the involvement of what he called amateurs.

'So you believe that Dr Armitage killed Miss St John and then himself?' Marcus asked him.

'That, of course, is for the inquest jury to decide,' Burns replied levelly. 'However, if you're asking my personal opinion, then yes, I think the evidence stands up.'

'His motive?'

'Sexual jealousy over her affair with Dr Callan.'

'Why'd you think Dr Armitage wrote his suicide note on a slip of paper rather than a whole piece?' Tom asked him.

'I've no idea,' Burns said. 'He was about to kill himself, so I don't suppose he was thinking very clearly at the time. I only know that the paper matched his own notepaper.'

'Why'd you ask?' asked Harris.

'Because that slip of paper could have been cut from a note he sent someone else,' said Tom.

'Now that *would* have been fortuitous,' said Burns. 'To have such a convenient postscript sent to you by someone you were intending to kill.'

'But doesn't it strike you as an odd way to kill yourself?' persisted Tom. 'To cut your own throat?'

'Not especially, no,' said Burns. 'There are precedents.'

'Really?'

'Yes, there was the doctor – I can't recall his name for the moment – who was blamed for the last case of smallpox in this country, he killed himself by cutting his own throat. Don't you remember that?'

Tom did, and gave a curt nod.

'What exactly are you suggesting, Mr Jones?' Harris asked him. 'That someone else killed them both?'

'I think it should at least be considered,' said Tom.

'Well, I simply don't believe it,' said Burns. 'And I doubt the coroner will either.'

Marcus said quietly, 'If Dr Armitage did kill Miss St John, is it possible that he did so because she was going to confess they'd been killing patients?'

'Is that what you think, Marcus?' Harris asked.

'I'm asking Superintendent Burns whether he's considered it as a possibility.'

'Doctors Singh, Tate and Stones have all stated categorically that nobody has been killing patients at the hospital.'

'They would, wouldn't they?' observed Tom.

'But there's no evidence,' said Burns. 'Oh sorry, I forgot – apart from an amateurishly doctored artificial saliva dispenser, provenance unknown.'

'Graham, you must admit that that does beg explanation,' Harris said to him.

'There's only one of them been found, we have absolutely no idea where it came from and two independent experts have said that it couldn't have harmed anyone.'

'What about the statistical evidence?' said Tom.

'What statistical evidence?'

'That there are significantly more deaths in that hospital than there should be.'

'Circumstantial in the extreme,' said Burns.

'The defence would almost certainly produce an expert witness to refute it,' said Harris. 'I do think you'll need more direct evidence for your theory to be taken seriously.'

'And that does not give you carte blanche to go on snooping,' Burns said, sensing victory.

'Probably best if you dropped it for the moment, Marcus,' Harris agreed.

Fraser, Jo, Marcus and Tom met the day after at Tom's hotel. Jo was available because she was off duty and Fraser because Ranjid's first act as Acting Consultant had been to sack him.

'I hold you personally responsible for Helen's death,' he told Fraser. 'And I shall say so at the inquest. I shall also say it to anyone who asks me for a reference. Now, get out.'

'So where do we go from here?' Marcus asked. 'Is there anywhere we can go from here?'

'Let's get something absolutely clear,' said Tom, looking round pugnaciously. 'Philip Armitage and Helen St John were killing off their patients. Furthermore, I find it impossible to believe that Armitage killed either St John or himself.'

CHAPTER 26

Jo stared at him. 'How can you possibly know that Armitage was involved?'

'Because he's dead, Jo. Do you really believe he and Helen were having an affair?'

'I . . . don't know.' She raised the ghost of a smile. 'It means she'd have had three on the go, which seems unlikely.'

'Then why did he kill her'? If he *did* kill her. . . .'

'Well, he might have realized what Helen was doing, killed her for it in a fit of anger, and then himself out of remorse.'

'D'you really believe that?'

'Why not? It's what the evidence says, isn't it?'

'Helen couldn't have killed those patients on her own, Jo.'

'Why not?' she said again. 'Substituting a Glandosalve dispenser isn't that difficult.'

'Maybe not, but what about the trifling matters of acquiring the resistant bugs, making them virulent and then manufacturing the doctored dispensers. She'd have needed help and I think it has to be Armitage.'

'Why not Edwina, or Singh? We know she was still seeing Singh, so why not him?'

'Fascinating though this may be,' Marcus cut in. 'What are we going to do about it? Bearing in mind that we've been ordered to stop?'

Tom turned to him. 'D'you accept what the police said, Marcus? No euthanasia, just a love affair that went tragically wrong – do you believe that?'

'You know perfectly well I don't. But what do you suggest we do about it?'

'Well, the first thing is to prove – to ourselves at least – that the euthanasia was real, and then find out who was in it with Helen.'

'How do we do that?'

'Is that a serious question?'

'Of course it is,' Marcus said impatiently.

'All right.' Tom gathered his thoughts. 'You and I go back to London and research the past careers of Armitage, Singh, Helen and Edwina. You find out where they worked, I'll go there and ask questions. OK?' Marcus nodded and Tom continued. 'Fraser, try and work out exactly how they did it, the capsule business. Doesn't matter whether you work here or in Bristol. Jo—'

'Sorry, Tom,' Marcus interrupted and turned to Fraser. 'It really would help, Fraser. It's the reason the police won't take us seriously. If you can find it, they'll have to listen. Go on, Tom.'

Tom nodded. 'Jo, you carry on at the hospital. Find out what people are saying about Armitage and Helen, they're bound to be talking about it. Look out for any more suspicious deaths, although I very much doubt there'll be any, and keep an eye on Edwina and Singh.'

'Anything else?'

'No, I think that's it.'

'I was being ironic.'

'I know.'

'Look,' she said. 'I've already aroused enough suspicion as it is – if I start asking questions now, it'll only make it worse.'

'You won't need to ask any questions, just listen. Anyway, you're not going to be there much longer, so it doesn't really matter what they think of you now, does it?'

'Oh, and Fraser,' said Marcus. 'One other thing – try and remember everything Helen and Armitage said that might be important, will you?'

The first thing that struck Jo when she went back was the silence. Oh, there were noises of course, and the staff still went about their business, speaking to the patients and to each other – when necessary. It was the loudness of all those other noises that emphasized the silence of the people who worked there.

Sister Jackie seemed to have changed from being a cheerful woman in her early forties to a careworn one in her late forties. She smoked more, usually in silence, and Jo knew better than to ask questions. Then she suddenly opened up of her own accord. 'I still can't believe it, Jo – oh, I know it happened all right, but I can't believe what the police are saying, that he was having an affair with Helen, that he killed her, for any reason.'

'But isn't that what they say about all killers?' Jo asked temptingly. 'The people who've known them, I mean?'

'You met him, Jo – do you believe it?'

'I didn't know him as well as you, don't forget.'

'But an affair with Helen? Killing her like that?'

'Well, it's difficult to imagine, I must admit.'

Which seemed to be the opinion of everyone else there.

But within a day or two, they had other things to worry about. The hospital, which had been running at near full stretch for a month, suddenly couldn't cope any more. Patients had to be turned away or referred to the main hospital and the staff became overworked, rather than just busy all the time, as they had been. They rushed around, impatient with the patients and each other, and the voice level rose again, although not its cheerfulness.

There was talk of bringing in agency staff and it occurred to Jo that quite apart from her work for Marcus, they really needed her there.

Fraser went home.

He was still slightly in shock, he supposed. He worked in a desultory way on the problem of the capsules, but without any result.

As Marcus had suggested, he also wrote down the things he could remember hearing Helen and Philip saying. This forced him to think about Helen, remember her ways, her mannerisms, the enigma of what she was. He felt an overwhelming sadness, and also guilt – had he somehow precipitated her death?

Marcus discovered that Philip and Edwina had worked together in Birmingham before they'd gone to Wansborough, while Helen was working in Reading. Tom went to both places, but learned nothing of interest about any of them, other than that they'd all left at about the same time, apparently headhunted.

Singh had worked in St James' for five years before moving to the new hospital. He'd been tainted by the stigma attached to the place, but other than that, there was nothing untoward in his past.

Before that, Philip and Helen (but not Edwina) had worked together in the care of the Elderly department at St Margaret's hospital in Southampton. Tom went down there and asked questions. Again, they'd both resigned suddenly, and together – but this time, Tom's antennae did pick up the miasma of something not quite right.

Most of the staff from the time had moved on. Tom tried pushing those who were left, but could feel them physically closing up. He traced two who'd moved, but with the same result.

In his experience, shellfish syndrome of this severity usually meant either hanky panky of the grossest nature, or something criminal. He contacted his old police boss in London and asked if he knew of anyone he could speak to in Southampton. He was given the name of DCI Ron Shawhurst, recently retired. He phoned and arranged to see him.

Ron Shawhurst was a cheerful, open-faced man who lived with his wife in a neat bungalow in the village of Hythe, on Southampton Water. He asked Tom in, sat him down and made him coffee, but when Tom told him why he was there, his face clouded over.

'No offence,' he said. 'But I'll just check with Andy Fox if you don't mind.' He went out and shut the door.

Tom didn't mind at all; he'd been expecting something of the kind.

He was back in five minutes.

'Sorry about that,' he said. 'But this one was a bit sensitive.' He sat down again and his eyes turned inwards. 'And I've got personal reasons for remembering it. . . .'

A young doctor had come to see him and told him she thought that patients in the Care of the Elderly department where she was an SHO were being deliberately killed.

'I was impressed by her,' Shawhurst said. 'Both by her manner and what she had to say.'

And maybe by even more than that, Tom thought, looking at him.

'She was very level-headed, didn't strike me at all as the type who'd imagine something like this.'

'Did she say who she thought was doing it?'

'She did, and it clearly gave her no pleasure. It was Philip Armitage and Helen St John.'

'Did she say how they were doing it?'

'Overdoses of diamorphine.'

She'd admitted straight away that it was difficult to distinguish between a high dose to alleviate great pain, and a high dose to kill, but she'd become uneasy about the frequency with which Armitage was prescribing such doses.

'She told me quite frankly that she'd very much admired Armitage when she'd started, but had become convinced that he was, in fact, practising euthanasia.'

'What kind of patients?' Tom asked.

'Oh, all those who were gaga, but also anyone with any kind of terminal disease.'

They'd set up a team and investigated the whole department very thoroughly, but had not been able to come up with enough to satisfy the CPS.

'What did *you* think?' Tom asked.

'That they were as guilty as hell.'

'Why? Gut instinct? Not that I've anything against gut instinct,' he added hastily. 'Truth be told, it's half the reason I'm here.'

Shawhurst took a deep breath. 'Yes, it was that,' he said. 'And more than that.'

Tom waited.

'As I told you just now, the young doctor impressed me, and I simply wasn't convinced by either Armitage or St John when I questioned them. But there was something else. During my investigations, I discovered that they both belonged to EXIT, the euthanasia group.'

'But EXIT's a perfectly respectable organization, isn't it?'

Indeed it was, Shawhurst agreed, but when he'd questioned some of its members, he'd uncovered the existence of a shadowy offshoot of EXIT called RELEASE, which held views of a rather different nature.

'Which were?'

'In a nutshell, that people who are in any kind of vegetative condition, or who have terminal disease, should be mercifully *released*, as they put it. Without option. Armitage and St John were both members.'

'But this wasn't enough to convince the CPS?'

Shawhurst shook his head. 'They said it was all too circumstantial.' After a moment, he continued slowly. 'I told you I had reason to remember the case.' He swallowed. 'I was officially bollocked for allowing myself to be unduly influenced by Emma, the young doctor, also for being over zealous, but she was sacked.'

'Sacked?'

'Yep. She had to emigrate to get another job. And we wonder why people are so reluctant to blow the whistle.' He sighed. 'Armitage and St John were both asked to resign, but no stigma was attached to them. I was told very firmly to keep my mouth shut and it was all hushed up.' He nodded grimly. 'Yeah, you could say I've got reason to remember that case.'

Marcus, meanwhile, was making a discovery of his own, He'd gone to see one of the department's statisticians to check Fraser's later figures from Glasgow and Bristol, the ones relating to pneumonia as a proportion of the causes of death. He'd realized they were crucial, because they showed that, once the rate had been corrected, Wansborough's higher death was entirely due to pneumonia.

Mike Fisher, the statistician, soon confirmed this as well, although using data from a great many more hospitals.

Marcus stood up to go when Mike stopped him. 'How many beds did you say that Wansborough had?'

'Forty-five – why?'
'D'you happen to know the size of population it serves?'
'Not offhand, no.'
They looked it up. . . .

CHAPTER 27

Tom looked round at the others. 'So can we agree now that Philip Armitage was involved in the euthanasia?'

Marcus and Fraser both nodded.

'Jo?'

'Oh, I suppose so.'

It was Friday and they were in Tom's room at the hotel.

She went on: 'You asked me to find out what people were saying at the hospital – well, all I've heard is complete disbelief that Philip Armitage could kill anyone. Especially stabbing Helen, I have to add – they just can't believe it, or in any affair between them.'

'There's a difference between giving an elderly person pneumonia and stabbing a young person to death,' said Marcus.

'They're both murder, Marcus.'

'So they are, but from the murderer's point of view, the former's a lot easier.'

'Oh, all right,' she said. 'I accept he was involved – what Tom's found does seem to clinch it.'

'Then let's move on to why they're dead,' Tom said. 'Are we agreed that the lovers' tiff is out?'

'The more I think about it, the less I believe it,' said Fraser.

'Then why are the police so keen on it?' said Jo.

'Because they didn't know them,' said Tom. 'Because Singh and Edwina agree with it and because it's the easiest solution for everyone.'

'But why are *they* so keen on it – Singh and Edwina, I mean? Especially Singh.'

'Because it's better than the alternative,' he explained. 'No one wants to believe in the euthanasia.'

She nodded slowly. 'Could he have realized – Armitage, I mean – that Helen was about to confess to Fraser? Is that why he killed her, to shut her up?'

'Why kill himself afterwards?'

'Remorse?'

'It just isn't in his character, Jo. They were both members of EXIT and RELEASE, they were committed to the cause, idealists. If they'd been caught, they'd have used their trial as a platform for their beliefs, not tried to murder their way out of it.'

Fraser said, 'I think that's right – in their own twisted way they were both ... well, honourable.'

Marcus nodded his agreement.

Jo said slowly, 'But if Armitage didn't do it, who did?'

'Whoever it was,' said Tom, 'they didn't do it for reasons of idealism. And I strongly suspect they employed a hit man, it's got a professional look about it.'

'But *who*? Edwina, or Singh, to hide what was going on?'

Tom shook his head. 'We've more or less ruled them both out of the euthanasia, so it wouldn't be that.'

'What about Singh out of sexual jealousy?' suggested Fraser.

'He'd have been more likely to kill you,' Jo put in.

'I can just about see him killing Helen in a fit of passion,' said Tom, 'But not Armitage as well.'

'Unless he was setting him up as fall guy.'

'That would be *very* quick thinking in a crime of passion.' He shook his head. 'I don't believe it.'

'Then who was it?'

'Who gains?' mused Tom. 'Who would gain from people dying in a hospital?'

'Only an idealist, or a nutter,' said Fraser.

Jo said with an edge of desperation, 'It's got to be one of the people we've already thought of.'

'Any ideas, Marcus?' Tom had turned to his boss with the polite smile of one who doesn't think so for a moment.

'I may have, actually,' Marcus replied with the satisfied smile of one about to confound his underling. 'For an area of its population Wansborough should have a community hospital with at least seventy beds. As we know, it only has forty-five. Isn't the question we should be asking ourselves: How have they managed for so long with so few beds?'

Tom and Fraser stared back at him. Jo said, 'Well, I can tell you how they're managing now, and that's bloody awfully.' She described the mess they were in. 'It was busy enough when I first arrived, but it's gone mad this last week.'

'It was getting worse before I left,' Fraser said. 'And yet it was fine when I first got there.'

Tom, who'd recovered a little, said, 'Well, it would be, wouldn't it? They were still bumping the patients off.'

Jo, looking at him, said, 'But that implies it was actually designed for killing people.'

'Who did design it?' Tom asked.

'Armitage,' said Fraser. 'They brought him in especially.'

'They? Who?'

'The trust.'

Marcus came in again: 'That wasn't all I found,' he said. 'After that little nugget, I decided to do some more digging. It seems that the trust wanted to build on the present spot, which was going spare on the Royal Infirmary site, but couldn't because it wasn't big enough for a seventy-bed hospital. They were about to buy a plot adjacent to the RI, but then they couldn't do that either, because of their mounting debts.'

Fraser got to his feet and started pacing around. 'St James' and the euro. . . .'

'Sounds like a parable,' said Marcus.

'You did tell me about that, didn't you?' said Tom. 'Remind me.'

So Fraser described again the saga of the St James' scandal, the committee of four and the disasters of the grade two listing of St James' and the euro conversion.

'So they were in the deepest of deep shit,' said Tom when he'd finished. 'But then along comes that nice Dr Armitage and shows them how to build a smaller hospital on the existing site.' His brain moved up a notch. 'The interesting question now is: Was it deliberate on the part of the trust? Did it happen that way because they wanted it to?'

Jo said, 'You're suggesting they deliberately employed Armitage knowing what he would do?'

'Can you think of a better idea?'

She turned to Fraser. 'Remember those papers of his you gave me to mug up on before the interview? How do we know that the trust didn't see them as well and employed Armitage in all good faith because of his efficiency?'

'No,' said Fraser. He'd gone over to the window and now turned so that he was silhouetted against the light. 'Do *you* remember when I was hauled off to that meeting with him – Armitage, I mean? You know, when Helen nearly caught you in my flat?'

She nodded.

'Well, he said something very strange to me when we were walking back – I told you about this as well,' he said to Tom.

'Remind me.'

So Fraser related how Philip had warned him about the dangers of being corrupted and manipulated.

Tom leaned forward. 'Can you remember his exact words, Fraser? It's important.'

Fraser frowned. 'It was something like: "All doctors are corrupted to an extent by economics." '

'He definitely used the word economics?'

'Yes. Then he said: "The thing is not to allow yourself to be corrupted beyond that extent, to be on your guard against being manipulated – by government, or anyone. . . ." '

'Did you take that to mean he was being manipulated by someone?'

'You're putting words in his mouth,' said Jo.

'It's all right,' said Fraser. 'I didn't at the time, but I do now.'

'So who?' said Tom. 'Who was doing the manipulating?'

Fraser thought about it. 'Well, the only thing I can think of is the committee, the gang of four set up to deal with the St James' scandal.'

'How did you find out about all that?' Jo demanded.

'Mostly from Helen, it was she who told me how they'd headhunted Philip to redesign and run the new hospital.'

'Redesign?' said Tom. 'She actually said that?'

He nodded.

'But is it enough to go on?' said Jo. 'I've no trouble believing in a couple of nutters killing off patients, but this I find very, very hard to believe.'

'I have to say that I don't,' said Marcus.

She turned to him. 'But would it be worth it financially? How much did the euthanasia plot actually save?'

'I did work that out,' he said. 'Costs in a community hospital are around £150 per patient per day. If we assume that Wansborough, by having forty-five beds instead of seventy is saving twenty-five patients a day, that comes to a million and a half pounds a year.'

Jo was visibly shaken by this, but ploughed on. 'How much were they in debt?'

'The figure I heard was twenty million.'

'That's what I heard,' said Fraser.

'But if they were in so much trouble,' she said, 'They'd have needed an immediate saving, wouldn't they? Not have to wait for year on year savings.'

'Yeah, I wondered about that,' said Tom. 'But Marcus gave us the answer just now. I'll have to work out the exact figures, but building a forty-five bed hospital on a piece of land you've already got is a hell of a lot cheaper than building a seventy bed hospital on land you have to buy. Certainly millions.'

There was a silence, then Jo said, 'And you think that's what this is all about, for the trust to get themselves out of the shit?'

'Can you think of anything else that fits all the facts?'

'Not offhand, no,' she said in a small voice. 'But it's a hell of a leap, isn't it?'

Fraser looked at Tom. 'D'you think it's all four of them, a conspiracy?'

'It's possible, although I doubt it. In my experience, it's unlikely to find four such criminally minded people thrust together by chance. I'd guess it was just one of them manipulating the others.'

'It's the way the upper echelons of administration work,' said Marcus. 'There's a problem, someone suggests a solution and everyone else agrees without looking too closely at the implications.' He shrugged. 'If it works, don't knock it.'

'And if it doesn't?' said Fraser.

'Nothing to do with me, guv.'

Jo said to Marcus, 'Is this what you've been thinking all along?'

He shook his head. 'Not until last night, when I found out about the shortfall in beds.'

'But since then?'

'I suppose so.' He paused. 'You see, I've been wondering for a while whether something like this was inevitable sooner or later.'

There was silence, while they waited for him to go on.

'I was at a seminar a few months ago and we were presented with figures showing that the average person has more money spent on them medically in the last year of their life than in all the rest of it put together.' He looked round at them. 'I've been wondering ever since how long it would be before someone came up with the bright idea of cutting that year out and saving some money.'

They had a sober lunch. Afterwards, Fraser said to Tom, 'If it is just one of them, couldn't you find out which by questioning them? Find out whose idea it was to employ Armitage in the first place?'

Tom nodded. 'Well, I'm going to try, but I don't mind betting it'll all be so tangled up by now that we won't be able to pin it on just one of them.'

'Who d'you think it is?'

He shrugged. 'You tell me, you've met them. What do you think are the respective strengths of their motives?'

'I suppose Fitzpatrick wants to keep his job, Matlock her political career. Otherwise, no idea.'

'Well, it's in the nature of chief executives to want to go on to better things and, as for Woodvine, I daresay he's in line for some pretty bauble or other for his chairmanship of the trust – his successful chairmanship, that is.'

Jo said, 'I'm still finding it hard to believe that any of it's a strong enough motive for this.'

'Then you obviously haven't met many ambitious politicians,' said Marcus drily. 'I sometimes think they'd do *anything* for another yard up the greasy pole.'

'Whichever, I don't see how we're going to prove it.'

'Doesn't mean we shouldn't try,' said Tom belligerently.

'But what are you going to do if you can't find out who's idea it was? 'Cos I'm betting you're right there.'

'I've been thinking about that.'

'I thought you were uncharacteristically quiet at lunch.'

He ignored her and went on. 'What I'd like to do is interview each one of them separately. We've got reason enough for that, and as Fraser said, it may even give us the answer, although I doubt it. Our bad boy or girl – shall we call them Ray, for Ray of Sunshine? – has almost certainly hidden him or herself by now, so what I propose doing is to leave all of them with something to think about. With your consent that is, Fraser.'

'Why my consent?'

'This is where I strongly advise you to run for your life,' murmured Jo.

Tom said, 'I believe that Ray had Armitage and St John topped not just to hide his or her part in it, but to try and hide the *existence* of the euthanasia plot itself. 1 think they're still hoping to hide its existence and I propose to offer them my help. If I'm right, then three of them won't believe in the euthanasia plot for the very good reason that they won't want to believe it. The fourth will know that it's true and will therefore react differently to what I tell them.'

'What are you going to tell them?' Fraser asked.

'That you came to us, Fraser, with the implausible tale of patients being killed, but that we were bound to look into it, even thought we didn't think much of either it or you.'

'Thanks,' said Fraser drily.

'And we *still* don't think much of you. We prefer the police version, that Armitage killed St John in a lovers' tiff and then killed himself. That Singh, Tate and Stones are right, that there has been no euthanasia plot and no cover up. Unfortunately however, we are still obliged to ask them some questions. The inquests have been set for Thursday the thirtieth. I'll talk to them not long before that and tip them off that you, Fraser, are planning to come out with the euthanasia story at Helen St John's inquest.'

'You're setting him up,' breathed Jo. 'They'll try and kill him.'

'They'll use that hit man again,' said Marcus. 'It's too dangerous.'

Tom turned to him and said with as much conviction as he could muster, 'Marcus, one of those four has deliberately engineered the murder of over 150 people in order to save their career.'

'A hundred and fifty?' said Fraser.

'That's what I make it. And then this person murdered the dupes they'd set up to do it. Are we really going to leave such a person running around in a position of authority?'

'We may have to,' said Marcus.

'Nobody's expressed any interest in my feelings about it as yet,' Fraser said pointedly. He turned to Tom. 'Is it inevitable he'll try to kill me?'

'No, that's what I was trying to get on to. I think that as a group, they'll try to persuade you to back off, but one of them will react differently from the others and that's how we'll identify them.'

'But what if it doesn't work?' said Jo. 'Fraser could end up being a target for . . . well, we don't know how long.'

'I agree,' said Marcus.

'And I agree with Tom,' said Fraser. 'We can't just leave this fucker to carry on.'

'I'm sorry,' said Marcus. 'But I think the risks are too great.'

Fraser said to him, 'I'm going to be called to give evidence at the inquest come what may, aren't I? What if I do tell them everything?'

'You won't be believed.'

'But enough shit would stick for there to be a bad smell around them for a while, long enough to screw up their careers, anyway.'

'Then they might just kill you for revenge,' said Jo.

'Which is why I'd rather go about it in a planned and controlled way.' He looked at Marcus. 'I remember you telling me that the purpose of your department was to stop corruption in the Health Service. Are you sayin' now that we should give in to it, because the opposition's too strong?'

Marcus pressed his lips together, then looked up. 'Are you really willing to go through with this?'

'Aye,' said Fraser. 'I am.'

CHAPTER 28

Whether it was because his mind had been jolted by the enormity of what he'd agreed to, Fraser didn't know, but he woke at home the next morning convinced he knew now how Philip had made the pneumococci virulent.

They'd forgotten to take his library pass from him when he'd left the hospital in Bristol and it was still valid, so he went there now to check out his theory. Then he phoned Tom, who was still at the hotel.

'Can you come to me?' Tom said. 'I'm still tied up trying to organize these interviews.'

He was with him in just over an hour.

'Well,' Tom said as he handed him a coffee.

Fraser took a sip, then said dramatically, 'Transformation.'

'What's that?'

'Briefly, it works like this. . . .' If he was disappointed with Tom's reaction, he didn't show it. 'If you inject non-capsulated pneumococci, like the ones found in the device, into a mouse, it lives, whereas if you inject the capsulated organism, it dies. OK?'

'Sure, although I don't suppose the mouse would agree.'

'But if you heat-kill those capsulated organisms before you inject them, the mouse lives.'

'So you need live capsulated bugs to kill a mouse – I think even *I* can work that out.'

The point was, Fraser told him, if you took live non-capsulated pneumococci, mixed them with a suspension of heat-killed, capsulated ones, and then injected the mixture, the mouse died. The live non-capsulated bugs somehow picked up DNA from the dead capsulated ones and became capsulated themselves.

Tom thought about this for a moment. 'And that's what you think they were doing?'

'It's got to be. They could have easily kept a culture of non-capsulated organisms going with next to nothing in the way of equipment. Then they mixed them with heat-killed capsulated bugs before putting them into the dispenser, and lo! Virulent pneumococci.'

'Where would they get the heat-killed ones?'

Fraser shrugged. 'Anywhere. They probably got them some time ago – once they're in glass ampoules, they keep for ever.'

Tom said, 'In the experiment, they were injected, here, the mixture would be inhaled – wouldn't that make a difference?'

'Well, I don't suppose anyone's ever actually *tried* it, but I don't see why it should.'

Tom nodded slowly. 'OK, but how would Armitage have found out about it? I mean, it's more your field than his and it took you long enough.'

'I've thought of that too. Remember when I got into his office?'

'And nearly buggered the whole—'

'Aye, all right. Well, he's got a collection of old pathology books in there and I'm wonderin' if he might have found it in one of them.'

Tom pursed his lips and drummed his fingers on the desk. 'Be nice if we could prove it,' he said at last. 'I wonder if Jo could bring it out.'

'It's huge, weighs a ton – and don't forget, they've tightened all the security now.'

'Yeah. . . .' More drumming. 'Jo's on nights at the moment, isn't she?'

'I think so.'

'Sorry, Jo,' Tom said as he picked up his mobile.

Even Fraser flinched at the stream of invective that spewed from the earpiece.

Nine hours later they were waiting in the shadows outside the main entrance of the unit. At exactly 1.00 a.m., they saw the orderly, whose office had been moved into the lobby, answer the phone. With a resigned expression, he replaced it, got to his feet and went over to the wards.

As soon as he'd gone, they walked over and Fraser keyed a number into the newly installed pad. The door opened. They quickly crossed the lobby to the admin corridor where Fraser punched in another number, pulled the door open and they were inside – Jo had found both numbers for them, and also a task for which she could call the orderly into the wards.

Tom produced vinyl gloves and they pulled them on. Fraser led the way to Armitage's office. The door was locked now, but one of the keys soon opened it. They went in and relocked it behind them.

Fraser sidled over to the window and, after checking no one was looking, gently lowered the blind. Tom switched on his pencil torch and they went over to the book cabinet. Fraser fumbled with the keys.

'Hold this,' Tom whispered impatiently, handing Fraser the torch and opening the cabinet himself.

Fraser pushed the glass aside, withdrew the Topley and Wilson and carried it over to the desk. Tom shone the torch on it and Fraser pointed to a piece of paper marking a place.

'That would be too good to be true,' Tom murmured.

But it wasn't. The book fell open and Fraser read: 'The transmutation of Strept. Pneumoniae in live mice.'

'It's a description of the original work,' he said in a low voice. 'It's all here.'

'Good. It would look better if we could leave it here, but I don't think we can risk that.'

'You think someone'll pinch it?'

'Well, it would screw us up if they did.'

Jo had said she couldn't get rid of the orderly twice, so they had to leave by the window. Tom held the book while Fraser cautiously raised the blind again.

'You weren't kidding about its weight,' Tom murmured.

Fraser cranked the window open, gingerly put a leg over the sill and did a sort of hop to get over the rose bush. He took the book from Tom, who then hopped out himself. He wasn't so adroit and hissed as a thorn ripped through his trousers.

He turned and fiddled with the catch a moment before pushing the window back and giving it a tap so that the catch fell back into place, then they vanished into the shadows.

'D'you realize,' Fraser said as they drove back in Tom's Mini, 'that this is the first time anything we've done has gone exactly to plan?'

'Well, you've got me with you,' Tom said modestly.

Fraser went home and Tom took the book with him back to London the next day.

Tom wanted the interviews of the gang of four to be as close together as possible, but the best he could arrange was to see them over the last three days of the week. Even this was tight, because the inquests had been scheduled for the following Thursday.

He hadn't planned them in any order, but was mildly surprised when the first turned out to be the Hon. member for Wansborough, Patricia Matlock. She'd had a cancellation, her secretary explained to Marcus, and would see Tom in her office in the Commons.

He'd been there before, of course, but had never failed to be impressed by the low murmured conversations, the quiet footfalls, the smell of power in Snow's 'corridors', even though he knew it was largely illusionary now.

Both her room and the lady surprised him; the former for its meanness, the latter for her sexuality; Fraser had told him about her, but he'd expected power dressing rather than pertness. However, once he started relating how Fraser had come to them with his story of euthanasia, her extraordinary blue eyes never left his face.

'Frankly, we found it very hard to believe,' he told her, 'But we were obliged to investigate it whatever we thought.' He paused. 'We hadn't got very far when the double killing occurred.'

'Something of a coincidence, that,' she observed. 'I'm rather surprised that Dr Callan wasn't suspected.'

'It did cross our minds,' Tom said. 'But the forensic evidence does indicate that Dr Armitage killed Miss St John and then himself.'

'A terrible tragedy.' She sighed and shook her head. 'But you say that Dr Callan still maintains they were – er – practising euthanasia?'

'He does and, as I said, we're bound to look into it.'

'Even though they can't answer for themselves now?'

'Even so.'

'So what exactly do you want from me?' She glanced at her watch. 'Sorry, but I did warn you that I'm pushed for time.'

'I need to understand the background to their employment. You remember the scandal over St James' Hospital?'

'I'm hardly likely to forget,' she said with a delicate shudder.

'I understand you were part of the junta set up to try and deal with it?'

She paused, then said deliberately, 'I don't think I care much for the word *junta*, but yes, there were four of us: myself, George Woodvine, Nigel Fleming and Patrick Fitzpatrick.'

'So whose idea was it?'

'George's, originally. Have you met him?'

'He's the next on my list.'

'Well, don't be fooled. He may look, even sound like a clown at times, but he's very shrewd, which is why the rest of us were prepared to follow his lead. It's the dandy who's the real clown,' she added.

'You'll have to enlighten me.'

'Mm. Well, perhaps I shouldn't have said it, although I'm sure you'll work it out for yourself. Patrick Fitzpatrick, the original Irish joke.'

'If he's that bad, why did you have him with you?'

Because, she told him, as Director of Community Medicine, St James' had been his responsibility. 'Why Nigel didn't sack him I'll never understand.'

He asked her whose idea it had been to sell the site for building and use the money for a new community hospital.

'Nigel's,' she said. 'It was he who saw the potential of the site – and of course he had the contacts in Town Hall.'

'But then came the grade two listing, not to mention the cost of the euro conversion?'

'You're very well informed, Mr Jones,' she said with a tight little smile. 'In fact, we'd known about the euro conversion for some time, we just hadn't realized how much it was going to cost.'

'So you were in trouble?'

'Yes.' Her eyes met his. 'We were.'

'Whose idea was it to employ Dr Armitage?'

'Why d'you need to know that?' she asked.

He shrugged. 'Because that person would tend to be the one who knew most about him.'

'As a matter of fact, it was Patrick's – I thought it redeemed him rather, at the time.'

'So it was his idea, and his alone?'

It was her turn to shrug. 'I assumed so. He showed us an article from a medical journal in which Armitage claimed that by caring for older people properly, you could cut costs, because they'd get better that much more quickly. And so it turned out.'

She described how Armitage had redesigned the hospital himself at a greatly reduced cost, and how Fleming had then had it built in record time on the smaller plot of land they had available.

'It's been a great success story up until now. Still. . . .' She sighed. 'I suppose every brilliant man has a flaw in his character somewhere.'

Ignoring this, Tom said, 'When the scandal first broke, you must have been worried about your political future?'

'I wouldn't have been human not to. But you know what they say – *If you can't stand the heat. . . .*'

He smiled. 'Dr Armitage's plan must have reduced the temperature somewhat?'

'Yes, somewhat.' She looked at her watch again. 'And now you really will have to excuse—'

'So a new scandal must be the last thing you'd want now?'

Another pause, then: 'Just what is it you're getting at, Mr Jones?'

He said mildly, 'Only that that's what you might get, a new scandal – if Dr Callan has his way. Are you going to the inquest?'

'I hadn't intended to.'

'You see, Dr Callan's told us that he intends to repeat his allegations there. He claims to have new evidence.'

'What new evidence?' Her eyes raked his face again.

'He won't say.' After a pause, he continued. 'The police, and the other doctors at the community hospital will try and refute him, of course, but as a witness at an inquest, he can say what he likes.'

'I see.' She seemed to be about to ask him more, then thought better of it. He thanked her for her time and left.

One down. . . .

CHAPTER 29

From the Commons, it was only a step to Whitehall, so he walked over and told Marcus about his meeting.

'So, employing Armitage was all Fitzpatrick's idea,' Marcus said. 'According to her, anyway. Is it really going to be that easy?'

'I somehow very much doubt it.' Tom paused. 'Have you found anything on them yet?'

Marcus shook his head. 'I have found something about Philip Armitage, though.' He'd managed to track down someone who'd actually worked with him when he'd been a junior registrar. 'It seems he was always a rather intense person, but what must have pushed him over the edge was the illness of his wife.' He paused. 'Motor neurone disease.' She'd been twenty-five when she'd been diagnosed and thirty-two when she'd died.

Tom grimaced. 'Enough to push anyone over the edge.'

During the last years, she'd been almost completely paralysed and in constant pain. Incapable by now of doing it for herself, she'd begged her husband to release her. Loving her, mindful of the Hippocratic oath, he'd demurred. By the time he changed his mind, it was too late – she was being kept alive in hospital.

'So when she got pneumonia,' Marcus continued, 'he made it clear he didn't want her treated, but she was, and lived a further miserable month.'

'I don't like to think what that would have done to me,' Tom said softly.

What it had done to Philip Armitage was to give him a complete nervous breakdown. On recovering, he'd specialized in community medicine, eventually becoming director of St Margaret's in Southampton 'Where, as we now know, he and Helen St John started *releasing* their patients,' Marcus finished.

'So how the hell did he manage to become director at Wansborough?' Tom asked.

'You ought to know the medical profession by now, when they decide to hush something up, it stays hushed. Meanwhile, he'd got a reputation for the excellence, and the efficiency, of his treatment of older patients, and published a lot on it, as we know. So he was a shoo-in for Wansborough, where he soon assembled his old team.'

Tom went back to his own home in Chiswick for the night. He phoned Fraser, who'd gone to stay with Mary now that the interviews had begun, and told him about Armitage.

From the window of his small manor house set in a hollow in the downs outside Wansborough, George Woodvine watched the figure of Tom the next morning as he emerged from the Mini Cooper and walked up the path. He stopped at the pergola and sniffed at the roses before continuing to the front door.

Cool-looking cove, Woodvine thought. Hard looking, too, although not particularly tall, and dressed rather casually for an investigator from London.

He heard the bell ring and Annie, his maid, go to answer it. A moment later, she tapped on the door and told him Mr Jones had arrived.

He went into the hall to find him perusing the portraits of his father and grandfather and, for some reason, the sight irritated him.

'Mr Jones?' he said a little more sharply than he'd intended.

The figure turned. 'That's right.'

'Do come through – would you like some coffee?'

'Please. Your father?' Tom said, indicating one of the portraits.

'Yes.' He asked Annie to bring them coffee, then led Tom into a light and airy drawing-room.

'I was admiring your pergola,' Tom said. 'They are roses, I assume?'

He had a distinct London accent which for some reason sharpened Woodvine's irritation. He suppressed it and smiled back at him. 'Old English Roses. They may not look as sensational as the cultured varieties, but the scent – well, I imagine you caught it yourself.' He ushered Tom to a chair. 'Now,' he said, sitting opposite him. 'How can I help you?'

Tom had sensed the irritation and wondered if he could use it. No, no point at this stage. He explained why he was there, taking in the ruddy face, thick white hair and moustache of his host as he did so Yes, he'd certainly captured the bluff countryman effect, except perhaps for the watchful grey eyes.

'I met Dr Callan several times,' Woodvine said, irritation firmly under control. 'And I have to say I was rather impressed by him. Is it possible that there's any truth in his story?'

'Well, we didn't think so at the time and subsequently found nothing to change our minds – until, that is, the deaths of Dr Armitage and Miss St John. That did make us wonder.'

There was a knock on the door and Annie came in with a tray of coffee. Woodvine thanked her and got up to serve it. He did, as the MP had said, Tom thought, look slightly clownish in his baggy tweeds.

He handed Tom a cup and saucer. 'You were saying?'

'That the deaths were rather a coincidence, coming so soon after Dr Callan came to see us. However, the police seem sure that Dr Armitage killed Miss St John, and then himself.' He told him about the forensic evidence. 'The question is,' he said, 'Why? Why did they do it? Was it star-crossed love, as the police think, or something worse, as Dr Callan claims?'

'What do you think, Mr Jones?' The tone was casual, the eyes shrewd.

'I think that the police usually know what they're talking about. However, Dr Callan still maintains they were involved in a euthanasia plot and I have to look into it. So what do *you* think, Mr Woodvine?'

'That the police usually know what they are talking about,' Woodvine replied with a smile. 'But I'm sure it's not just my opinion you've come here for?'

Tom hesitated, as though trying to decide what to say. 'I need to under-stand the background,' he said at last. 'I believe it was you who set up the junta after the St James' scandal broke?'

Woodvine smiled again. 'Junta, I rather like that – it's exactly the right word.'

'I'm gratified you should think so. Ms Matlock was quite offended by it.'

'Oh, take no notice of Patricia.' He drank some coffee. 'The purpose of a junta is to get things done quickly, without dissent or red tape, which is exactly what we had to do if we were to restore any confidence in the trust. We all had a strong motivation to find a solution as quickly as possible, which is what we did.' He explained the decision to demolish St James' and make a fresh start. 'Nigel got the finance sorted out, Patricia used her clout over planning regs, and when the going really got rough, it was Patrick who headhunted Philip Armitage.'

'When you say the going got rough, you mean the grade two listing and the euro conversion?'

'Indeed I do. Of course, we ought to have been more prepared for the cost of the euro, but I'd gladly garrotte the good citizen who suggested the grade two listing – if you'll forgive the figure of speech,' he added with a grin.

Tom grinned back 'You said that it was Fitzpatrick who discovered Dr

Armitage – d'you know that for a fact?'

'I suppose not, strictly speaking – I just assumed it was when he came to me with the idea.'

'You mentioned that the other three had a strong motivation to overcome the crisis, but what about you? What was your motivation?'

He raised his eyebrows. 'I'd have thought that fairly obvious – I'm the chairman of the trust and have responsibility for it.'

'But you're non executive chairman, no one could have really blamed you.'

'Couldn't they?' He looked quizzically at Tom. 'I think they could, and would have. And they'd have been right – my job is to oversee the affairs of the trust, to anticipate problems such as this.'

'How long have you been chairman?'

'It'll be six years at the end of this year. I'll step down then.' He hesitated. 'I'd like to leave things tidy if possible – d'you really think there's a chance of another scandal raising its head?'

Tom pursed his lips as though in thought.

'It comes down to what Dr Callan says at the inquest,' he said at last. 'If he just raves about a euthanasia plot, he'll be discredited by the experts. If he *were* to have any evidence, though. . . .'

'Has he?'

'He *says* he has. You'll gather our relationship with him has become rather difficult of late, so we don't really know.'

'From what you tell me,' Woodvine said slowly, 'I wonder if he's really fit to give evidence. Couldn't he be stopped?'

Tom shook his head. 'Difficult, since he's the one who found Miss St John's body.'

'I mean stopped from expressing his wild theories?'

'The coroner could order him to confine his evidence to the discovery, I suppose.'

'Then I wonder if perhaps someone ought to have a word with the coroner,' mused Woodvine. 'Sorry, forget I said that.'

CHAPTER 30

Marcus's delving into Home Office records, meanwhile, had brought forth fruit – bitter fruit, in the form of Helen's past, or at least, her mother's. He phoned Tom with it after he'd got back from seeing Woodvine.

Tom felt he had to tell Fraser face to face. He phoned him at Mary's and said he'd be with him in an hour.

Fraser had given Mary an abridged version of what was going on and she greeted Tom rather warily before leaving them alone.

'I needed to talk to you about Helen anyway,' Tom started, then paused. 'The thing is, Marcus phoned me just before I left with some information about her. Do you want to hear that first?'

'It would be bad, I take it?'

Tom nodded.

'Aye then, maybe I should.'

'All right.' Tom paused. 'Well, some of your guesses about her were remarkably accurate.'

Helen's mother, Ruth, had indeed been from a wealthy county family. She'd been precociously artistic and also a sixties wild child. Both talents had been nurtured at art college. She'd become pregnant, although unaware of the fact until it was too late for an abortion. Her parents had tried to make her have the baby adopted, but she refused – they were convinced just to spite them rather than from any maternal feelings. They'd responded by refusing to support her at college or to help with the baby, although they had later helped with the child's education.

'Jesus, what a brew,' said Fraser.

Ruth had been always been manic depressive; this had worsened after Helen's birth and had not been relieved by Helen going to boarding school. She'd hanged herself during the school holidays when Helen was fourteen. Helen had been the one to find the body.

'With an upbringing like that,' Tom finished. 'It isn't so hard to under-

189

stand her take on life. Nor to imagine what happened when she and Armitage met and started mixing philosophies.'

'Poor wee girl,' Fraser said softly. He could remember as though she were standing in front of him how she'd prevaricated over her past, her contrived gaiety, the fact that she'd loved him. 'She needed help,' he said. 'And all she got from me was pretence.'

Tom could see from his face that it wouldn't do any good telling him not to blame himself. He waited, wondering how, or even whether he should broach the other business now, then Fraser spoke again. 'What was the other thing you wanted to talk about?'

Relieved, Tom asked him if he could remember anything Helen had said about any of the gang of four. 'Now I've started interviewing them, I need everything I can get on them.'

Fraser thought for a moment. 'She knew Fitzpatrick and Woodvine a lot better than the others,' he said. He told him about Patrick and Fleming's loathing for each other and the reasons, how Patrick had left his first family for the pregnant Marie, also his world-weary cynicism.

'I haven't met him yet,' said Tom. 'He's tomorrow. What about Woodvine?'

He smiled as Fraser described the chairman's extrovertism at the party, his later concern about Philip and what Helen had said about his father and grandfather.

'Interesting,' said Tom. 'I wonder if that's a sensitive point.' He told him about Woodvine's irritation when he'd found him staring at the family portraits.

'She never mentioned anything like that to me,' Fraser said.

'What about the Hon. Patricia Matlock, did she say anything about her?'

Fraser shook his head. 'I had a funny experience with her, though. . . .' He told him about her curious behaviour and enigmatic remarks at the party and later. 'I got the feeling she's a bit of a power freak.'

'Yeah, that was my impression.'

'Any ideas which of them it is yet?'

Tom laughed. 'I'm not even thinking about it until I've seen all of them.'

After Tom had gone, Fraser went up to his room and shut the door. He sat on the bed and thought about Helen. 'Poor wee girl,' he said again.

Patrick Fitzpatrick realized who Tom was the moment he saw him from his window the next morning, striding purposefully up to the trust HQ. No point in putting if off, he thought, and when the receptionist called to say that Mr Jones had arrived, he went downstairs to meet him.

He was standing in the entrance hall, smiling as he looked round at the elegantly proportioned ceilings, the polished furnishings and the pictures on the walls.

'Mr Jones? Patrick Fitzpatrick.' He pumped his hand. 'Would you like to come up?' He added quickly, 'And would you care to share the joke?'

'Oh,' said Tom, still smiling. 'I was just reflecting on how administrators always seem to bag the best buildings for themselves.'

'Along with the best salaries to go with them, I expect? But then, I'm thinking that you're in the way of being an administrator yourself, Mr Jones. In a manner of speaking.'

Tom laughed as they reached the stairs. 'And you'd be right. In a manner of speaking.'

Patrick took him to his office and offered him coffee, which he refused. 'Then of what service can I be?'

Tom, as he gave him the story, could see what Patricia Matlock had meant about him, his clowning and his clothes. He went beyond being merely smart: his soft grey suit looked brand new and his shirt so crisp it could have shattered, if Tom had been able to get a grip on it through his ripe plum of a tie.

'So you're tellin' me that you decided to investigate Dr Callan's story even though you didn't believe it?'

'Oh, we had to – the one we ignored would be the one that turned out to be true. Murphy's Law would see to that,' Tom added.

'Ah yes, Murphy's Law,' Fitzpatrick said, still smiling faintly. 'You know, I've always wondered why it shouldn't be Smith's Law, or even Jones' Law.'

Tom grinned back, not displeased with the reaction, then explained how he needed to understand the background to the affair. 'You remember the business over St James'?'

'Now, if you've done your homework, as I suspect you have, Mr Jones, then you'll know that I'm not likely to forget.'

'Who was actually in charge of St James'? Medically in charge, I mean.'

'The late and quite unlamented Dr Peter Holway. And now you're goin' to ask me how it was that *I* didn't know what was goin' on there, aren't you?'

'Something like that.'

'After all, it was my responsibility and I should have known, shouldn't I?' Fitzpatrick paused, then continued more quietly. 'I did know it was bad, although not quite *how* bad. I'd been saying for some time to anyone who'd listen that we had to do something about it, but it was put off, and then put off again. Always something more urgent.' He shrugged. 'I should have put it in writing, of course. Then the scandal broke and we *had* to do something. Which as you know, we did.'

'Who actually set up the junta to deal with it?'

'Junta, I like that – your own? It was George Woodvine,' he said without waiting for an answer. 'Although Patricia was the front woman, so to speak. But I'm sure you know this already.'

'But it was you who discovered Dr Armitage, wasn't it?'

'*Discovered*, now there's an interestin' word. It was me who suggested we approach him, but it was Nigel who brought him to my attention in the first place.'

'Nigel Fleming, the general manager?'

'The same.'

'But I understood from Ms Matlock and Mr Woodvine that it was you who actually found out about him.'

'Probably, to be candid, because I allowed them to think that. But it was Nigel who showed me the article Armitage had written in *Community Care*, the one in which he said you could save money by giving older people better treatment.'

'It didn't occur to you that it might be too good to be true?'

'No, that didn't occur to me,' he said, his eyes fast on Tom's face. 'What is occurrin' to me now, however, is that *you*, Mr Jones, give Dr Callan's story a soupçon more cred than you've led me to believe.'

Tom said slowly, as though still thinking about it, 'I did begin to wonder, when Dr Armitage and Sister St John were killed so soon after Callan came to us.'

Fitzpatrick's brow furrowed. 'But I thought Dr Armitage killed her and then himself?'

'That's what the police say, and who am I to argue with them?'

'Would you *like* to argue with them?'

Tom shook his head. 'No, it's what the evidence seems to say.' He continued quickly. 'You didn't lose your job in the fallout from St James'?'

'I thought I would.' He let out a sigh. 'You know, in retrospect, perhaps it would have been better if I had.'

'Why d'you say that?'

He met Tom's eyes. 'Because I'm sick to death of the whole damn business, Mr Jones.'

'Well, if Dr Callan were to be successful in stirring up another scandal, you probably would lose it this time, wouldn't you?'

'Oh, I expect so. But I wouldn't be losing any sleep along with it.'

'What about your pension?'

'What about it?'

'You'd lose a chunk of that, wouldn't you?'

'You know something, Mr Jones?' He leaned forward conspiratorially. 'I'm beginning to think it might be worth it.'

'So, if I were to tell you that Dr Callan is still convinced that Dr Armitage and Sister St John were bumping off their patients and is threatening to say so at the inquest, it wouldn't bother you?'

'Is he?'

Tom nodded slowly. 'And he claims he has new evidence.'

After a pause, Fitzpatrick said, 'You know, what really interests me is what *you* think of it, Mr Jones. Do you think they were bumping off their patients?'

Tom paused for effect before saying, 'No, I don't think so. But as I said, some of the facts did make me wonder.'

'Such as?'

'It's a funny thing, but when I came in, I thought it was supposed to be me asking *you* the questions.'

'Humour me.'

'Well, as I said just now, Armitage and St John's deaths. Then there's the device Dr Callan found and the statistics he produced.'

'Ah yes, the statistics. . . .' He lingered long and lovingly over the word.

'You're not a believer, then?'

'Oh, I'm a great believer when I can get them to say what I want them to say. Otherwise. . . .' He shook his head. 'No.'

It may interest you to know that Ms Matlock referred to you as a clown.'

'And I don't imagine she intended flattery.'

It was Tom's turn to shake his head. 'I don't share her opinion, though.'

'Ah, now that would be the Celt in you, Mr Jones. You are Welsh, I take it?'

'My grandfather was. The other three quarters is English.'

'Never mind, there's still hope for you. Don't give up.'

Tom laughed. He realized that they were going round in circles, so he stood up. 'On that happy note, I shan't keep you from your work any longer.'

'You weren't.' He insisted on coming down to the front door to see Tom off.

CHAPTER 31

His network on full song now, Marcus rang Tom later in the afternoon with the lowdown he'd gleaned on the junta.

'First Patricia Matlock. She's up for a junior minister's post in the next reshuffle and the grapevine suggests that any new scandal in her constituency would dish her.'

'Which gives her a motive.'

'It does,' Marcus agreed. 'But does it for two years ago, when – if you're right – this must have been set up?'

'I don't see why not. You're the one who made the crack about ambitious politicians.'

'Hmm, all right. Next, Nigel Fleming. . . .'

It seemed that the general manager's contract finished at the end of the year and, by mutual agreement, was not being renewed. It was rumoured he was going for a management post in Lisco's, the supermarket chain.

'Bit of a comedown, isn't it?' said Tom. 'A management post in a supermarket, after being top honcho here?'

'A management post with a salary of 250 grand instead of the 120 he's on now.'

'Ah. . . .'

'So I don't imagine a new scandal is what he wants either.'

'No,' said Tom, scribbling.

'George Woodvine is up for a KBE in the next honours list when his period of office finishes.'

'A knighthood? Now that *is* a bauble of some pulchritude, isn't it?'

'Have you been at that dictionary again?'

'Yeah. Is he really worth a knighthood?'

He already had an MBE for various services, Marcus said; he was a chief magistrate, president of the Wiltshire Conservation Trust and chairman of governors of the local comprehensive.

'The chairmanship of the Health Trust is the jewel in his crown, so to speak. He's also got plenty of money and friends in high places.'

'What sort of high places?'

'Governmental.'

'Would that be political or administrative?'

'Both, but mainly civil service.'

Tom drew a box round Woodvine's name and connected it to another with a pound sign and the word clout in it. 'What about Fitzpatrick?'

The Original Irish Joke, it seemed, wasn't up for anything, except perhaps the order of the boot. He was generally regarded as a waste of time and space and would certainly be the first to go in any new scandal.

'However,' Marcus said. 'He's got money of his own as well, so maybe it wouldn't bother him too much.'

'How much? Money, I mean. . . .'

'He's said to be comfortable.'

'How comfortable?'

'Comfortably comfortable.'

Tom repeated the money box sign for Fitzpatrick. 'That changes things, doesn't it?'

'In what way?'

'Well, we thought that Woodvine had the weakest motive and Fitzpatrick one of the strongest. Now it's the other way round.'

'Only if you think a KBE's as strong a motive as Fleming's supermarket job, or Matlock's ministerial post. And whereas *comfortable* might be fine for you and me. . . .'

'Mm,' Tom mused. 'It's funny, isn't it, the way some people collect a reputation. Everybody seems to think Fitzpatrick a complete tosser, but when I was with him an hour ago, I thought he was as sharp as. . . .' He searched for a word.

'Greek Chardonnay?'

'I had something more intellectual in mind.'

'Ah, but people with money are like that sometimes, aren't they? Clever but unambitious, even lazy.'

Nigel Fleming had been tempted to refuse to see Tom at all when Marcus first rang him, but then he'd sensed Marcus's own clout and reluctantly agreed. He'd been tempted to cancel the appointment after Patricia had rung him the day before and told him what it was all about, but then thought better of it.

Now, as he watched from his window Tom smoking a cheroot outside, his irritation bubbled over – *the bloody gall of it*. They'd sent someone who wasn't even properly dressed. So when his secretary rang through to say that Tom had arrived, he made him wait for a quarter of an hour.

His feelings were not soothed by Tom's explanation of his presence. He said coldly, 'Why are you telling me all this now?'

'Because as I explained, Dr Armitage and Sister St John's deaths—'

'I mean, why wasn't I informed earlier about these allegations of Dr Callan's?'

'Because we didn't give much credence to them. If we raised the alarm over every story we—'

'Are you saying that you do give credence to them now?'

'No, I'm not saying that.' Pause. 'Not necessarily. But we do have to look into them, especially in view of the deaths.'

'Isn't that the job of the police?'

'Not in this case, no. They're not looking for anyone else in connection with the deaths, and they're not interested in Dr Callan's story.'

'But you are?'

'We have to be, it's our function.'

Fleming stared back at him a moment more, then said, 'All right, what do you want to know?'

Protest registered, thought Tom. He said, 'I'd like to go back, to the St James' crisis and the junta you set up to deal with it.'

'Why? What relevance does that have?' Patricia had told him about the J word, and he ignored it.

Tom patiently explained why he needed to understand the background and Fleming briefly and factually described the setting up of the committee and its subsequent actions. His account didn't differ much from those of the others.

Tom said, 'Whose idea was it to sell St James' and use the money to build a new hospital?'

'Mine, originally. I have contacts in the construction industry and I put them to use.'

'So you'd done all your sums and were about to spend twenty million on a new hospital, and then St James' was listed. Hadn't it ever occurred to you it might be?'

'It most certainly had not – it's a hideous building.'

'Granted,' said Tom, who'd seen it. 'But the euro conversion, surely you knew about that?'

'We did, although the actual cost was a huge shock to us. Even so, it wouldn't have been a problem but for the grade two listing.'

'So you were in trouble?'

'We were at risk of a considerable overspend.'

'Which following the St James' scandal, would have been something of an embarrassment?'

'We wanted to avoid it, if possible.'

'Whose idea was it to employ Philip Armitage?'

'Fitzpatrick's,' Fleming said. 'I know you spoke to him this morning and I imagine he's told you that I showed him a journal article by Armitage. And so I did. At the time, we were all searching for ideas and that was one of many.'

'How did you come to see the article?'

'By coming across it in the journal, I imagine.'

'It was published in *Community Care*, which isn't the most widely known of journals. I was wondering how this particular article came to your attention.'

Fleming shrugged. 'The trust takes all journals that might have relevance to our work.'

'The trust didn't take *Community Care*, not at that time, anyway. I've checked.'

'Then I don't know.' Or care, his expression added. 'We're always leaving articles and such like on each other's desks and I can only assume that's what happened here.'

'Didn't anyone say anything to you about it later, ask what you thought of it?'

'Not that I can remember.'

After a pause, Tom said, 'I imagine that the last thing you want now is another scandal.'

'You imagine correctly.' He paused. 'Before you came here this morning, I had no reason to think there would be. Are you telling me now that there is?'

Tom took his time answering and Fleming felt his gorge rise again.

'The only answer I can give you,' Tom said at last. 'Is that I don't know. As I told you earlier, it was only at Dr Callan's insistence that we investigated this matter as thoroughly as we have. We haven't found any hard evidence to back up his story.'

'Well, I'm glad to hear that, at any rate.'

'However, he still doesn't accept this and intends to make his allegations public at the inquest.'

'But surely he won't be taken seriously?'

'Oh, I'm sure the other witnesses such as Dr Singh, Dr Tate and Dr Stones will do their best to refute him, but. . . .' Another pregnant pause. 'He does claim to have more evidence.'

Fleming asked quietly, 'And does he? Have more evidence, I mean.'

Another breath. 'Well, the only evidence we know about is the statistics and the doctored aerosol device I mentioned earlier. On their own, they're refutable, but...' He shrugged. 'It all depends on what this further evidence is. Since he refuses to tell us, we have no way of knowing.'

'So you're saying that he might?'

'Yes,' agreed Tom. 'He might.'

When he got back, Tom ordered a pot of coffee, sat down and thought. Then, before starting on a tabulation of everything he'd heard, he wrote each of their names down and tried to think of a word or phrase that summed each one up: 'Matlock. *Coquettish with Hauteur*. Woodvine. *Bonhomie with Bullshit*. Fitzpatrick. *Bullshit with Bonhomie*. Fleming. *Imperious? Pompous? Arrogant?*' All of these, certainly at first, although not so much latterly.

He smoked a cheroot while he thought about it, twiddled his thumbs and then called Marcus. 'Well, I've seen them all now.'

'And sown the seeds of doubt?'

'Yes. I've got no idea which of them it is, though.'

'But?'

'How did you know there was a *but*?'

'Because I know you.'

'All right, there is a *but*.' He tried to pull his thoughts together. 'It's just that I'm finding it hard to believe either that the motives you found out about are strong enough, or, now I've met them, that any of them have got the sheer balls for something of this scale.'

'So you're thinking it's none of them, or all of them, or what?'

'No, I still think it's one of them, *but*....' He took a breath. 'Could there be someone else beyond that?'

'Wheels without wheels, you mean?'

'Yeah. Oh, don't tell me, you'd already thought of it – you *had*, hadn't you?'

Marcus took his time answering. 'You know how it is at meetings,' he said at last. 'People say all sorts of things, things that are obviously meant to be taken as a joke, but then afterwards, you wonder: joke or kite? Maybe, they're not sure either. Anyway, I've been aware lately of one or two people saying that if we go on living longer and filling up the care homes and hospitals the way we are now, then we'll have no choice soon but to start bumping a few off. That sort of thing.'

'And what you're wondering,' Tom said softly, 'is whether someone decided to take it seriously and try an experiment?'

'Exactly.'

'Any idea who?'

'Possibly.'

With which answer Tom had to be satisfied.

CHAPTER 32

Fraser, more or less incarcerated at Mary's, was bored stiff. He was also, although he and Mary were very fond of each other, conscious of the fact that guests, like fish, tend to go off after a few days. He had to get out for both their sakes, so he phoned Tom and asked if it was all right to go to his own house to pick up the post.

'Mm . . . not sure about that,' Tom said.

'They might have sent me a note or something.'

'Can you get in the back without being seen?'

'Easy.'

'All right. In and out, don't hang around and don't let yourself be seen from the front.'

It was a relief just to be outside again. The sun was shining, so he dropped the hood, savouring the feel of even the city air on his face.

He parked in the road at the back of his house, slipped down the alley and climbed over the gate into his garden. He'd already knelt down to pick up the letters in the hall when he heard the board creak upstairs. Not very loudly, but he knew that floorboard – it was in the main bedroom, between the bed and the door and always made that noise if you trod on it. And the book by the phone had been moved, he saw as he rose to his feet.

Get out, quick . . . Not too quick, don't let them know that you know.

He was moving now, walking as fast as he could without seeming to hurry . . . back along the hall, through the kitchen, listening.

No sound.

Through the back door, pull it shut across the lawn to the gate. *What if there was someone on the other side?* No, they wouldn't have had time – would they? He slid back the bolt, slipped the latch, eased the gate open. Nothing.

He ran lightly back up the alley to the car – should he phone Tom now? But they could already be out looking for him.

He got into the car, started up and drove to the junction, turned left. There was nothing in the mirror; he'd beaten them. Then a dark saloon pulled out. But cars pull out all the time. He turned right, accelerated . . . and just as he thought he was clear, it reappeared.

Got to lose him but make it seem accidental.

He drove to the city centre. With the hood down, he felt completely exposed – it would be so easy for anyone in a car to stop beside him and lean over with a gun. He kept glancing in the mirror, but the dark saloon always stayed two or three cars behind.

It wasn't until he was in Broad Quay that he got his chance – a light on amber he could jump and leave his tail stranded behind the more law abiding citizens. Round past the cathedral, up Park Street, then left up a side road toward the Cabot Tower. He found a large van and tucked the MG behind it. Double yellows, but so what? He phoned Tom.

'Are you sure you've lost them?' Tom asked.

'Sure as I can be.'

'Trouble is, your car's rather conspicuous, isn't it?' He thought for a moment. 'Phone Mary now, tell her to bolt her back door, put the chain on the front and not let in anyone she doesn't know.'

'You think she's in danger?'

'Very unlikely, it's just a precaution. Do it now and phone me back.'

Mary was not amused. 'Fraser, what is going on?' she demanded as soon as he'd said his piece. 'Is this connected with Tom?'

'I promise I'll explain soon,' he said. 'Please, just do as I ask.' He rang off and was about to ring Tom again when he became aware of a shadow behind him. He jerked round – it was a traffic warden.

'You can't park there,' she said.

'No, sorry. Can I just make a phone call, please? It's very urgent.'

'Sure,' she smiled. 'But if you do, you'll get a ticket.'

It was almost worth it, but he didn't want to attract attention. 'Is there anywhere near I can park?'

She sucked on her teeth, shaking her head. 'Difficult at this time. And not really my problem,' she added.

He drove off. If he stopped anywhere near, she'd get him. If he kept driving, his tail could pick him up again.

His mobile rang. Probably Tom. He kept driving. Found another side street. He parked at the end, still on a yellow line, but hopefully far enough away. He phoned Tom again.

'I think you'd better come to me,' Tom said.

'What if they pick me up again?'

'Could you recognize the car if you saw it?'

'I . . . think so.'

'Only think?'

'I'm fairly sure.'

'All right. Have you got a map?' He found it. Tom said, 'Don't use the motorway. Can you see the A road that goes to Wansborough from quite near the centre?'

'Yes – Oh, God. . . .'

'What?' It was the traffic warden, she'd spotted his car and was walking purposefully towards him.

'I'm on my way,' he said. He took off before she could reach him.

He had to stop to check the map again, but then found the road quite easily. No sign of his tail. It took an hour and a half to get to Tom's hotel.

'So there's absolutely no doubt in your mind that someone was actually in your house?' Tom said as he handed him a coffee.

'None whatever. I wasn't expecting anyone so soon.'

'Neither was I, or I wouldn't have let you go.'

'Presumably, it lets Fleming off – they must have been put on to me before you spoke to him.'

'No, I'm certain one of the others had already told him, so he could have set it up yesterday.'

After a pause, Fraser said, 'D'you have any idea yet who it is?'

'Not really.'

'Not *really*?'

'Maybe the shade of a suspicion, but nothing more.'

Fraser pressed him, but he refused to say anything else. 'So what do we do now?' he asked.

'We wait. Sooner or later, one of them is going to contact you.'

'Then what?'

'Depends on what they say.'

Fraser drank some of his coffee. He said, 'You think it was the people who killed Helen who were in my house?'

'Probably.'

'Does that mean they're out to kill me?'

Tom thought for a moment. 'I hadn't thought so – not yet, anyway . . . I thought the junta would try and change your mind first, or maybe discredit you in some way. But the fact they were in your house does make me wonder.'

He phoned Marcus and Jo to let them know what was happening. Jo asked if there was anything she could do, but Tom said he couldn't think of anything. After that, while he went out to buy Fraser a toothbrush and a few other basics, Fraser phoned his house to check for messages, and then Mary to try and put her mind at ease.

Tom came back and they began the waiting.

After dinner, in the bar, Fraser said, 'D'you have to do much of this?'

Tom glanced down at his beer. 'Drinking?'

Fraser grinned. 'No, waiting around for something to happen.'

Tom grinned back. 'Quite a bit.'

'How did you get into this?' Fraser asked, genuinely curious, and Tom told him how he'd joined the army to get away from his family, then the police, where a bad marriage had wrecked his career.

'So when Marcus offered me this, I jumped at it.'

'Ever regretted it?'

'Never.'

The next day, Saturday, Fraser read every section of the paper, swam in the hotel pool, read a book from the hotel library, played chess with Tom (who won) and watched a mediocre film on TV. There were calls from his mother and Rob, but not the one they were waiting for.

The only item of interest was that someone had called on Mary asking for him. Polite and charming, Mary said, told her he was a colleague from Wansborough, but didn't leave a name.

'What did you tell him?'

'Only that I didn't know where you were.'

He was about six feet, well built and mid-thirties, but she couldn't remember anything about his face, except that it was 'ordinary'.

By Monday, Tom and he were beginning to invade each other's nasal spaces. The inquest, on Thursday, was drawing nearer.

'Yeah, but what happens if they *don't* phone?' Fraser demanded.

Tom swallowed and bit off the retort he was about to make. 'I thought they would by now,' he admitted. 'If they don't by tomorrow, I'll think of a way of stirring them up.'

'How?'

'I said I'd think about it, OK?'

Jo rang again. 'D'you want me to come down?' she asked when Tom told her how things were.

'It might help actually,' Tom said slowly 'Might get Fraser off my back, anyway.'

She joined them twenty minutes later.

'What worries me,' she said after they'd brought her up to date, 'is that they don't want to talk to Fraser, they just want to kill him. Hence the men at his house.'

'Even if that were true,' Tom said quickly. 'Which I *don't* believe, they've got to find him first.'

'They will, if they look here.'

'They still think he's in Bristol, that's where they'll be looking.'

'As long as they don't go back to Mary,' Fraser said.

'Does she know you're here?' Jo asked him.

He shook his head. '*My* worry is that they'd try and get at me through her.'

'They won't,' said Tom.

'How d'you know that?'

'Because it would give them away – Ray, I'm talking about. He, she, wants to *hide* the fact of the euthanasia, and that would confirm it.'

'I wish I could be so sure.'

'C'mon, Fraser,' said Jo. 'Didn't you say this place has got a pool? Give Mary a ring, and then we'll go for a swim.'

Tom found them later that afternoon and took them to his room. 'I've just had an interesting phone call,' he said. 'One of the people I wanted to speak to at Southampton had left the hospital without leaving any forwarding address. Also changed her name, which didn't help – anyway, we've traced her to Bournemouth, but she won't speak to me on my own. Doesn't trust men, apparently.'

'Can't really blame her there,' murmured Jo.

'But she will talk to you, Jo. I said we'd meet her at seven, so we'd better get going.'

Fraser said, 'What if they contact me while you're away?'

'Stall them and phone me.'

'And if they want to meet?'

'Agree, but stall. Say you've got something else on you'll have to rearrange, then call me. Don't, *whatever* you do, tell them you're here.'

Fraser let out a snort. 'What d'you take me for?'

'OK, sorry.'

'When'll you be back?'

'Depends . . . say two hours to get there and find the place, an hour with her – say around ten.'

Five minutes later, they were gone. Fraser mooched around, then rang Mary again, and then his mother. He checked the messages on his land-line – nothing.

To try and work off his frustrations, he went down to the gym for an hour, and then to the swimming pool again, where he swam alternate lengths on the surface and underwater until he was exhausted.

A touch of cramp suggested he'd overdone it, so he showered and went to dinner.

It wasn't until he was on his way back up that he realized he hadn't taken his mobile with him. It was ringing as he unlocked his door.

'Fraser? It's Patrick,' the voice in the earpiece said. Electricity crawled over his head and down his neck. 'You're a hard man to get hold of, are you back at home now?'

'No, I'm staying with a friend – in Bristol.'

'Ah.' Pause. 'Listen, Fraser, I know it's late, but is there any chance you could you come and see me tonight? It really is important,' he added.

'Why tonight?' Fraser asked, trying to keep his voice level.

'If we left it till tomorrow, it would have to be at the trust with the others and I'd really rather not.'

Don't seem too eager. 'What's it about, Patrick?'

'Well, to be honest with you, I've been put up to it by the others.'

'What others?'

'George, Patricia and Nigel – but the point is, I've been thinking all weekend about what Mr Jones told me, and there are some things that really bother me.'

'What sort of things?'

'Well, it comes down to the fact that an intelligent man such as yourself should be thinkin' the things Mr Jones says you're thinkin'.' He sighed. 'I'd meet you halfway, but Marie's out tonight and I'm babysitting. It wouldn't take you much over an hour to get to me if you use the motorway.'

'You're probably right there, except that I've already arranged to go out tonight.'

'It *is* important, Fraser. To you as much as me.'

He pretended to consider a moment, then said, 'All right. Let me talk to them and I'll come back to you in ten minutes, OK?'

He rang Tom, who answered almost immediately. 'Is this it?' he said.

Tom hesitated. 'I think it probably is. He wants to sound you out and set his weasels on you if you won't play.'

'What do we do?'

'We were about to start back – is there anywhere we can meet near his place?'

Fraser thought quickly. 'He lives just outside a village called Cotlake, there's a square with a war memorial in the middle of it.'

'Hang on.' There was the rustle of a page being turned. 'Yeah, got it, can you meet us there? Better make it an hour and a half, say nine?'

'Yeah, but what are we going to do then?'

'I'll work that out on the way – ring him now and tell him you'll be with him at 9.30. That'll give us half an hour to sort something out.'

CHAPTER 33

Patrick, smooth as snakeskin, instantly agreed and Fraser, putting the phone down, found he was shaking. He felt hot and clammy – it had been close all day (which might account for the irritation, he reflected) and now it was sultry.

He showered again, finishing with a spell on cold, then dressed in the jeans and dark sweatshirt Tom had bought him. He went down to the car.

So it was Patrick, he thought as he drove out of the hotel. Good ol' Patrick, he thought, the Original Irish Joke. And yet what he'd said on the phone was plausible, that the others had put him up to it, that he was worried about what Tom had said.

But what was it Tom had said to him, Fraser? 'One of them will act differently from the others.' and that was just what was happening.

Another thought occurred to him, how the first of the attacks on the hospital playing field had been just after he'd taken Patrick into the social club and told him how he regularly used it.

It had to be. Was Marie in on it too, he wondered? What reception had they planned for him?

By now, he'd reached the outskirts of town. He crossed the motorway and took the Marlborough road. Ten minutes after that, he was on the narrow twisting road to the Wansdyke.

The murk had brought on an early darkness and the bushes and trees not directly in the beam of his headlamps were like the blobs in an impressionist painting, although there was still enough light in the sky for him to make out the ridge of the hill ahead. The car purred and seemed to float through the turbid air.

He braked as a sheep blundered into his path. It trotted up the road in front of him for a few moments before veering away to the left.

Would Tom be there yet? He glanced at the clock – no. What was he going to do?

The headlamps of another car flickered in his mirror as he approached the ridge, caught up with him.

By now he was nearly at the car park, so he slowed to let it pass, then another car pounced in front of him from the verge. He knew instantly what it meant and slammed on his brakes – the car behind punched into him, shunting him forward. He rammed the gear stick into first gear, spun the steering wheel and pushed his foot down, lurching into the park. He accelerated to the far end, jumped out and started running ... over the stile and onto the Wansdyke and it wasn't until he'd gone fifty yards that he realized he had the car keys in his hand – he must have turned the engine off.

Now, why had he done that, he wondered? It must have wasted nearly half a second. He glanced back, saw two figures about fifty yards behind, dressed darkly like him, not shouting, just running after him.

He realized he was panting and tried to control his breathing, filling his lungs with each breath – then his foot caught a stone and he nearly fell. He recovered, kept going, his trainers hitting the hard dusty ground with a muted scratch-scratching. He kept running because he had to, like Old Man Kangaroo in Kipling – now why was he thinking about *that*?

He glanced behind again – they were closer now and the first rawness was whistling in his windpipe. There was a thick bank of conifers on the right – the path down to the shepherd's hut! Where was it?

A shadow loomed ahead, bigger than the other shadows between the rows of pine.

He lurched right, down into the ditch, up again, over the stile and into the silent trees, his footfalls intimate as they bounced among the trunks.

As he heard the hit men reach the ditch, he swerved into the bracken lining the path, but it was tougher than he'd thought and he had to tear his way through – then he ran, his feet making no sound at all now on the layers of dead pine needles.

He ran, the soft needles robbing his legs of energy, they felt like plasticine after all the exercise he'd had – then, through the darkness, he made out a fallen tree, altered course and fell behind it.

Silence.

Save for his breathing. And his heartbeat. And his blood shushing through his neck and head. An image of Helen with her slashed throat flickered in his mind and he pushed it away as he peered round the trunk of the fallen tree.

The rattle of a stone on the path, the glimmer of a torch moving down.

Keep going, keep going. Then the torch stopped, moved back – surely they couldn't see where he'd come off the path. Could they?

The bracken. The path was long and straight and they'd realized he was no longer on it and seen where he'd forced his way through – and now the torch light was coming straight towards him. When you disturb a bed of pine needles, the darker layer underneath shows up very clearly. They were tracking him.

No ordinary hit men these, not like the nerds in the hospital grounds.

Gotta move. Maybe work his way back to the path. He pushed himself up and crept away, keeping low, treading carefully so as not to leave a trail, watching the flickering beam of the torch. A twig cracked beneath his foot, but not loud enough for them to hear . . . forty yards, fifty.

A telephone rang and he froze. It was his own *feckin'* mobile.

Shouts from the hit men.

He snatched it from his pocket, threw it as far as he could and ran. Shouldn't have done that, he thought. Too late now.

He ran, trying to dodge the trees as the thin lower branches flicked spitefully at his face, ran as his breath grew heavy. He *had* to. . . .

A break in the trees ahead and more bracken – the path? No, the ground opened beneath him and with a cry, he fell into a ditch . . . and on to something that squealed, kicked him in the face, jumped up and bolted away. He crawled further along the ditch, heard the hit men jump over it, following the noise of the animal's hooves. A sheep? A deer? How long had he got?

Not long. He crawled as fast as he could, the ditch was dry and dark, the bracken curled over the top shutting out the light – he stifled a cry as a thorn dug into his palm. He stopped and tried to pull it out.

Silence.

Why not just stay where he was? They'd never find him here, would they? But they must have realized by now they'd followed an animal, that he must still be in the ditch.

He raised his head, straining his ears.

No sound. Absolutely nothing.

They could be a couple of hundred yards away, or just a couple, waiting for him to move.

He found himself picking at the thorn in his palm, made himself stop.

How long should he wait? Sweat trickled from his pits down his sides and he itched to move, to get himself as far away as he could.

He started crawling again, very slowly, hand over hand along the ditch. The thorn jabbed and pricked. The bracken scratched faintly over his back. He kept going, feeling ahead in the darkness for anything that might make a noise.

Was that light ahead? The path?

Without warning, the ditch came to an end, it was above the level of the path and he fell into it with a clatter – a shout came from behind and the flash of a torch.

He jumped up and ran downhill, the trees flickering past, the torch flickering behind him.

He ran, trying to empty and fill his lungs with each breath, trying to ignore the sand-blasting in his windpipe, his mercury-filled legs, the stitch like a needle in his side.

A dog barked; had to be the shepherd's dog. He burst into a clearing, saw the caravan in front of him as the dog barked again, saw the door swing open releasing the light inside and a voice. ' 'Oo's there?'

A torch shone in his face, blinding him.

' 'Oo's there, wha' d'you want? Stop or I'll shoot.'

'It's me,' Fraser croaked. He could see he was holding a shotgun. 'Doctor . . . the path . . . me and the girl, you gave us tea.'

'Wha—?' the shepherd began. Then the dog started barking again and he swung the torch round. ' 'Oo's that?'

'They're after me,' Fraser managed.

' 'Oo?'

Then there was a flash and a noise like someone spitting as the torch disintegrated and the shepherd let out a yell, then he raised the gun to his shoulder and a rod of light speared into the darkness. In the aftermath of the blast, Fraser thought he heard the shepherd say 'inside' because he turned and jumped for the door.

Fraser followed him, tripping over the dog which was trying to get in too. The shepherd grabbed Fraser's collar, hauled him in and slammed the door.

'You all right?' he said.

'Yeah. You?'

'Me 'and.' He held it up, it was dripping blood. ' 'Oo are they?'

How the feck do I explain that? 'They killed my boss, he was in charge of the community hospital where I work and now they're trying to kill me.'

'Why?'

'Because I know about them.'

The shepherd grunted. 'We'd better get these lights out,' he said. He crawled a little way along the floor, stood and turned a tap under one of them and Fraser realized they were gas lamps. He got up cautiously and doused one himself.

A window smashed and they dropped to the floor. Then the shepherd started moving along the length of the caravan, reaching up to each light only when he was sure he was out of sight.

One left, in plain sight of a window. He grabbed a broom and poked at the mantle until it went out. 'I'll turn 'er off in a minute,' he said. 'Don't want no gas in 'ere.' He grabbed his gun, quickly stood and fired a shot out of the window before dropping down again. The blast in the confined space deafened Fraser.

Then the shepherd bobbed up again and deftly turned off the tap before ejecting the spent cartridges from his gun and stuffing in two more.

As Fraser's hearing came back, he was aware of the whining of the dog. 'Have you got a phone?' he asked.

The shepherd shook his head. 'Nah.'

'Is there another door?'

'In the kitchen. I bolted 'er when I turned out the light.'

'Can we get out of it?'

'Faces the same way as this one.' He nodded at the door they'd come through.

Fraser pressed his lips together, then said, 'Can we get through the floor?'

Another shake of the head.

'Oh, shit.' The enormity of their situation hit him – the men out there were armed, they could be anywhere and they knew exactly where he and the shepherd were. He swallowed. 'So we can't get out?'

'An' they can't get in,' the other grunted.

As though in answer to this, a voice called from the outside: 'We don't want to hurt you, throw out the gun and—'

'Cunt!' The shepherd got up and fired in the direction of the voice before dropping to the floor and replacing the shell he'd used. The dog was barking.

Fraser said, 'We can't just stay here.'

'Why not?'

The dog was whining again, looking towards the kitchen.

'Are they trying to get in down there?'

'They do, they gets this,' the shepherd said grimly, looking at his gun.

But nothing happened and after a few minutes, Fraser said, 'I'm sorry I got you into this.'

The other shrugged.

Bloody stupid thing to say, Fraser thought, so why did I say it? I'm going to be killed, he thought and dizziness prickled over his scalp and face. The dog went on whining.

There was a noise from the kitchen. The shepherd heard it too, he lifted his gun and fired, then fired another out of the window before reloading.

They waited.

Silence.

Then Fraser smelt smoke. They looked at each other, then at the kitchen where smoke drifted out and a yellow light flickered behind it.

CHAPTER 34

'Can we put it out?'

' 'Old this.' The shepherd pushed the gun at him and scrabbled on his hands and knees toward the glowing smoke. He looked like a spider against it, Fraser thought. He could hear it crackling now.

He held the gun, glanced round. Could he fire it? Did it have a safety catch?

The shepherd came back. 'They've done something with the fuckin' gas,' he said, taking the gun back. 'Looks like we 'ad better find a way out.'

The voice came out of the darkness again, strangely disembodied against the rising voice of the fire: 'Come on out, we don't want to hurt you.'

The shepherd started to get up again, but Fraser grabbed his arm. 'I'll keep him talking,' he said urgently. 'Can you get out there?' He pointed to the back window. 'With the gun and circle round?'

The shepherd thought about it for a second and nodded. Crawled to the other side of the caravan and looked up.

Fraser called out, 'How do we know you won't shoot us?'

'Because we need you alive. We could have shot you several times over by now if we'd wanted.'

The fire had spread to the next room to them now and Fraser could feel the heat of it. He also felt a sudden compulsion to believe what the man outside was saying.

No! He glanced at the shepherd, who'd levered the window open with the broom. He looked round at Fraser and nodded.

'All right,' called Fraser. 'We're coming out of the door.'

'Throw the gun out first.'

He looked round desperately, then the shepherd handed him the broom.

'All right,' he called again, shouting over the roar of the fire. 'It's coming out of the door now.'

He turned the handle and pushed it open – and the flames leapt in the draught. He dropped the broom through as low as he could, hoping they wouldn't notice what it really was. The shepherd lowered the gun through the window, then in one quick movement, rose up and pushed himself out head first. His legs upended, he wriggled . . . then he was gone.

The flames were nearly at the door now, roaring, reaching for Fraser in hot licks. The dog ran to and fro, whining, yelping, licking Fraser's face.

The voice again. 'Well, are you coming?'

'All right,' he called. The shepherd should have got round by now. Was he waiting for him . . . or dead?

Had to go, another minute and it would be too late.

He somersaulted out of the door, over the steps and rolled under the caravan.

Tom and Jo got to the war memorial at five to nine. They waited till nine, then Tom called Fraser's mobile. No answer. At the message prompt, Tom snapped, 'It's me, Tom, where the bloody hell are you? Not answering,' he said to Jo as he cut the connection. 'He should've been here before us.'

'Perhaps he can't answer because he's driving.'

'He should've stopped.' He turned to her. 'D'you know which way he's coming?'

'I think so.'

Tom tried the mobile again, then Jo directed him out of the village and up through the chicane. As they went past the car park at the top, she said, 'Tom, stop. It's his car.'

He reversed, then drove up to the three cars at the end.

'They must have jumped him but he got away,' he said. 'But where is he?'

She said, 'I know,' and told him about the shepherd's caravan.

He found a torch, then dropped the compartment under the dash and took out his gun. 'I'm going after them,' he said, opening the car door. 'Phone the police and tell them how to get there – is there another way to it they can drive?'

'He's got a truck, so there must be.'

The boom of a shotgun came quivering through the night air.

'Make that an ambulance as well.' He jumped out and started running along the Wansdyke. The shotgun boomed again.

He found the path, jumped over the stile and then let gravity take him down through the trees. He tried not to use the torch, then he tripped and fell. He rolled over, got to his feet and went on, flashing the torch occasionally. Then he saw the fire. Tried to go faster. Fell again.

He heard the hit man shouting for Fraser to come out as he got there, saw him silhouetted against the fire, then saw the caravan door open and something drop out, not a body.

He looked round for the other hit man, couldn't see him. Then a body did drop from the burning caravan and roll underneath it. The gunman started forward and Tom, not daring to leave it any longer, levelled his gun and shouted, 'Stop!'

The gunman spun round, brought up his own gun. Tom let off three quick shots – the gunman staggered and fell and Tom ran forward, then his eye caught a movement to the left . . . a flash, something hit his head.

Under the caravan, Fraser started crawling . . . molten fire dripped in rivulets from the floor to the ground as the heat closed around him. He heard a shout, shots – then the whole kitchen section collapsed and the flames whooshed, licking his face. The section of floor he was under began to sag, pressing on to his back. He dropped on to his face and squirmed like a snake, reached the other end, grasped and pulled at the nettles at the verge, barely aware of the pain as they stung his hands. He pulled, then flexing his body round, rolled out as the whole bottom section collapsed on to the ground. He rolled into something – the body of the shepherd.

He staggered up. The burning caravan was threatening to topple over on them. Getting his hands under the shepherd's shoulders, he pulled him away . . . and something gleamed – the shotgun!

He grabbed it and ran round the caravan. In the light of the flames, about twenty or thirty yards away a figure was standing. One of the hit men. As Fraser watched, he walked slowly forward, stopped and pointed his gun at something on the ground.

Fraser lifted the shotgun and pulled the trigger. Nothing. He shouted 'Oi!' as he scrabbled with his fingers.

The hit man spun round, let off a shot . . . a female voice screamed, 'No!'

The hit man glanced back. Fraser felt something click under his fingers and he hauled on the trigger again. A double spear of light shot out and the recoil knocked him backwards. He scrambled up again, ran to where the hit man had been standing. He was dead, his face and upper body a mess of blood. The figure at his feet was Tom.

The woman came running up – Jo.

'Is he all right?'

'I think so . . . You see to him, the shepherd's round there, worse.'

A siren cut through the noise of the fire.

'Police,' she said. 'I called them. You'd better put that down.' She indicated the shotgun.

Fraser dropped it and went to look for the shepherd. He found him where he'd left him. The dog, which had jumped out after Fraser, was whining and licking his face. He was still alive, but in a worse state than Tom – at least two bullets to the body that Fraser could see, almost certainly bleeding internally.

The siren suddenly grew louder and then stopped. Blue lights pulsed. Fraser stood up as two policemen ran over to him. One knelt by the shepherd, the other said, 'Was it you who phoned us?'

Fraser shook his head. 'She's round the other side.' He looked at the shepherd. 'He's bad.'

'There's an ambulance just behind us.'

CHAPTER 35

It arrived in time to save the shepherd, but both contract killers were dead. They were never identified. (They had, as the shepherd thought, done something with the gas – cut the pipe from the cylinder, lit it and pushed it back through the hole into the caravan.)

Tom was taken to hospital and Fraser and Jo spent the rest of the night answering questions, as did Patrick Fitzpatrick, once Marie returned home – he'd been telling the truth about that, at least.

Patrick simply stuck to his story, that the others had persuaded him to approach Fraser and offer him an internal enquiry in return for his silence on the euthanasia plot at the inquest. No, of course he knew nothing of any ambush. And yes, of course he'd kept the others informed of what he was doing.

The other three were questioned the next day and confirmed what Patrick had said.

'There's one thing that still puzzles me,' Fraser said to Tom that same day at his hospital bed. 'Those hit men, they could have shot me easily, several times over. Why didn't they?'

Tom thought for a moment. 'If you'd been found dead with bullets in you,' he said, 'it would've confirmed that you'd been silenced. If, however, you'd been found dead in your burnt out car at the bottom of the scarp, it would have just been a tragic accident.'

A few days later, Tom, his head still bandaged, found himself pressing the bell push of George Woodvine's house again. The girl answered and said she'd see if Mr Woodvine was available. He came to the door.

'Can you give me one good reason why I should speak to you?' he asked coldly. He made no comment on Tom's bandaged head.

'Because, with your help, I think I can clear this mess up.'

Woodvine pursed his lips and slowly nodded. 'I suppose that comes under the category of good reasons. You'd better come in.'

He stood aside to let Tom through, then closed the door and indicated the drawing room.

'Well?' he prompted when they'd sat down.

Tom said, 'You know about the attempt on Dr Callan's life last week?'

'I ought to,' he said drily. 'I've been questioned at length by the police about it.'

'The point is,' Tom said, 'why? Why should anyone want to kill Dr Callan?'

'I'm assuming the question is rhetorical?'

'Not entirely, no – I'd be interested to hear what you think. Bushwhackers, perhaps?'

Woodvine smiled unwillingly. 'Frankly, I'd have said that was just as likely as the police's suggestion, that one of us, the – er – junta, set him up to prevent him speaking at the inquest.'

'Speaking about what, did they say?'

'His obsession with the idea that Philip and Helen were killing off their patients.'

'Well, I suppose all four of you could be said to have motives for not wanting him to do that.'

'Naturally.' Woodvine shrugged. 'As servants of the trust, we have no wish to see, or hear, it slandered. That's why we were going to guarantee Dr Callan an internal inquiry into the matter if he agreed not to say anything at the inquest That's why Patrick asked him to come to his house.'

'I meant personal reasons.'

Woodvine drew a breath, then released it. 'I suppose that's true as well, to a greater or lesser extent.'

Tom said curiously, 'Why was Fitzpatrick the one asked to speak to him? Why not you, for instance?'

'They'd had a good relationship in the past and we thought he might be more responsive to him.'

'Did you really think that Dr Callan would agree to an internal inquiry?'

'Why shouldn't he?'

'Well, as we both know, internal inquiries can be postponed, delayed, frustrated in a hundred ways, and when they do eventually come to a conclusion, it's usually meaningless.'

'Oh come, that's rather cynical, isn't it?'

'Is it?' Tom paused for a moment, then said quietly, 'I still think that the key to all this is the identity of the person who had Philip Armitage employed in the first place.'

Woodvine snorted impatiently. 'The key to *what*, for God's sake? We've been over this before anyway – it was Patrick, after he'd read Philip's article.'

'He says it was originally Nigel Fleming who noticed the article and gave it to him.'

'Does it matter?'

'Does it surprise you that neither of them knew about Armitage's record?'

'What record?'

'The fact that he'd been suspected by the police of practising euthanasia at his unit in Southampton.'

Woodvine blinked. 'Is that true?'

Tom nodded slowly.

'I see . . .' He looked up sharply at Tom. 'Suspected, you said, was he ever charged?'

'No. The CPS said there wasn't enough evidence.'

'Then he didn't have a record.'

'Let's say his history, then.'

'Why should any of us have known about that?' He looked at Tom carefully. 'Mr Jones, it was originally my understanding that you didn't believe this theory of Callan's either – are you now saying that you do?'

'No, I'm not saying that,' Tom replied. 'What I'm saying is that I know it to be the truth.'

A heartbeat's pause, then: 'A remarkable conversion, if I may say so.'

'Not really. I always believed it. Now, I know.'

Woodvine looked at him askance. 'Then it would seem that you've been less than honest with me – with any of us, in fact. I'd be interested to know exactly *how* you know.'

Tom said, 'As well as Dr Callan, we've had a nurse working undercover for us at the hospital.' He told him how they'd isolated the ampicillin resistant pneumococci from a dying patient and then saved the life of another by giving her cefataxin.

'You *have* been underhand, haven't you?' Woodvine said when he'd finished. 'However fascinating it may be, that doesn't amount to anything like proof.'

'Possibly not, although it's very strong circumstantial evidence, as is the doctored artificial saliva device we found, the one used to give Mrs Stokes her infection. Definitive proof has been more difficult to come by.'

'Perhaps for the very good reason that there isn't any.'

'That may have been the case before,' Tom said easily. 'But not now. After the attempt on Dr Callan's life, the police took his story more seriously and yesterday, they searched Armitage's and Miss St John's houses a little more thoroughly and found a cache of the doctored devices. Now, that really is strong circumstantial evidence, wouldn't you say?'

Woodvine spoke carefully. 'What I would say is that I only have your word for that. And also no guarantee that if this evidence exists at all, it wasn't planted there by Dr Callan. Or even yourself.'

'You're clutching at straws. We can also show that Armitage and St John were killed on the order of the person who arranged for them to come here in the first place.' Tom wasn't completely sure about that, but felt the time was right to say it.

'This is surreal.' Woodvine was still smiling. 'What possible motive could anyone have for that?'

'The trust, of which you are chairman, was at grave risk of over-spending two years ago, due to the St James' debacle and the euro conversion. Philip Armitage's plan saved nearly ten million pounds, which was enough to get you out of the immediate trouble. His redesigned hospital was only about half the original cost, and since then, has saved about a million and a half a year. That's the motive. The ostensible motive. Of course,' he continued before Woodvine could say anything, 'Philip Armitage and Helen St John weren't in it for the money. They were idealists who genuinely believed that euthanasia for the hopeless cases was the only way forward. And when they realized they were going to be caught, they planned to confess and use their trial as a platform for their ideals. Armitage even wrote and told you he wasn't going to involve you, which is how you were able to use his post-script when you had him killed.'

After a pause, Woodvine said, 'I think that you're seriously deranged, Mr Jones.' He stood up. 'I'd like you to go now, please.'

'Your father was called Robert, wasn't he?' said Tom, not moving. 'Sir Robert. And your grandfather Henry? Sir Henry. Both knighted for services to the state.'

'Are you seriously trying to suggest that as a motive for me?'

'Certainly. You wanted this knighthood more than anything in the world, and you knew it was yours *ostensibly* for guiding the trust through troubled waters without scandal or overspending. You wanted it so much,' Tom said slowly, trying to control the anger he still felt, 'that you were prepared to connive at the deaths of 150 people to get it.'

Woodvine gave a short laugh. 'How could I have possibly known about Armitage's activities in Southampton?'

'You met Armitage five years ago there on one of your fact-finding trips. Mrs Peacock, who was a manager there at the time, remembers introducing you to him.'

Woodvine shrugged. 'I may have met him, but—'

'As for his activities, you were told about them in your capacity as a chief magistrate, by Superintendent Hayes, who was in charge of the case, as an example of justice not done. Later, you made it your business to find out everything you could about him. You saw his article in *Community Care* and it gave you an idea. You sought him out and put a proposition to him, which he foolishly accepted. You left the article on Fleming's desk, knowing that it would end up with Fitzpatrick. Then all you had to do was congratulate him on his brilliant idea when he suggested headhunting Armitage.'

Woodvine shook his head pityingly. 'And I suppose I somehow arranged for Callan to visit Patrick so that I could set up the – er – bushwhackers.'

'Indeed. You did that as you've done everything else, by suggestion and manipulation, so that you were always in the background.'

Woodvine went over to the door and opened it. 'Mr Jones, I shall be reporting you to the authorities. And now, I should like you to leave my house, please.'

Tom still didn't move. 'I shall be reporting to the authorities as well. The police know that it's you and are actively looking for proof. They'll almost certainly find it. Even if they don't, you will not be getting your knighthood, not ever. You will be eased off the Bench and all the other positions you hold; in fact, you will never hold any position of influence again in your life. And those around you will gradually become aware that there is something unwholesome about you. You will become a nothing.'

Woodvine said, 'You don't have the power to do any of those things.'

'You're absolutely right,' agreed Tom. 'I don't.' He smiled wolfishly. 'But my boss does.'

'Even if you're right, which I very much doubt, you will be giving me a non-punishment for a non-existent crime.'

Tom leaned forward. 'We both know that what I've said is substantially true, and that one way or another, you're going down for it. But we also know that it was not originally your idea, that someone in the department put you up to it, someone who knew your—'

'What department are you talking about?'

'The Department of Health.' It wouldn't hurt to say that much. 'Where you have friends. Are you going to let this particular *friend* get away with it? Getting you into this mess and leaving you to braise in it.' He was studying Woodvine's face as he spoke, but there wasn't the flicker of a suggestion that any of it meant anything to him.

He said, 'For the last time, will you leave my house, now, or am I going to have to phone the police to eject you?'

Tom got to his feet and walked to the door. Woodvine followed him into the hall as Tom opened the front door and let himself out. He walked down through the scented pergola to his car, got in and drove away. He drove to where Marcus and the police were waiting in the van.

'Hard luck,' said Harris. 'You couldn't have done any more.'

Tom nodded. 'He probably guessed I was wired.' He divested himself of the bug and handed it over. 'And now I'm going outside for a few minutes if you don't mind.'

He walked a little way from the van and lit a cheroot.

Marcus joined him. 'He was right, Tom. You couldn't have done any more.'

He shrugged. 'Maybe. God,' he said. 'I hate the thought of them getting away with it.'

'They won't. Or at least, Woodvine won't – I can deliver most of what you promised him. And you never know, our friends back there might find something to nail him with.'

'I don't think they will, though,' said Tom. 'And the other bastard'll get off with nothing.'

Marcus said quietly, 'I'm hoping that won't be entirely true, either. I shall drop words into selected ears and then frame the kind of report that'll let him know that I know.'

'You'd better watch your back, then – we both had,' Tom added reflectively.

'That's where the choice of ears and the words I use in the report come in,' Marcus said. 'Chosen with discretion, I hope it'll stop him, and anyone else, contemplating anything like this again. And also bugger up the promotion or any other hopes he may have had. We both know how that hurts the great and good.'

Tom smiled. 'What about your own prospects? It won't do them a lot of good, either. Shoot the messenger and all that.'

'Fortunately, it doesn't bother me.'

Tom nodded. He knew that was true.

George Woodvine watched Tom go, his face still devoid of any expression, then he shut the door, turned and walked slowly back to the drawing room.

There seemed to be cloud forming round his head. He poured himself a drink to dispel it, then another. The cloud swirled round and round and he heard a voice calling from the hall: 'George, come here. . . .'

His feet dragged him unwilling into the hall and over to the portrait of his father. He looked up at him. His father raised his hand, pointing, his lips moved and he spoke in his cold, unemotional voice.

'I told you that you were a failure George, that you would let us all down, and I was right.'

When the girl came to see what all the noise was about, she found George Woodvine jumping up and down and shrieking as he beat the image of his father's face with a marble figurine.